AFTER MIDNIGHT

SARAH GRIMM

Cover Art by Arial Burnz

Publishing History
First Champagne Rose Edition, 2011
Print ISBN 978-0-9899361-1-8

Published in the United States of America

Dear Reader,

Allow me to introduce myself. My name is Noah Clark, the lead singer/songwriter for the rock band Black Phoenix. Perhaps you've heard of us. About ten years ago we topped the Billboard charts—a multi-platinum band whose last album was the most successful of its century. But that was before everything went to shit. Back before the sex, alcohol, and rock and roll took away my best friend and drummer, Danny Treybourne. Afterwards, I gave up the lifestyle, the world tours, hell, I gave up the band. I headed back home to London and committed myself to leading a normal life, one without music as its driving force.

For ten years, I was miserable.

So I'm back to making music. I crossed the pond, settled in a place called Auburn, California and began the preparations to reunite Black Phoenix. We hired a new drummer, set up a meeting with the record company, and I went in search of a private, reputable studio to record a demo. I found one in Long Island City, just up the road from a pub named Izzy's Bar. Where one night, after midnight, I wandered in and set eyes on its namesake.

Damn...Isabeau Montgomery, child prodigy pianist, hiding behind a lie of her own making. She has the most pale, haunted eyes I've ever seen, and dark, golden skin. The first time she set those eyes on me and smiled, I was lost. I'm a songwriter, but the way she affected me, I haven't words.

A detail about me you should know, I was born with a one track mind. I want something; I go out and get it. From the moment I first laid eyes on Isa I wanted her. I wanted to show her what she was missing, ignoring her music the way she did. I wanted to share with her everything I spent all those years figuring out: Denying who you are is nothing but a waste of time, time a person can never get back. Problem is my one track mind got me in trouble. I became so focused on saving her from herself, I didn't see the whole picture. I pushed her too hard. And in the end, I pushed her away.

Hopefully, one day she'll forgive me for being such an ass, because Isabeau...Isa completes me.

In a way even my music never could.

Noah Clark

CHAPTER ONE

Isabeau Montgomery sat in the dimly lit bar and shook like an amateur before her first recital. Her gaze, blurred by the sudden threat of tears, settled on the keys before her. Her stomach cramped painfully, yet the need was too great to ignore.

With ability as natural to her as the color of her skin, she began to play. The waterfall of music filled the air, washed over her, completed her in a way nothing or no one else ever had. Against the razor sharp sting of memories, she fought...

She was young, vibrant, and born with a raw talent rarely seen. Classical, jazz, or rock and roll, she played it all. Loved all the genres— loved to create. All that mattered was her joy, her love for the instrument beneath her fingers and the music she was so skilled at creating.

For a good ninety seconds, joy returned, the rush of adrenaline and, conversely, the sense of belonging. In those seconds, time slowed, the lines between the past and the present blurred, and she was a child again. There was no longer pressure to be something she couldn't be, no fear of what her future would hold.

And with the innocence of youth, no idea that everything she held dear could be lost in the blink of an eye.

The song built to a crescendo then quickly faded as pain, her old friend, returned with enough force to quash her joy. Her stomach roiled. Her breath caught.

Tears gathered in her eyes, and she dashed them away. Isabeau ran her hands up and over her face, pushing her long mass of ebony hair away from her forehead. She struggled to pull herself back together. Her fingers were chilled, cooler than normal, yet perspiration pooled at the small of her back. She closed her eyes, took a deep, slow breath

"I didn't expect that old thing to be in tune."

Sweet Jesus.

She jumped at the deep baritone voice, slamming her knees into the piano. The key cover abruptly closed, and she startled again. Heart racing, she rose and faced the double doors she'd obviously forgotten to lock.

She swept her gaze around the bar's dim interior until she spotted a dark, male frame. "The bar is closed."

Her tone was sharp, curt, and left no room for argument. Under different circumstances, she wouldn't inflict such rudeness on a customer, but he intruded on her privacy, her pain. Her emotions were too close to the surface for niceties.

His voice rang with a clipped British accent and the tone of someone unaccustomed to being questioned. "I was here earlier."

She remembered the voice and didn't need him to step out of the shadows to recognize him, which he did anyway. She'd served him a few hours ago—dark lager, no glass—and shared with him a smile as powerful as it was sexy. "We were open earlier. Now, we're closed."

His eyebrow shot up. His mouth shaped itself into an ironic curve. "So you have said."

"Then perhaps you should leave." Hands unsteady, she bussed the table closest to her and carried the glasses to the bar. His words stopped her cold.

"You're very talented. How long have you played the piano?"

No, no, no. This wasn't happening. She closed her eyes on a wave of emotion, doing her best to will him away. But even then she knew. The man at her back was not going away.

She focused her gaze on his reflection in the mirror that ran the length of the bar. He was tall and lean, with eyes that shone with intelligence, even in the dim light. His hair was a mix of medium and dark blonde, worn long enough it fell across his forehead, nearly into his eyes, and brushed the collar of his shirt. Dark

3

stubble shadowed his jaw.

The fine hairs on her arm stood on end as he crossed to her. She edged to the side and turned to face him. "I don't play."

"Of course you do. You were playing when I entered."

"You're mistaken." She countered his step forward with one in retreat, ensuring that she remained out of arm's reach.

With a frown, he stopped. "You have nothing to fear from me."

It never occurred to her to fear for her safety, even though the bar was empty but for the two of them, the lights dimmed in deference to the late hour.

"Let me start again by introducing myself."

"I know who you are."

"You do?"

Of course she did. He was the person who brought back her desire to create, whose presence in the room made something inside her sing out. He was the reason she'd been driven to play tonight, after years of resistance. The reason the siren song continued to play in her head, louder than ever before. "Yes, I do."

"And I frighten you?"

"Of course not."

"Then why do you tremble? You've gone pale and look as if you're ready to bolt."

She dodged his hand when he reached out

as if to touch her. Her breathing grew shallow. She waited for him to comment. Instead, he casually tucked his hands into the back pockets of his jeans and rocked back on his heels.

His gaze moved around the room before settling on the piano. "What is the name of the song you were playing?"

The walls were closing in on her. Her body trembled so violently she was surprised her teeth didn't chatter. "I don't play," she reminded him.

She desperately needed to put some space between them. However, so far he'd countered every move she made. He moved again, stepped close enough she could make out the intense green of his eyes. It was difficult to hold her ground and not flinch as he took his time studying her features, his gaze lingering on her eyes.

She was not a beautiful woman. Taken separately, her features held the potential for beauty, but together, with her mix of cultures, she had a face like a jigsaw puzzle whose pieces didn't fit together. Her cheeks were too sharp, her lips too large, and her eyes, pale enough they all but disappeared beneath the dark tones of her father's heritage. Neither blue nor gray, her eyes brought her the most displeasure. Most people spoke of her eyes as "peculiar" and "haunted."

Isabeau couldn't handle such a reference

from him. "What do you want from me?" she inquired before he could comment.

"That's a good question," he replied, more to himself than in answer to her. "How about your name?"

The way he looked at her made it very, very hard for her to look away. "Isabeau."

"Isabeau." His voice brushed across her senses like a lover's caress. His hand settled upon her arm. His very large, very warm hand.

She opened her mouth, but no sound came out. Trapped by the contrast of his pale skin against her darker, golden tones, her mind blanked. He dwarfed her, which at five foot three wasn't all that difficult to do. Her heart raced. His scent snaked into her lungs with each breath she took.

The scent of him broke her from the spell and filled in the gaps. She shifted away from his touch, understanding what brought him back after closing. She'd found it, tossed carelessly into the corner of a booth—his black leather jacket. Soft as butter, it held his scent. Subtle, masculine, and just enough to stir her blood as she'd carried the garment into the kitchen for safekeeping.

Where, with no one to witness the act, she'd pressed her nose to the lapel and inhaled him.

Her cheeks grew warm. She shot him a look from under her lashes. "Wait here, I'll be right back."

She felt his eyes on her as she returned from the kitchen, and crossed to stand before him, his coat in hand. Felt them still as, without asking how she'd figured out what he needed, he removed the garment from her grasp and slid his arms into it. Finally, she lifted her gaze to his.

"I like your place, Isabeau." His tone hinted he liked more than her place. And even though everything inside her screamed to get him out of there, it was impossible not to get a little bit lost. He was so inherently sexual that any woman would have to be blind not to be affected by his virile good looks and confidence. "Maybe I'll see you again sometime."

She watched him go, pressing her fingers against her pounding temples. As the door shut behind him, the pain eased, the noise in her skull dropped to a more tolerable level. Five minutes passed before she dared draw a deep breath for fear his scent lingered. She didn't need further reminders of his visit. The music that pulsed through her system was reminder enough.

He thought he would see her again, but she knew he wouldn't. Not because the chances of him returning were too slender, or even because a man like him could never truly be interested in a woman like her.

Because she'd been waiting thirteen years

for someone to truly see her.

So far, no one had.

****

Isabeau knew it was him before he cleared the second set of doors. Her stomach fluttered. An overture sprang to life behind her eyes. She stepped out of the kitchen as the inner doors swung in and *he* stepped through. Noah Clark—the front man for the famed rock band Black Phoenix. Who ten years previously topped the charts, dominated the industry.

Until the sudden, tragic death of their drummer.

Noah Clark, who two nights prior walked into her bar and tipped her world on its axis. Not because he was famous, or had been in his day. Because he made her yearn for more. To be whole, complete.

Something she could never be.

She wanted to retreat. Instead she stepped behind the bar, grateful for its barrier between them. No matter how minor. "I don't suppose it would do any good to tell you the bar isn't open yet?"

The slap of plastic against wood echoed like a shot in the large room.

"You lied to me," he accused, his accent made stronger by his irritation.

"I didn't."

"You haven't even looked at what I

brought you. Why don't you take a look?"

"No, thank you."

He plucked something off the bar, waved it across her field of vision.

A compact disc.

One of hers.

"You told me you didn't play."

Her insides clenched. She kept her face blank even as her nerves scrambled. "I don't play. Not anymore."

"Why?" He sounded so bewildered she nearly answered him. But what exactly did he question? Why she didn't play anymore, or why she'd lied to him? Neither answer was simple or painless enough to share with him.

Silence stretched between them. He finally broke it. "Why, Isa?

His voice was low, intimate, and set off a stirring deep inside. "Don't call me that."

"What would you have me call you?"

"Izzy."

He stared at her, his gaze probing, pinning her in place. She couldn't look away. He wouldn't look away.

"No," he said with a shake of his head. "Izzy doesn't fit you."

Nothing fit. Not even her skin. Not since the accident.

Desperate to escape his penetrating stare, she looked down at the bar, at the three CDs stacked before her.

"You're missing one," she said absently. "The most important one." Unable to keep from touching them, she lined them up in chronological order. "People lie all the time, Noah, about any number of things. I would think being a recognized musician you would know that better than most."

"So you do know me."

"I know your name, what you do for a living. I don't presume to know who you are."

"You would be the first," he mumbled under his breath.

She shifted her attention from the bar to his cool green eyes.

He flashed her a knock-out smile. "How did this conversation turn to me? We were talking about you."

"We were?" She pretended nonchalance as panic reigned. Two days had passed since he'd first stepped through those doors, two days during which she'd almost managed to write off her reaction to him as a silly adolescent crush. Except that the music playing in her head remained so loud she couldn't sleep, and the electric charge in the air was real, not the by-product of decade-old girlish fantasies.

He should have forgotten her the moment he'd stepped into the night. She was nothing special or memorable. Just a girl in a bar. Only, he hadn't forgotten her. And he looked at her as if she *was* special.

She'd waited her whole life for a man to look at her like that.

"Isabeau?"

God, this was hard. She wanted to be seen, held, to be special to someone. Without the music.

"Why don't you play anymore? Didn't you enjoy it?"

"It was like oxygen." The admission slipped out unintentionally and all too heartfelt, exposing more of herself than she meant to expose. Already he could see far more in her than anybody else. If she wasn't careful, he would see the truth.

He locked his gaze with hers and everything inside of her softened, reacted to him in ways she'd never before experienced.

"Oxygen. I like that. I know that. Not many people do."

She fought the flash of understanding, of connection she felt with him. She couldn't soften. She couldn't change the past, and she refused to relive it. Not even for a man who would understand her on a level no one before him ever had. "The girl you're looking for no longer exists."

"What girl am I looking for?"

"The one who lived to create music. She died thirteen years ago. The woman who's left, she's just a bartender."

"I don't believe that."

11

She stacked the compact discs and pushed them a few inches away from her. "It's true. I no longer make music. I leave that to others."

"You can't ignore it, you know." He sounded as if he spoke from experience.

"No?"

"Music is everywhere. It's inside you, you can't ignore that."

The comment hit her like a slap in the face. She covered her mouth to keep a startled cry from breaking free. Pain, sharp and blinding, knotted her stomach.

She should have known, guessed it when he strolled into her bar carrying her music. Her pain-filled past could be uncovered with a few keystrokes in any Internet café. Her entire life spelled out in black and white, and a bit of it in all too vivid color. He'd seen it all—the truths as well as the lies.

Old fears and uncertainties returned. Her hand dropped away from her mouth to fist against her thigh. "Tell me something, Noah. Is it morbid curiosity that brings you in today, or something else?"

"I don't know what you're talking about."

Of course he did. Not for a minute did she believe the confusion that flashed across his face. "I don't play anymore because the music is no longer inside of me. It's gone." Except it wasn't. It cantered through her skull like a

12

caged beast finally set loose. "Now if you want to know anything else, you'll have to go back to your source."

"What if I want the truth? Will I find it there as well?"

He couldn't possibly know of the lie that burned her tongue like acid. "Since when does anyone care about the truth?"

"I care."

She shook her head in denial. He sounded so sincere she almost believed him. Almost.

"Leave." She paused at the emotion in her voice. "There's nothing for you here."

He hesitated.

Desperate to have him gone, to quiet her painful memories as much as her mind, she shoved the compact discs across the bar top. The stack tipped, one slid off the other and spread out as she'd arranged them a few moments ago. Three unblemished, cherubic faces looked back at her, reminding her of how much she'd lost. "Please go."

Noah plucked the CDs from the bar without taking his eyes off her face. He didn't understand that she clung to the slippery edge of control. But then, he didn't need to understand. He needed to leave her.

Then he did. Just like she'd wanted.

So why did she suddenly feel empty?

13

CHAPTER TWO

The place hadn't changed at all. It remained as memory recalled. But the woman behind the polished, chestnut bar was better.

Noah Clark slid into the booth in the far corner, his gaze drinking in the dark-haired beauty. Her hair was parted in the center and framed her face in layers that started at her chin and continued to the base of her shoulder blades. Sometime over the past two months she'd cut it, for he remembered it longer, all one length and hanging to her waist. Although he couldn't see them from this distance, he knew her eyes were the most remarkable shade of gray-blue—pale and misty. Set in a complexion that appeared darker now, kissed by the summer sun.

She wore faded jeans that hugged her slender hips. A black tank top revealed arms sleekly muscled in a feminine way that told him she was stronger than she looked. Her legs were surprisingly long for a woman her height. His gaze lowered, lingered on her legs before arriving on her boots—a pair of those high-heeled, pointy-toed boots that made him wonder

14

how she kept her balance as she approached a nearby table with a tray full of drinks.

While classic rock blared from the speakers, he took a moment to study the profile that looked both soft and angular. She wasn't beautiful in the traditional sense, but compelling. She had a way of looking at a person as she spoke with them, like they were the most important person in the room. And a wide, friendly smile that could steal a man's breath. He'd been on the receiving end of it once, just once, and he'd yet to fully recover.

Keeping his eyes on her, he settled more comfortably into the booth and thought about what brought him back to her bar on a Monday night, after midnight. Ten weeks before, a meeting with the record company already set and nowhere to begin work on their demo, he'd gone in search of somewhere to record. The studio had to be small, private, and reputable, somewhere outside of the mainstream recording industry, where they could make their own hours and work at their own pace.

He'd had his mind made up, his eyes set on a private studio near Sacramento when he'd come to New York. The man who ran the studio in Long Island City was a friend of the band's manager, Tony, so heading back home without seeing this final place hadn't seemed right. Still, even with the scheduling problem that would need to be worked out, California felt like the best fit.

Until the night he'd decided he didn't want to spend his birthday alone in some strange city. The night he allowed the flashing neon to lure him through the doors into Izzy's and he'd set eyes on its namesake.

She'd stolen his breath. One look and every nerve ending in his body stood at attention. One smile and he'd been lost.

Right then, that first night, he'd made the decision and started the ball rolling. Later he asked Pete Knowles, the man whose studio he'd signed on with, if he knew the woman who owned the bar down the street and learned her name.

Isabeau Montgomery.

He went back, to the bar and the woman who irresistibly drew him. Only to discover that what she felt for him was anything but pleasant. So here he sat, ten weeks later, living out of a hotel because of a woman he couldn't forget. A woman he felt a connection to despite the fact that, by all accounts, she couldn't stand the sight of him.

Noah sighed. He tracked Isabeau's smooth glide across the hardwood floor. On her tray remained one lone bottle—his preferred brand. He didn't want the lager, but kept that information to himself.

"Isabeau." A jolt of electricity arced through him. Stronger than he recalled. "You look well. You cut your hair."

Surprise flickered across her features. The corner of her mouth began to tip up, then stopped. Her gaze, carefully cleared of emotion, moved slowly over his face, down his body. Heat flared, followed the path of her eyes. Desire curled in his stomach.

"I did," she verified, her voice pitched to be heard over the sudden burst of laughter from a raucous group at the far end of the bar.

He shot the group a cursory glance. "Busy place tonight."

"They're celebrating a job promotion. Although that group never needs much of an excuse."

One glance told him as much. "No?"

"They've convinced me to keep the kitchen open, so if you're hungry let me know."

"I didn't know you offered food."

"Just soup and sandwiches. Everything is homemade by me using only organic ingredients."

"Not sprouts and tofu?"

"Who doesn't enjoy a good bean sprout sandwich with their lager?"

He shuddered; caught the barest hint of a smile before she controlled it.

"Organic as in no chemicals used in the growing process," she corrected. "Today's special is roast beef on rye. Having food available helps to keep the level of inebriation under control."

17

As if on cue, the sound of a glass shattering carried to them. It was immediately followed by more laughter. Isabeau sighed. "Well, usually."

She turned her head, her gaze settling on a waitress carefully picking up the larger shards of glass. "I apologize if they're disturbing you. They'll be gone soon."

The group didn't look eager to leave. "How can you be sure?"

"I called their wives and girlfriends."

"Smart."

"Yeah, well they're a bit too grab happy for me tonight. It's time for them to go."

The muscle in his jaw began to tic double time. He leveled his gaze on the men across the room, while the urge to teach them some manners flared.

"I should get back to it. Let me know if you need anything else."

Fighting the foreign compulsion, he could only nod as she turned and walked away. A knot settled in his gut as she skirted the tables, taking a wider than normal path around the noisy group. He scrubbed his hand over the back of his neck, eased out a breath.

There'd been no note with the package she'd sent him, no way of knowing why she'd taken the time to mail him the compact disc. There'd been no return address either. Only the disc itself told him the identity of the sender— her disc, the one he'd been missing.

He'd thought of her often in the weeks since receiving the gift. Why did she send it? What did it mean? He wondered again tonight, as he watched her, unable to gauge her reaction to his sudden reappearance in her bar.

"Nick said I'd find you here. It seemed out of character enough that I had to check it out."

Noah shifted his attention to the man leaning against the wall at his right, hands tucked in the front pockets of his jeans. Dominic Price was tall and wiry, with wavy black hair that hung just past his shoulders and a face women swooned over. Today that face was lined with fatigue. The wall appeared to be the only thing keeping him upright.

"Dom, how was your flight? Did you get settled into the hotel yet?"

"Yeah." Dominic eased into the booth with a sigh. "This one's better than the last hotel we lived out of. At least the art is recognizable." He paused, but only briefly. "You're not falling back on old habits, are you?"

"Of course not."

Dom's gaze settled on the bottle of lager. "You're certain about that?"

Before Noah could reply, a shadow fell across their booth.

Isabeau slid a napkin before Dominic. "What can I get you?"

"I don't suppose you have any tea?"

"Sorry."

19

"How about bottled water and something for a headache?"

"Certainly." Her fingers dipped into her back pocket and removed a thin object about the size and shape of a credit card. Her thumb moved across the top of a tiny remote unit, and the speakers above their table and along the back wall went silent. "Is that a little better?"

"Yes, luv, thank you."

"You're welcome," she replied, gifting Dominic with the smile she'd denied Noah.

Noah clenched his jaw. "Isabeau Montgomery, my band mate and bassist Dominic Price."

"Nice to meet you," she said as she returned the remote to her back pocket. "I'll be right back with your water and ibuprophen."

Noah watched her departure, fascinated by her smooth stride in those skinny heels and the way her small, shapely bottom swayed. His gaze stayed with her as she pulled a bottle of water from the cooler, snagged something from beneath the bar, and started back.

She settled the water onto the napkin before Dominic, tore open a small white packet, and dropped the contents into his upturned hand.

Dom tipped the bottle to his lips and swallowed the pain reliever. "Your name's Isabeau, as in Izzy? Is this your pub?"

"It is."

"I like it."

"Thank you."

"You have unique features. What nationality are you?"

A brief shadow crossed her face. Her eyes changed color, from pale blue to dusky gray. "My father was Mohican."

"Your mum, I bet she has blue eyes."

"Yes. She was a blue-eyed blonde."

"Ah. Noah fancies blondes."

The light went out of her eyes the moment her attention turned to him. It appeared the passage of time had not lessoned her animosity toward him. He'd read too much into her sending that disc to him, had hung his hope on the idea that she'd meant the gesture as an offering of peace between them. Hope died, replaced by disappointment.

Her gaze slid to the still full bottle at his right hand. She picked it up, gesturing with it as she spoke. "Is something wrong with your beer?"

"I guess I'm not in the mood."

"Can I get you something else?"

Because he was tempted to reach out and smooth his fingers across the white-knuckled grip she had on the lager bottle, Noah balled his hands in his lap. She eased back a step, obviously anxious to leave.

"I'm okay for now."

The moment she was out of earshot, Noah

turned to Dom. "What was that about?"

"She does have unique features."

That's not what was going on and they both knew it.

"She spoke of both her parents in past tense."

He'd noticed. Noah straightened in his seat, frowned at his closest friend. "What's on your mind, Dom?"

Dominic turned and gave him a level-eyed look. "This isn't like you."

"What?"

"It explains a lot, though."

"What the bloody hell are you talking about?"

His eyes flicked from Noah to a retreating Isabeau, back to Noah. "She's why we're here."

"We're here to make a demo," Noah replied tightly.

"Yeah? How long have you been sitting in her bar?"

Noah didn't like the awareness in Dom's eyes. "A bit."

"This isn't like you," Dominic repeated. "You're usually not one for self-deception."

They fell into an uncomfortable silence. A silence Dominic broke. "We're supposed to be starting over. The guys and I trusted you to choose the best place for that to happen."

Noah let out a controlled breath, and pushed his fingers through his hair. Anywhere else and he would be on his feet, pacing. "I did, damn it. This place has everything we're looking for."

"Including a woman close by who happened to catch your eye."

"This studio is quality. It has a fantastic reputation and is private."

"Yeah," Dom agreed, setting his elbows on the table and leaning forward. "But let me take a wild stab. It wasn't the only one."

"No, it wasn't the only one."

Dominic began to swear, slowly, steadily.

"It's only temporary. Before you know it we'll be back in California."

Not a fan of California, the information didn't make Dom happier. "Fantastic."

"At least you won't have to live out of a hotel room. You can have my guest bedroom."

"I wouldn't be living out of a hotel right now, if you hadn't decided to let your dick think for you."

Noah set his teeth. "Do you actually believe that I would do anything to jeopardize our future?"

Dom closed his eyes and pinched the bridge of his nose. "I don't think you would consciously make a decision that would jeopardize our future."

"What's that supposed to mean?"

"Women have a way of fucking up a man's decision making."

Exhaustion pulling at him, Noah sighed. "Becca," he said. It was all he needed to say, the bleakness in Dominic's eyes said everything. Rebecca Dahlman, the woman Dom hadn't managed to move beyond even after all the time they'd been apart.

Dominic slid out of the booth. "I hope you're right about this place, Noah. I'd hate to think I hopped the Atlantic for nothing."

So did he.

"Do me a favor," Dom continued. "Don't bring this up again anytime soon. I'm going to pretend we didn't have this conversation." He turned his back, mumbled under his breath. "Maybe after a few days sleep, I'll see the humor in this."

As Dom walked away, Noah looked to the ebony-haired beauty behind the bar. He hoped he hadn't made the biggest mistake of his career.

****

Isabeau leaned against the bar, eyes closed, absorbing the welcome silence. The total, absolute silence...that wasn't. For the first time since she'd reopened the bar, no music played while she prepared for the lunch crowd. It would have been too much to handle what with the music in her head already at an earsplitting level.

The relentless, unavoidable rhythm kept

her from getting sleep the night before. Today, it threatened to sour her mood. Nothing helped, not her morning run, a hot shower, or even the tapping of her fingers against the polished chestnut bar.

The source of her pain was obvious. The return of the man brought the return of the music. It ebbed and swelled, adagio to allegro, pianissimo to fortissimo. It wouldn't stop and it was not to be ignored. But ignore it she must. She had no choice.

She raised her hand, pinched the bridge of her nose and pleaded with whatever God listened to make it stop.

The door squeaked as it swung inward. The echo of boots upon the wood floor drew nearer then stopped.

What had she done to deserve this?

"I'm not going to say it," she mumbled before gaining the strength to open her eyes and focus on him. "You never listen anyway."

His mouth curved into an irresistibly devastating grin, and everything female in her stood at attention. He strode the rest of the way to the bar, his every movement fluid and easy. Confident. Naturally sexy. His lean, rangy body was clad in snug jeans and a black tee. Jeans so worn and faded that only their seams gave hint to their original color. Jeans that rode low on his hips, cupping his sex as tightly as a hand.

Her body reacted before she could steel

25

herself against it. A burst of heat snapped along her nerves. Her pulse raced. She was staring. She knew she was staring but she couldn't stop.

He moved, sliding onto the stool directly before her, so that suddenly their gazes locked. She waited for him to speak, to say something to break this spell that had come over her. He remained silent, sitting there watching her with those eyes that seemed to see right into her.

As he leaned forward, casually resting his forearms atop the bar, she took a step backward. Already a warm, masculine scent, which she recognized as uniquely his, swirled around her, muddling her thinking.

"Would you—" Was that her voice, all husky and breathless? She cleared her throat. "Would you like something to drink?"

"Water."

He did things to her, made her wish for things that could never be. Whether it was his effect on her body or his effect on her head, his sudden reappearance in her life was not going to be easy for her to handle. She would have to come up with a way to discourage these impromptu visits of his. Maybe discourage all visits altogether. Let him find a different place to unwind.

"Headache?"

She raised her eyebrow as she placed his water before him.

"You keep rubbing your temple."

She did? "Is Dominic feeling better today?"

"I haven't seen him. We're meeting at the studio up the street in about an hour."

"You're in town to record?"

"Noon to midnight, six days a week for the next few months."

"It's a nice studio. Pete's a good guy." Why was she making conversation when she was supposed to be working on a plan to get him to leave?

Mentally rolling her eyes at herself, she started to turn away when he held up something in his hand. A compact disc, her name in bold script across the front.

He placed the disc atop the bar. "You sent this to me."

"I did."

"Why?"

She didn't know why, hadn't taken the time to think about the reasons behind her actions. Just slipped the case from her collection upstairs, boxed it up, and sent it to his manager. She was surprised that he'd received it.

"You didn't have it" was the best she could come up with.

A look of contemplation crossed his face. "And I needed it because...it's the most important one?"

"It's hard to find. They didn't make many of that one."

He nodded as if he accepted her simple answer, even though she was certain he didn't. "Thank you."

"You're welcome."

He studied her for a moment before his gaze dropped, came to rest on her hands so near his atop the bar. She held her breath, waiting for him to comment or question, as people were inclined to do when they first noticed her scars or two missing fingernails. He did neither. His hand shifted closer, settled next to hers. His thumb lifted, ran along the pale, jagged line of the largest of her scars.

The trembling started in her legs and worked up her body. She recoiled, tucking her hand into her front pocket and out of view.

He frowned. "You look tired today, Isabeau."

"I didn't sleep well last night."

"Do you ever take a day off?"

With the abrupt change of subject, she was able to regain a bit of her composure. "Yes."

"What do you do on your day off?"

"What do I do?"

"Do you go to the movies? Do you go shopping?" His lips curved when she wrinkled her brow in confusion. "It's not a trick question, Isa. What do you do to relax?"

"Why do you ask?"

"I'm curious."

"I like to go to Astoria, to the

restaurants," she confided.

He cocked his head and regarded her for a moment. "Isn't that a lot like being here?"

"No. I don't have to cook the meals there, just enjoy them."

"You never feel like getting away from the noise and the crowds?"

"I like the noise."

"Do you?" he asked quietly, his voice edged with disbelief. "Or do you hate silence?"

The room was suddenly devoid of air. She couldn't breathe. She could barely speak. "Why would I?"

"That's a good question."

She stood motionless, her palms damp, muscles stiff as cardboard. She let out a pent-up breath, praying the answer to that question was something he never discovered.

Immediately on the defensive, she asked tightly, "Why are you here? It's not for the water, and I doubt it's for the company."

"Why wouldn't it be for the company?"

She swallowed and looked at him. "I can't be the person you want me to be."

"I prefer people to be who they are."

She wanted to believe him, longed to lose herself in his eyes and forget everything else. For once in the thirteen years since her mother's death, to just be. No more lies. No more secrets.

She couldn't. She'd lived the lie for far too long to go back now. Her entire life was built

29

upon it.

"I can't be the person you want me to be," she repeated.

"Isabeau—"

"There's nothing for you here."

He ran his gaze over her features. "You said that once before. I didn't agree with you then, and I don't agree with you now, but I can take a hint."

He stood, picked up the disc and started for the door. When he stopped and looked back at her, his voice was lowered. "You know, I'm not asking for much, just the chance to get to know you. I wish you'd give me that chance."

He stood before the doors, waiting. Hand clenched against her thigh, Isabeau struggled to absorb his admission. By the time she found her voice, he was gone.

CHAPTER THREE

"Look, Hannah, I don't like to be rude, but this is the second time this week that you've failed to make delivery." Isabeau tightened her grip on the phone as the infuriating woman continued to argue with her. "No, I did not cancel my order. Of course I'm sure."

"What's your name again?" the nasal voice on the other end of the line asked.

"Isabeau Montgomery," she supplied for the third time. She did her best not to scream aloud in frustration. "My customer number is three seven five, five four six."

"One moment."

Isabeau pushed her fingers through her hair and held onto control. She cringed as the teeth-grinding din of bad music, the signal that she'd been placed on hold, blasted from the earpiece. After propping the phone against her shoulder to keep from going deaf, she waited.

The digital clock behind the bar read six p.m., and already she wanted to crawl beneath the covers and put this day behind her. Who knew facing the man who made her insides quake would be the highlight of her day? Sure, he was a fine male specimen, but the pounding in her skull and the war of emotions? She could have gone all day without those things. Follow that up with her best waitress skipping out on work to run off to Vegas and get married...Isabeau had a full-blown migraine.

And that was before she realized her organic vegetable order hadn't been delivered.

Now it was happy hour. At least for her patrons. The music from the telephone competing with the game highlights on the high definition television in the corner, felt more like hell to her. She shook her head just as Clint caught her eye and smiled. Tall and slender, his dark hair and eyes held more than one woman's attention as he manned the bar with his usual aplomb. Early, as usual, his arrival meant she caught her first break of the day. She'd used it to call about her missing vegetables. What she'd expected to be a quick telephone call was turning into a major pain.

As the song on the handset turned from sappy and overly emotional to a poorly mixed remake, she groaned aloud. She closed her eyes against the pounding ache in her temple and absently rubbed warmth back into her left hand. Although she'd regained total use of her hand after the accident, the extent of the damage left her circulation poor. Which meant that even on days like today, when it was warm enough outside she had to bump the air conditioner to a lower setting, her fingers were chilled.

Except, she recalled as she followed the raised scar with her fingertips, when Noah traced his thumb along the back of her hand. She hadn't felt chilled then, but a shock of warmth that stole her breath. All she had to do was recall that feeling and every muscle in her body tensed, including some that she preferred not respond to Noah that way. Rocked by unbidden images—images of her and Noah together, of his large, warm hands tracing other parts of her anatomy—she wondered...

Would he invoke that spark of electricity everywhere he touched her?

"What's that?" she asked into the phone, realizing she had missed something during that little jog her mind had taken. Isabeau turned her irritation on the woman on the other end of the line. "Look, I need that delivery."

"Ma'am, we show you cancelled those deliveries."

"No, I didn't."

"Ma'am—"

"Listen to me," she interrupted. She'd had enough of this woman's impertinence. "I did not cancel any orders. I don't know who you're taking these cancellations from, but I assure you, it is not me."

"What are you insinuating?"

"I'm not insinuating anything. I'm telling you that someone in your company is not doing their job. I believe it is your company's policy that all orders and cancellations be verified with an account number. Since I'm the only person who has that number, and I am not canceling my orders, you have a problem."

"How would you like me to correct the problem?"

Isabeau took a deep breath. She chose to ignore the woman's condescending tone. "I need my delivery. I'd appreciate it if you could get that rescheduled for me as soon as possible."

"Of course, ma'am."

"Thank you." More irritated than when she'd dialed the number, she hung up the phone with a thud.

"Rough day?" a deep masculine voice asked from behind her.

She spun around and bounced off a solid male chest. Warm hands gripped her elbows to steady her. She pulled back enough to look up, met ocean blue eyes. Dominic Price.

"You all right, luv?"

She gave the darkly handsome Dominic a smile, relieved that he was the one Pete had sent to pick up the studio's supper order and not the man who'd occupied her thoughts far too much since his mid-morning visit.

"Yes," she assured him as she stepped out of his grasp. "Sorry about that."

"No worries. You're having problems with deliveries?"

His accent was much stronger than Noah's, something she hadn't noticed last night. "Yes."

"Did you get it straightened out?"

"It's more likely that I guaranteed I'll never receive another delivery from them."

He eased onto the stool nearest him as she slipped behind the bar. "Was it worth it?"

"Definitely."

His grin was irresistible. She imagined he didn't long for female companionship. Even she wasn't unaffected by his charm and good looks, and she wasn't one to succumb to a man's magnetism.

"I'm afraid your order won't be ready for a few more minutes. Can I get you something to drink while you wait?"

"Whatever you have on tap."

She retrieved a frosted mug from the cooler below the bar and filled it, leaving it on the drip tray before sliding around Clint and pulling a long neck out of the beer cooler. Topping off the mug, she turned and placed it before Dominic—the long neck went to the customer on his left.

"Thanks, Izzy," the man mumbled as she swapped the full bottle for the empty before him.

"You're welcome, Bill."

She turned back to Dominic. "How's the recording going?"

"How do you know we're here recording?"

"Noah told me."

"Ah."

"What's that mean?"

A smile played at the corners of his mouth. His eyes sparkled with something she couldn't name. "Not much happening yet, we're still settling in. You know the owner, Pete?"

She stepped aside as Clint reached over her head for a wine glass. "I do."

"He seems like a decent bloke."

"He is. He's also good at what he does. He's got a good ear."

He nodded, watching her thoughtfully. "You say that as if you speak from experience. How long have you known him?"

Most of my life. "Years."

"How long have you had this place?"

"I reopened it four years ago after a substantial renovation." She continued when he quirked his eyebrow. "It's a long, boring story. The bar is an inheritance I didn't initially want."

"Was part of the remodel the addition of food?"

"It was."

He took in the room and its occupants before returning his gaze to her. "Is it always this busy? If not, that would explain the harried look you're wearing."

"I'm short-staffed tonight. I had a

waitress quit today."

"Why?"

"She got tired of the customers asking so many questions."

He grinned. "You going to replace her?"

"Why? Are you looking for a second job?"

Dominic's grin widened as he continued to watch her. He held her gaze for so long that, despite his easygoing words, a spark of apprehension raced down her spine. "I'll go get your supper."

She returned a few minutes later and placed the bagged order atop the bar.

He stood and reached for his wallet. "You're okay, Isabeau."

"I'm glad I passed the test."

He didn't react to the hint of sarcasm in her voice, just continued to smile at her like a child with a secret. "What do I owe you for the drink?"

He hadn't touched his drink. "It's on the house."

His smile remained in place as he returned his wallet to his pocket and lifted the bag off the bar. "I guess I'll see you again."

Unable to shake the feeling that there was more behind his visit than supper, she replied dryly, "I guess you will."

****

Noah stood with his hand on the door and

thought better of entering. Inside the bar, music played—David Bowie singing about changes. It was a song he could relate to.

For two weeks, he'd come here after putting in a twelve-hour day at the studio. Two long weeks of watching, aching. And for what? Isabeau Montgomery wanted nothing to do with him. She had him completely at her feet, and she didn't even know it. Hell, had she known, she most likely wouldn't care.

Noah closed his eyes, wondering why he bothered. She'd barely spoken to him after the day he accused her of fearing silence. He lost track of how many times he'd berated himself on the subject. Yet it remained on his mind since that day. Even now, as the song drifted through the double set of doors, he wondered why she chose to hide from the music in a place full of it. If only she could see what was so clear to him. That denying who you are is nothing more than wasted time. Time you never got back.

No matter how much you wished otherwise.

Releasing the door handle, he considered his options. The prospect of leaving, of spending the evening alone in his hotel room, didn't tempt. Even when weighed against spending the evening alone in a bar, wanting something he couldn't have.

"Damn it!" He scrubbed a hand over his face. He needed to get over his obsession with her. He didn't even want a lager, he wanted to see Isabeau—smell her, relish the way his blood moved a bit quicker through his veins when she was near.

He let out a long, slow breath. He should have invited Dominic along. At least then he had a chance in hell of talking to her. Isa liked Dom, enjoyed his company, enjoyed herself when he was around. It was a given that, had he invited Dom, her smile as he stepped through this door would show bright and genuine.

For Dominic.

Not for him.

Laughter drifted out the door. *Isabeau.* His mind made up, Noah reached for the handle. He couldn't walk away. Not when there remained the slightest possibility she may turn that joy upon him. Tonight, if the stars aligned right, she would laugh with him the way she did her other patrons. He believed that. Just as he believed she would eventually forgive him for whatever the hell he'd done to her. She had to.

Even for a Tuesday night, there wasn't much of a crowd. Besides Isa, Adam the bouncer, and himself, there were only two other people in the place. Both sat at the far end of the bar, watching Isabeau with rapturous looks on their face while she chatted on, totally oblivious to her appeal.

Tonight she wore her usual hip-hugging jeans. Her shirt, a pale blue that matched her

39

eyes, had tiny straps that held it up. Made of fabric that clung to her like second skin, it emphasized the perfect shape of her breasts and her slender waist before ending at her belt. As she reached above her head and slid glasses into the rack, her shirt inched up revealing a flash of smooth, golden skin.

For a moment, he forgot to breathe.

Because of a minuscule glimpse of her stomach. Shit. How ridiculous was that? Certain his face now mirrored the other men's, Noah sat on the barstool closest to the door. "Pretty quiet in here tonight."

"It is." She held up a bottle of his preferred brand, opened it and placed it before him when he nodded. "I've already sent everyone else home. Well, except for Adam, his wife's expecting, so I told him he could work through his shift."

"That's very generous of you."

She shrugged. "You're here earlier than normal. Slow day at the studio?"

"We hit a small snag and decided to call it off early."

"I closed the kitchen already, but if you're hungry I could warm something up."

"I don't require special treatment, you know."

"All my customers receive the same treatment," she assured him, then settled her hands atop the bar.

Settled in, instead of running off. Interesting.

He looked her over, noting her relaxed posture. He took in her beautiful face, her golden skin, and the way her fingers danced atop the polished chestnut. She wore no rings, no jewelry of any kind. Why hadn't he seen that before? She had nice hands, slender fingers with eight unpainted, well-manicured nails. The last two nails on her left hand were missing, something that wasn't readily apparent unless you looked closely, as he did now. Scars littered the back of the hand, a large one that extended from the base of her ring finger to her wrist, and a multitude of others of varied size. Too many to count, he was shocked to realize.

He had read a few of the articles about the accident that claimed her mother and ended her career. Every one mentioned a debilitating injury—one severe enough she would most likely never recover full mobility of her left hand. If the scars were any indication, the reports about her injury weren't that far off. With one exception—she had regained the use of her hand—enough that she could still play the piano.

Isabeau stepped back. Noah caught the flash of uncertainty in her eyes as she tucked her hands into the back pockets of her jeans.

"Let me know if you decide you want something to eat," she said, then glanced over her shoulder to the customers at the other end of the bar. Her cheeks were colorless, her eyes a pale gray. "I need to see if they need anything."

He reached out, slid his hand across the top of the bar as if he could keep her from walking away. "Isabeau."

Her gaze dropped to his hand before rising to meet his. "Yes?"

He wasn't ready for their conversation to end. Not after her silence the past few weeks. Hoping to keep her from running off, he said, "We didn't place our supper order with you tonight."

"No, you didn't."

He curled his hand around the lager bottle. "What did I miss?"

"Creamy garlic potato soup."

"And the sandwich special?"

"Izzy's Secret."

Did he dare ask?

"Marinated chicken breast on a whole wheat bun," she supplied.

Okay, he had to know. "What's the secret?"

"The marinade. Don't order it unless you like it hot."

"As a matter of fact, I do like it hot."

"You do."

"Yes."

A small smile tickled the corners of her lips. "Are we still talking food?"

"You are. I'm not."

She stared at him for a long, silent beat. Then, the most amazing thing happened—she smiled at him. Her eyes sparked as she broke into an open, friendly smile that ended in a laugh. And in the way you only read about in one of those sappy paperback novels, his world shifted.

He stared back at her, a little stunned. "So you can do it."

"What?"

"Smile at me."

"I smile at you."

"No, Isabeau, you don't."

Her smile faded. A curious mix of emotions flashed in her eyes. She lifted her chin a fraction, opened her mouth as if to comment, and was interrupted by a drunken bellow from the other end of the bar.

"Izzzzy," it slurred, drawing out the name in a way that set his back up. "Another!"

She closed her eyes and sighed. "It's time to go, Tommy," she replied, her voice pitched so that he could hear her. "You've had enough for tonight."

"Another," the man growled as he slammed his empty glass down with enough force the resulting reverberation overpowered the music.

Isabeau drew herself up to her full height, summoning a smile that didn't come close to reaching her eyes. "Excuse me, Noah. I've got to take care of this."

Spine straight and looking six feet tall, which she was nowhere near even with the three-inch heels she habitually wore, Isa turned and crossed to stand before Tommy. She removed his empty glass and placed it in the tiny sink before her with one hand, while the other ran a cloth across the bar.

"Whiskey," Tommy commanded. The menace in his voice matched the gleam in his eyes.

Noah glanced over his shoulder, relieved to find Adam no longer sat comfortably by the door, but stood, his focus on the drunken patron.

"No," Isa replied to the demand for more whiskey. "I can either get you coffee, or a cab. Which will it be?"

Hands clenched, the man surged to his feet. He was tall, taller than Noah's own six-one, and twice as wide as Isabeau, but she didn't seem to notice. She kept her eyes leveled with his as temper caused his body to vibrate. "You've had enough, Tommy."

"Who are you to tell me when I've had enough?"

"I'm the woman who owns this bar."

Anger flashed in his eyes. His jaw ticced. "Bitch."

She held her ground. A few seconds passed, then a few more.

The drunk staggered off in the direction of the restrooms.

Muscles coiled, Noah kept his eyes on the man until he disappeared from view. Realizing he held a crushing grip on the bottle, he forced his fingers to relax.

"Sorry about that, Larry," Isabeau said to the man remaining.

"Tommy never could hold his liquor."

"I know," she replied softly, then picked up her rag, rounded the bar and began to wipe down the tables.

Larry stood, tossed a few bills on the bar and headed for the door.

Noah pinched the bridge of his nose and closed his eyes. He forced tense muscles to relax. The song on the stereo changed, smoothly transitioning from one chart topper to the next. As the first few chords rang out, the sound of breaking glass split the air.

Noah jerked around in time to see Tommy vise his hand around Isabeau's upper arm and slam her against the wall. He pressed his body intimately against hers, muttering something meant for only her ears. His hand tightened on her upper arm. Pain flashed across Isa's face, yet she made no sound.

Noah came off the stool like a shot. Halfway to her, Adam stopped him.

"I'll take care of this," the bouncer growled. He crossed the room faster than Noah thought the big man capable. They were about the same size, Adam and Tommy, but the bouncer had the advantage of being sober. He grabbed the arm not holding Isabeau and twisted it behind Tommy's back. "Let her go."

Tommy released Isabeau. Adam released Tommy. He stepped in front of the big man, using his body as a shield. "Izzy, you okay?"

Adam never took his eyes off Tommy, but Noah did. Isabeau remained against the wall, her right hand wrapped protectively around her left upper arm. Her voice was even and controlled as she replied, "Yes. I'm fine."

Her eyes told a different story.

"You want me to have him hauled in?"

"No. Just, on your way out, see that he gets into a cab."

Adam checked over his shoulder. "Izzy?"

"It's okay. I'm going to call it a night. Turn the lock for me, will you, Adam?"

"Sure, Izzy, no problem."

Adam might not have a problem leaving Isabeau alone, but Noah did. Was he the only one who could tell her calm was only an illusion?

"Consider yourself lucky, Tommy," Adam continued, guiding the man toward the door with a hand to the back of his neck. "Left up to me, I'd have you strung up by your balls."

Tommy continued walking toward the door without comment. Adam stopped, motioned to Noah, "You, too, let's go."

Isabeau leaned against the wall, staring without focus at the far side of the room. Her color was bad. Her breathing shallow.

Noah shook his head. "I don't think—"

"No thinking. It's closing time. Let's go."

"It's all right, Adam," Isabeau assured the big man. "Noah can stay. I need to talk to him."

Noah waited until they were alone. "Isabeau, are you really okay?"

She nodded.

"Why do I get the feeling that you're not being completely honest with me?"

"I'm fine." She hugged herself and closed her eyes. Her right hand moved against her left arm, her long, slender fingers massaging. "I just need a minute."

"Can I do something?"

"No."

Noah shoved his hands in his pockets and gave her the time she asked for. He felt helpless, and he didn't like it one damn bit. The urge to envelop her in his arms was powerful. Isabeau didn't like him to touch her, and if she didn't like him to touch her, she definitely wouldn't want him to hold her.

Minutes passed before she whispered, "I never saw him coming."

"Neither did I," he replied tightly. He should have kept an eye on Tommy. He knew the guy was angry and drunk—a bad combination under any circumstance. "How bad did he hurt you?"

Her eyes opened. The fingers on her upper arm stilled. "It's nothing."

"No? Then you won't mind if I have a look." He closed the space between them, and stared down at her, his chest tight. "Let me see your arm, Isabeau."

She dropped her hand, exposing an angry red ring left by a man holding her with great force. At the back of her arm, he could clearly make out the mark of each individual finger. He swore under his breath. "You're going to have a bruise."

"I've had worse."

She wouldn't look at him. He found that as unsettling as her admission.

"You've had worse." He had no idea what to think. "You mean from a fall or an accident of some kind?"

Slowly her eyes rose to meet his. In them was something he didn't want to see. Alarm clanged in his skull. Sweat gathered at his lower back. His body tightened like a bow. "What are you saying?"

She dragged the heel of her palm across her forehead. "Nothing."

"Nothing?" A hard knot settled in his gut. "Who are we talking about? A friend? A lover?"

"It's not what you think."

"What is it?"

Her eyes held his, pale and full of things he couldn't name. Turning away, she started across the room.

"Tell me what it is. Explain this to me."

She went still for a beat, then turned back. "Let go of me, Noah."

"Let..." He followed her gaze down to where his hand grasped her elbow. When had he reached for her? "Isa."

Her skin was cold. Shivers wracked her body. He eased her closer to his warmth.

"Please let me go."

Because she looked like she was about to come apart at the seams, he released her elbow. "I would never hurt you."

"It's not that." She glanced up at him, then quickly away.

The tears in her eyes killed him. "Isabeau."

"I can't, Noah."

"What can't you do?"

A tear slipped down her cheek, and she dashed it away with a swipe of her hand. "I can't have you touch me."

He balled his hands against the ache in his gut. He wouldn't have guessed her admission could cause such pain. "Fine. I won't touch you."

Shaking her head, she took an audible breath. Then another. "You don't understand," she replied, her voice barely above a whisper.

"I want to. I want to understand."

She blinked, spilling tears down her cheeks. This time, she made no move to wipe them away. "I didn't mean for this to happen."

"Isabeau—"

"I didn't want to cry in front of you." She looked up at him, and the misery in her eyes made his throat tighten. "I knew I would...if you touched me."

He didn't know what to say to her. He did know that there was no way in hell he was going to stand there and watch as she shook apart in front of him.

Reaching out, he folded her in his arms. Her back went rigid, and he braced himself, prepared for her to pull away. She didn't.

"It's all right," he murmured, stroking her back with his hand. "It's over."

Slowly the rigidity went out of her spine, and she swayed against him, pressing her face against the center of his chest as she wept softly.

His hand made a gentle pass over her hair. He couldn't help himself. "It's all right now."

She melted against him, and the tension in his own body began to ease. Finally she was right where he'd wanted her from the beginning. With a sigh, he rested his cheek against the top of her head.

"No one is going to hurt you again."

CHAPTER FOUR

Isabeau didn't know which she found more comforting, the husky baritone of Noah's voice or the slow, steady beat of his heart in her ear. In contrast, her own heart raced with residual fear and disgust. Even now, she could still feel the pain of Tommy's hand brutally clamping around her arm. The panic as his body pinned hers to the wall.

Without warning, the terror slammed into her. She shuddered, then melted into Noah, pressing her face to his chest. Her fingers fisted his shirt.

He hugged her closer, his voice a whisper against her temple. "He's gone." A big hand cupped the nape of her neck. "It's over."

Gradually, her tears ebbed. Her shivers eased as she soaked up the warmth of his body, the security of his embrace. She drew in a ragged breath meant to fill her lungs with oxygen and restore her equilibrium. Instead, it filled her with his provocative scent.

She turned her face to his throat and absorbed the sensations. He held her so close, her breasts molded against his chest. His thigh rested between hers, his left hand spread wide against the skin of her lower back. Her nerves hummed as she became aware of the tips of his fingers beneath her waistband. A whisper of desire slashed through her.

Easing back, she tipped her head and looked up. She sucked in a breath when she found his eyes locked on her. An electric current ran through her. Her heart climbed into her throat. A kiss. She wanted just one kiss. To close the space between them...

She took a step sideways, out of his arms.

"Isabeau."

God, she loved the way he said her name, how it rolled off his tongue like a sigh. It stirred something inside her, dropped the bottom out of her stomach. The same way the thought of learning his taste did.

She took another step in retreat.

"Isa?"

His fingers worked the buttons of his chambray shirt loose. She could only stare, heart securely lodged in her throat as each one popped free, revealing a bit more of the T-shirt he wore beneath.

"Are you still with me?"

She'd never felt more lost. Still trapped in the web of desire for him, she didn't know what he was talking about, or why he was removing his shirt.

He moved behind her, and her eyes slid

closed. She started when he touched her, eased the shirt up her arms. The soft cotton carried his scent. Still warm from his body, it felt like being enveloped in his arms again.

"To chase away your chill," he explained, as he lifted her hair out from beneath the shirt. His fingers brushed her neck and every nerve ending went on high alert.

Oh God, how was it possible that hot on the heels of revulsion could sneak lust? Her eyes snapped open. A rush of heat moved down her chest.

His hands settled on her shoulders, and he turned her to face him. Unable to look him in the eye for fear he would be able to see what path her thoughts veered down, she concentrated on the shirt he still wore.

Although sleeveless now, she didn't believe it originally had been. Navy, worn and on the comfortable side, it clung to him in all the right places, emphasizing his broad shoulders. Her gaze wandered to the play of muscle in his arms and the tattoo on his right shoulder as he began to roll up the sleeves of the shirt she swam in.

The image of a skull decorated his upper arm. As a woman, she didn't understand the male attraction to skeletons and skulls, but as the honorary daughter of a talented tattoo artist, she recognized quality body art when she saw it. Off center and primitive in design, this was not it.

"I know someone who could fix that for you."

He glanced in the same direction as she before switching to the other sleeve. "You know about tattoos?"

"A bit," she understated. Her eyes flicked downward. "Do you do this often?"

"I have a niece who liked to play dress up in her younger years."

"And you would oblige her?"

Finished with her sleeve, he tucked his hands into his back pockets. "Does that surprise you?"

She considered him for a moment. "Yes."

"Why?"

"I'm not sure. I guess I never thought of you as an uncle."

"How do you think of me?"

As the man who made her body hum with one look. Whose presence in the same room set off a symphony in her head, and whose touch sparked an electrical current. But also, as a man who wanted something from her she didn't have in her to give.

His eyebrow arched. "Is it that bad?"

"No. It's that complicated." He hadn't moved his gaze from her face, and her pulse kicked up a few beats. She stared back at him, curling her hand around the spot on her arm that continued to throb. "I'm sorry I cried all over you."

"You have nothing to apologize for. You were frightened. Hurting. You should press charges."

"I can't do that." She turned, started for the bar. "I'm going to pour myself a cup of coffee. Would you like one?"

"Sure."

Isabeau slipped through the pass thru and retrieved two mugs while he sat on the stool in front of her. She filled the mugs, moved back around the bar, and handed him one. "I didn't ask you how you take it."

"This is fine. Why can't you press charges?"

"I can't cause him any more pain."

"Who?"

She blew across her mug, then sipped. "My father."

"Your father? I thought your father had passed."

She eased onto the stool next to him and curled her chilled hands around her mug. "My biological father has. I mean the man who was a father to me in every other way, Thomas Cahill."

"It's not a coincidence that they share a name, is it?" His voice held no hint of the frustration that she could see in the tight set of his jaw.

"No, it isn't." She shifted her hold on the

mug, welcomed the warmth slowly seeping into her hands. "Thomas is Tommy's father. Thomas and his wife divorced when Tommy was a boy. Tommy's mother raised him."

"Let me guess, you were raised by his father?"

She nodded. "My mother and Thomas met when I was two. We moved in with him not long after. They were together until her death."

"What was your mother's name?"

"Nicole," she supplied, smiling as the image of her mother flashed through her memory. "She was kind and beautiful, a cellist with the New York Philharmonic."

"So you came by your talent naturally," he said, his voice quiet, matter-of-fact.

"My gift, she would call it." Only it had turned out to be her curse. Wrinkling her forehead, she set her mug aside and changed the subject. "Tell me about your niece."

"I have a nephew as well. They're my brother's children."

"What's his name?"

"My brother? His name is Paul."

She tilted her head. "Older or younger brother?"

"Older by two years."

"Are you alike?"

"Total opposites," he replied with a grin as he set his untouched coffee aside. "Paul is business suits and loafers; I'm worn-out Levis and boots. The only music he listens to is classical. Or yours—he's a big fan of your music."

"You don't consider my music classical?"

"No. It's...I don't know what I'd call it, but not classical."

She thought for a moment but couldn't come up with an accurate description of her music either. "Is Paul married?"

Slowly, his grin became an all-out smile. "It's one of the greatest mysteries in life, how Paul managed to woo Anne." Despite his mocking words, his love for his brother was obvious. "The kids, they take after her. Good looking. Smart."

Did he know how lucky he was? To have the love of a family whom he loved in return? She'd never had more than her mother and Thomas. Taking a deep breath, she allowed herself a moment to wonder what it would be like to have Noah talk about her the way he spoke of his family—with obvious love and connection. Her heart pounded. Or maybe that was her head. Was the stereo still playing?

Tucking her hand into her back pocket, she retrieved the remote she carried with her habitually, aimed it at the wall behind the bar and powered off, enveloping the room in silence.

"What are their names?"

"Megan and Robert. Megan's the oldest at twelve, and Robert's ten."

Her eyebrow went up. "I'm impressed. There are a lot of fathers out there who can't tell you the ages of their children. You're an uncle."

He shrugged as if it wasn't a big deal. To her it was.

"Your father, could he tell me your age?"

"Depends on which one you asked. My biological father never bothered with such trivial details."

"What would Thomas say if I asked?"

"He'd tell you I am twenty-five. He'd be right."

Noah scrubbed a hand down his face. "Jesus."

"What?"

He shook his head. His laugh was soft, and not necessarily amused.

"What is it?"

"It just occurred to me that...I'm old."

He didn't look old to her. He looked like the most beautiful man she had ever seen with his leanly muscled body and those gorgeous green eyes. "How old are you?"

"Old enough to know better."

She gave him a look.

"Forty-one."

"You're right, that's old."

"Thanks."

She laughed aloud and it felt good. She was enjoying herself, his company and conversation. He had worn her down, come in night after night over the past few weeks. Never discouraged, no matter how little attention she gave him, or how rude she was. He always sat in the same booth, the one in the darkest corner, remaining long enough to order two beers before slipping away as quietly as he appeared.

She'd grown accustomed to him and to the effect he had on her system in that time. At least, to the music continually dancing through her head. She doubted she would ever get used to the way one look from him made her entire body tremble.

As it did now.

"You're talking more than usual," she observed, in a desperate attempt to distract herself from her body's reaction to him.

"How do you mean?"

"I've watched you. Even with Dominic, you're more of a quiet observer."

"There's only so much you can learn about someone watching them," he said simply. "If you want to know someone, eventually you have to talk, ask questions, give of yourself."

"And you want to know me?"

"I do."

"Because I made music once."

"Partly," he admitted.

"Partly," she repeated. She didn't know how she felt about his admission. She feared he wanted something more from her than she could give him. "Why else?"

His eyes narrowed and he leaned forward, resting his elbows on his knees. The move narrowed the distance between them considerably. "Does there have to be a secret agenda? Dom's managed to befriend you. What's the difference?"

Isabeau fought the urge to lean back. Her gaze moved from his eyes to his mouth and back to his eyes. "Dominic doesn't...He doesn't..."

"Dominic doesn't what?"

Dominic didn't melt her bones with a glance. He didn't make her senses spin by stepping in the room. "Dom's in love with Rebecca."

His eyebrow shot up. "I'm impressed. He doesn't normally talk much."

"Dominic? He never stops."

"He doesn't say much of Becca," he corrected.

Actually, Dominic had told her quite a lot. That Becca loved him once, until he got scared and hurt her. That he loved her still—missed her desperately. She considered that for a moment, how Dom would talk with her for hours about a subject he usually avoided. "Maybe he wanted a woman's opinion."

"Did you give him one?"

"I did. I told him not to give up so easily. That personally, there is nothing I wouldn't do for love."

"Good advice." He gave her a long look.

"So what you're saying is you don't find Dom threatening."

"I don't."

"And me? Do you find me threatening?"

God, yes. She needed to be careful with him. "Very."

Triumph surged in his eyes. A satisfied smile curved his lips. He reached for her hand. "Good."

"Noah..." Her throat tightened. Her pulse skipped.

He turned her hand over, traced his thumb across her palm. "There's something I want to ask—"

"Please don't."

"Don't what? Touch you?"

Her gaze moved from his face to their hands. She withdrew her left hand from his, cupped it in her right. Her heart beat erratically. Her stomach trembled. "Don't ask."

"And if it's your favorite color I want to know?"

"That's not what you want to ask me."

"Are you sure?"

Slowly her eyes lifted.

The warmth of his smile echoed in his voice. "You do have a favorite color, don't you?"

"Red," she admitted. She knew what he was doing, and she let him do it. He was gentling her again, as he had done when she cried. Only this time, it was in pretending something as innocuous as her favorite color was what he'd wanted to know. "Not hearts and flowers and Valentine's Day red, but deep, rich, brick red."

"I've never seen you in red."

"I don't wear it, I decorate with it. I like rooms to have lots of color. I don't know how you live out of a hotel—so drab and institutional. Don't you find it depressing?"

"It's not so bad. The bedcover is...colorful."

"I bet," she replied with a smile. "But the walls are white, aren't they? And the bath—also white." She cringed.

"You'd hate my house. Every room there is white."

"On purpose?"

She seemed so genuinely horrified Noah couldn't help but laugh. Truth be told, he never paid much attention to such things. It was only four walls and a roof, a place to sleep.

"A place to unwind," she continued as if reading his thoughts. "To relax. To entertain. A home should be an expression of self. What does yours say?"

"That I only just bought it and haven't gotten around to having it painted?"

"Will you get around to it?"

"Honestly? Probably not. Once the studio is complete, I'll spend most of my time there."

"Studio?"

"I'm having a recording studio put in the basement."

She tilted her head. "When will this happen?"

"It's happening right now. Construction started before we came here."

"And when it's done, you'll leave here."

Her words weren't a question, but he answered her anyway. "Yes."

"For where?"

"Auburn, California."

She fell silent for several long moments. Her gaze swept around the room, looking everywhere but at him. Her hand rubbed absently at her upper arm, at the bruises forming beneath his shirt.

He was afraid to read too much into her quiet, afraid to hope that the thought of him leaving would disturb her. Finally her eyes returned to his, carefully neutral.

"How's your arm?" he asked.

"It aches." Her hand stilled, dropped to her lap. "Can I ask you something?"

"You can ask me anything."

"Every night you come in you order a dark lager but never drink it—not more than a few swallows. Sometimes you order a second, and that one goes untouched as well. Why?"

Surprised, he straightened. Whatever he'd expected her to ask, this was not it. It was no simple question, with no simple answer. Of course, maybe she'd sensed that.

"I'll make you a deal. I'll tell you, the whole ugly story, if you answer a question in return."

"Is it that bad?"

"It is."

"What's your question?"

"No. Not until after you agree."

Her war of emotions played out in her eyes. Those pale, wide, expressive eyes of hers. They got to him. Nodding, she took a deep breath. "All right."

"How come I order drinks I never consume, is that your question?"

"Yes."

"Because at one time, I had a problem with alcohol," he replied, oversimplifying.

"A problem?"

"One I prefer not to repeat."

"Then why order anything? Why come in at all? Are you testing yourself?"

"It's not a test." He avoided answering her, put off revisiting the ugliest time of his life for as long as she'd allow him to. He wondered how long she'd let him get away with it.

"I don't understand. What happened to make you change?"

Not long.

"Something must have happened. Most people don't stop drinking without a good reason."

She was right about that. He had a reason, a damn good one. "Are you sure you want to hear this? You might not like my answer."

"Yes."

Noah leaned forward, resting his elbows on his thighs. He rubbed at a day's worth of stubble on his chin with his palm before dropping his hands to hang between his knees. "My best friend died."

"I'm sorry," she stated quietly.

"Danny Treybourne, our original drummer?" He waited to see whether she knew the name, continued his tale when she tipped her head in acknowledgment. "We grew up together, around the corner from each other, raising hell, chasing girls. We always dreamed of playing in a band, making it big. Though I don't think either of us ever truly believed it would happen."

He couldn't believe he was actually going to share his story with her—tonight of all nights. The night she'd finally broken her silence and talked with him, given him the chance he'd wanted for weeks. Sharing with her the ugliest time of his life wasn't likely his smartest move.

He did it anyway.

"We were fifteen when we first put the band together—Dominic, Nick, Danny, and me. We spent six years playing the local clubs before we got any recognition, two more before we were signed."

He recalled the day they signed that first contract—the excitement, the belief in their dream and their music. He could recall exactly what he and Danny had done to celebrate that day—they'd gotten pissed. It was a tradition that continued for years.

"The sudden jump to fame is a hard one. You work your whole life for something, go nowhere fast, and then one day, you're labeled an overnight success. Anything we wanted was suddenly ours for the taking. Drugs. Alcohol. Women. Bloody hell, the women. Each of us handled it differently, some of us better than others. Me, I took advantage," he admitted, chagrined. "After all, I wasn't stupid. Okay, maybe a bit stupid."

Incredibly stupid. Of course, years later, he saw the mistakes, the risks. He knew how differently his story could have ended. "I was reckless, I admit, we all were. But we never considered the risks. Nothing was going to happen to us, we were invincible."

She remained silent, allowing him to tell his story in his own way.

"It got out of hand—the drinking, women, and touring. We were touring steadily, city after city after city. After a while, it all blurs together. There were times I don't know how I functioned, how I got through a show. It got so I couldn't get out of bed in the morning without a shot of bourbon to get my blood moving.

"One night, I can't tell you where we were—I put my glass down and looked around. I looked at the mass of people crowding the room and I asked myself, 'who are these people?' The room suddenly came into focus. For the first time I realized I didn't know half of the people about me and those whose names I did know, didn't know the real me."

He had her complete attention. She chewed thoughtfully on her lower lip, eyes sober as she looked at him.

"They only saw who they wanted to see. They didn't see that I was miserable. That I hated the turn my life had taken and was drowning my sorrows in alcohol and meaningless sex."

"What did you do?" she asked softly.

"What could I do? I got pissed."

Her mouth thinned. "You got drunk."

"I did. The night Danny died, I was drunk. Not a big surprise. By that time, I had a bottle in my hand day and night. I didn't know Danny had started using, that he was mixing drugs and alcohol."

He'd been too busy fighting his own demons, dealing with his own disillusionment to notice his friend's.

"I didn't know...until it was too late. I found him," he said, his voice tight with anguish. "It was so unreal. It didn't seem possible that he could be dead. I mean, how could he be dead? He was always so alive. But he was cold when I touched him, pale and unresponsive."

Danny!

"I tried to bring him back, to will him back to me."

Don't do this, Danny.

"I was too late."

Her eyes glimmered with sympathy. She offered no meaningless platitudes, and he was glad.

"That was it for me. I stayed long enough to fulfill our contractual obligation, then I quit. Quit drinking, quit making music. I went back to London, found a real job."

"Which you hated."

"You've heard this story?" He brushed his knuckles down her cheek, ridiculously pleased when she didn't shift away. "I found I could not deny what I am. I'm a musician. So I'm back to making music. Only, this time, we're older, wiser. It's about the music now, not the fame. I'd sing to a group of ten as eagerly as a sold-out stadium."

She studied him for a minute before stating, "I have one problem with your story."

"Just one?"

"You still drink."

"It's not something I do with regularity."

"I see you in here pretty regular."

He grinned. "I order lager, but I don't drink it. Isn't that what sparked your question?"

"Then why do you come here?"

"It's not for the alcohol."

"I don't...understand."

She really didn't. "Isabeau." He cupped her chin, smoothed his thumb across her bottom lip. "I come here to see you."

Her breath hitched. "Oh."

"Yeah. Oh." She got to him, dammit. He wanted to kiss her. Pull her off her stool and onto his lap in one fluid motion. Bury his hands in her hair and kiss her until she forgot her name.

Instead, he stood, backed toward the door. "You look tired. I'll let you get some rest."

"You're leaving?"

"Yes." Before he ruined everything by giving into his impulses. "As long as you're feeling steadier."

She blinked. Something he couldn't identify sparked in her eyes. "You never asked your question."

"It'll keep," he assured her, turning the lock.

"Noah." She rose, walked the few steps to where he stood and put her hand on his forearm.

Her fingers were chilled.

The jolt that arced through his system

was red hot.

"You don't need an excuse to come here, Noah."

Emotion swamped him. He managed to turn and leave, but once on the sidewalk, he stopped, tipped his head to the sky, and checked the alignment of the stars.

CHAPTER FIVE

It wasn't what he expected.

Noah stood in Isabeau's doorway, having come up the back steps, as instructed by Clint. Her door was wide open. She was nowhere in sight.

He could see pretty much the entire upper level of the building that housed her bar. It had an open floor plan and wooden floors with a long rag-rug runner that started at his feet and ran down the center of the space. "Isabeau?"

He stepped onto the rug, into her home.

Directly to his left, on the other side of the bar-style counter, was a galley kitchen. The kitchen segued into the dining area, where a long, scarred table sat surrounded by mismatched wooden chairs of varying color. In the center of the table was an oversized vase filled with wildflowers.

An entire wall of bookshelves started just past the kitchen and continued around the end wall to stop opposite him, at a large set of windows. The shelves were covered in books, photos and whimsical knick-knacks. At the far left corner of the room, surrounded by those shelves, was a large, wooden-based bed.

An old brick fireplace occupied the center of the wall to his right. More flowers, red this time, filled the hearth, artistically spilling out into the room. Before the fireplace a brown leather couch with a low back and rolled arms faced a tan fabric couch of modern design. He'd never seen anything quite like it—tan walls and mismatched neutral furniture —tied together with deep, red accents. It was warm, comfortable.

Like Isabeau.

At the far right end of the room, near the windows, a grouping of three theater chairs caught his interest. He started down the rug for a closer look.

"Noah?"

She stood behind him, back where he'd just been. Turning around, he faced her, prepared to ask how she'd suddenly appeared.

His brain went soft.

The rest of him went rock hard.

Isabeau was wearing a bikini. Two bright white triangles covered her breasts, attached with a string that tied around her neck and around her back. Large amounts of sun-kissed golden skin lay between her tiny top and her equally tiny bottoms. They weren't much in the way of bottoms. Slung low on her hips and tied at the sides, he had the feeling that the suit required grooming in an area he probably shouldn't think about.

"I didn't hear you come in," she said, oblivious to her effect on him.

"Clint sent me up." He couldn't take his eyes off her. Petite, yet curved in all the right places, she took his breath away. His loins gave a painful lurch, and all he could do was stand there and absorb the shock.

"Does he need something?"

"Ah..." He kept his eyes on her face, away from all that smooth skin. "Who?"

"Clint."

He cleared his throat. "Right. Clint." And then because he had to know, he asked, "How can you be darker? The sun's only been up for—"

"Hours," she supplied, her eyes bright with amusement. "Of course, with your work schedule as unconventional as mine, perhaps you didn't know that."

She smiled at him with an ease she'd never shown around him before. "It's the Mohican in me. Did it work?"

"Work?"

"To conceal the bruise."

"I can still see it."

"Yes, but you know it's there."

She turned and studied her arm in the trio of large, decorative mirrors that hung on the wall and his stomach tightened. He was staring again, and suddenly as uncomfortable as a horny teenager. No doubt about it, Isabeau

73

had a great ass.

She was trim, toned, a runner; she jogged past his hotel every morning. He'd never seen the appeal of running without being chased or chasing something. Until now. Her legs, God, her legs were almost as beautiful as her ass. They were long and smooth, and he couldn't help himself as he traced them all the way to her toes and back again.

"My father is not going to be happy. I'd hoped..."

In the mirror's reflection, their gazes locked. Even if his mind hadn't already gone blank, it would have as he caught the look in Isabeau's eyes.

Heat.

Desire.

She was not as immune to him as she pretended.

"I, um, hoped to camouflage the mark. I didn't want Thomas to find out about last night." She faced him, features carefully schooled, and pulled a throw off the back of the couch, securing it around her hips.

Her actions drew his gaze to her middle, and for a moment he stood mesmerized. He'd been wrong about her not wearing jewelry. She wore it all right, in a spot that usually remained hidden from view. Isabeau Montgomery had her navel pierced.

He broke into a sweat just looking at her.

His gaze veered to the scar that bisected her abdomen from just to the left of her navel to somewhere beneath the top of her bikini bottoms. It was old—barely noticeable—faded so that it appeared only slightly paler than the rest of her skin. The type of incision made quickly, in an effort to save someone's life. The type she might receive after an automobile accident severe enough to have ended her mother's life.

"He's bound to find out, sooner or later," he said, as he returned his gaze to her face.

"I'd prefer later, rather than sooner." Her smile was apprehensive. The pulse at the base of her throat racing. "Are you thirsty? I can get you something to drink."

Dry mouthed, he shook his head while the image of her sprawled across the top of that big bed sprang to mind. Longing filled him, along with the need to fill his hands with her incredible ass while his tongue explored the bloodstone in her navel—right before following that scar to the groomed treasure hidden beneath those tiny bottoms.

"Hungry? I can...Actually, unless you went downstairs, I can't offer you anything to eat."

I wouldn't say that.

He swore beneath his breath as the image already forming in his mind sharpened.

"I'm going into the city for lunch," she explained, then tipped her head. "Is something wrong?"

Hell yes! He pushed his fingers through his hair and pulled in a breath. The scent of her tanning oil made his head spin. All that golden skin...Christ. She drove him crazy.

It was a damn good thing she didn't know what was going through his mind. How easily he could have her naked. His hands on her. His mouth. If she knew, she would shove him out the door and down the flight of stairs.

Even that wouldn't ease the throbbing in his groin.

"I'm fine, Isa. You're off the clock. You don't need to serve me."

A frown line appeared between her pale eyes. "I do that," she admitted candidly. "It's not something I can turn on and off."

Damn, he hadn't meant to make her feel bad. Guilt filled him.

"You never said what Clint needed."

"He didn't need anything. I went into the bar looking for you. He told me I'd find you up here." He had. More of her than he'd been prepared for. Turning away before she noted his erection, he crossed to the far corner of the room, where the theater chairs sat.

There were three of them—wooden with burgundy velvet seats. The center seat had a sign draped across its back that read "reserved." Black and white photographs in a variety of sizes covered the wall behind the seats. Some matted, some not. Some landscapes—a few places he recognized. Most of the same subject. A tiny, dark-haired girl with the face of an angel.

Isabeau.

Her age varied from picture to picture—from six months of age to ten years. In one, she was a baby, lying stomach down on a mirror, studying her own reflection. Another, barely past toddler years and sitting at a piano large enough to make her already petite form appear downright puny.

Cartwheels in a field of green grass at the age of five.

Standing center stage and looking out over an empty symphony hall.

He leaned closer. Instead of happy and smiling, she appeared strangely disheartened.

"My mother's work," she explained from just behind him.

"She was very good."

"Yes, she was. Why were you looking for me, Noah?"

The largest photograph held him transfixed. Were he to hazard a guess, he would say she was about ten. She sat before a concrete bench, the type you'd see in a garden or park, her legs drawn up under her. Her white ruffled dress was arranged around her, her dark hair pulled back away from her face and secured at the base of her neck. Her steepled hands rested atop the bench, her cheek against her hands. Her eyes were closed, as if she were sleeping. The absence of color in the photo made it all the more dramatic. The white of her dress against her dark skin. The black of her hair against the pale bench.

It was pure, ethereal.

"I was wondering how you were doing today," he replied, distracted.

"So you stopped in on your way to the studio?"

"I'm not going in today."

"You came by to check on me?"

"Yes." He faced her. "Who's it reserved for?"

Her eyes moved from him to the middle chair and back again. "It's silly."

"Tell me anyway."

She sighed, pitched her voice lower than normal. "My mother. It's reserved for my mother."

The mother she'd lost thirteen years ago. He couldn't begin to understand what losing a mother at such a young age must have been like for her. He did understand the desire to keep a loved one alive in her heart. "Do you still have her camera?"

"Mom's camera? Yes, I do."

"You should place it in her seat. So it's there for her when she visits."

She stared in silence, surprise written all

over her face. "I'm not sure she needs it any-more."

"That doesn't mean she wouldn't appreciate the sentiment."

She gifted him with a smile that could melt a glacier. Her eyes went soft and sweet. "Would you like to have lunch with me?"

He blinked. Had he heard her correctly? "You're asking me out?"

She drew herself to her full height, which, without her heels, was barely to his shoulder. "Yes, I'm asking you out."

"You and me? A meal you didn't have to cook?"

"Not exactly." She shifted, brushed a few wisps of dark hair off her cheek and tucked them behind her ear. "You, me, Thomas, and a meal I didn't have to cook."

He lifted an eyebrow.

"We have plans to meet for lunch before my shift at the bar begins. He wouldn't mind if you joined us."

He returned her smile as his pulse kicked into overdrive. No way was he passing up the chance to spend an afternoon with her.

"I don't do this with everyone," she explained unnecessarily. "I thought..."

"You're sure he won't mind?"

"Thomas? Of course not."

"Then I'd love to."

"Good." She started across the room,

walking backwards. "Let me rinse off in the shower and throw something on, and I'll be ready."

Noah glanced at the dark bruise still visible on her upper arm. "Something with sleeves," he suggested.

She scowled at the reminder, her fingers gently brushing across the mark. "That would only make him suspicious. I don't wear long sleeves unless I'm cold and I'm not cold."

Self-preservation had him biting his tongue. He scrubbed his hand over the back of his neck and waited until the *click* of the bathroom door assured him she was out of earshot. "Trust me, I noticed."

****

One hour later, Isabeau pushed through the door of her father's shop with the jingle of bells, Noah a step behind her.

"Izzy, is that you?" a voice called out from somewhere out of sight.

"Yeah, Dad, it's me."

"I'll be out in a sec."

"No problem."

Noah shifted. His shoulder brushed hers as he leaned in. "So you know someone who can fix my tattoo, do you?"

His mouth was inches from her ear, his breath a cloud of warmth against her cheek. A burst of heat snapped along her nerves, tensed every muscle in her body.

She forced herself to breathe evenly. "I do."

His eyes amused, he glanced around the shop, from the two private rooms where the body piercings and tattoos were done to the large wall of snapshots that showcased Thomas's work. "Is he any good?"

"He's exceptional."

"Exceptional, that's high praise."

The warm masculine scent of him drifted into her lungs. For a brief moment, she closed her eyes and absorbed. Her heart pounded in her head, masking the sound of the music that looped through her with the annoying persistence of a commercial jingle. "It's well earned." She gestured across the room. "See for yourself."

Hands in his pockets, Noah strolled around the room. Pausing in front of a glass display case, he turned Thomas' open sketchbook and studied the drawing before him. Then he moved to the wall of snapshots.

"Tell me something." He leaned in for a better look at one of the pictures. "Why am I here?"

His hair was wind tousled after their brief walk from the parking garage. He wore jeans that molded his butt and hips, his long legs, and a black T-shirt that stretched taut across his chest.

She would have replied, if there'd been any air left in her lungs. God, he was attractive. Strong. Male. Capable. And for a moment today, he'd wanted her. She'd seen the hunger in his intense green eyes while he'd studied her backside. Saw it, just didn't understand it. Men didn't look at her like that. Ever.

Her heart beat wildly against her ribs. Her throat went dry as dust. She felt the hot, reckless pull of need and pondered for a moment what it would be like to give in to it. Press her lips against his tempting mouth, and finally discover the taste of him. To feel the warmth of his flesh beneath her palms as her hands cruised over his mouth-watering body.

"Isabeau?"

She jolted. Her eyes remained on his as she pushed her fingers through her hair.

What was she thinking? A man like Noah Clark wouldn't be interested in her, at least not for long. Anything he felt for her was about the music, his drive to get her to play again. His need to show her that she wasn't complete without the piano.

That fact was blatantly apparent after the story he'd shared last night. How he'd given up his career only to learn, years later, that he couldn't live without music. It was crazy to think anything else. She was neither blonde nor beautiful—two things she imagined he looked for in a woman. The desire she'd glimpsed in the mirror's reflection this morning had been nothing more than a natural male reaction to her near naked state.

Her stomach tightened into a painful knot. She breathed a sigh of relief when her father chose that moment to join them.

"I had a visitor this morning," Thomas said as he entered the room. "He asked how you were doing." The pleasure so apparent in his eyes dimmed a notch as his gaze settled on Noah. "You should have told me I had a customer."

Isabeau smiled broadly at the man she'd always called her father—welcomed the swift rush of love for him. "He's not a customer, he's with me. I invited him to lunch with us."

"I see," Thomas murmured. His gaze left her and locked back onto Noah.

"Thomas Cahill, this is Noah Clark."

Noah offered his hand. "Mr. Cahill."

"Thomas," he corrected, not smiling.

Noah tipped his head. "You have a nice place here, Thomas."

"It pays the bills."

Isabeau laughed. She bumped her shoulder against Thomas's side. "Knock off the scare tactics, Dad."

The beginnings of a smile tipped the corner of his mouth. Well, she knew it was a smile, to anyone else it looked more like a sneer. Thomas Cahill was tall and broad of shoulder, well-muscled with a bald head he usually hid beneath a skull cap. He wore his pale blonde mustache a bit too long and preferred sleeveless tees and a black leather vest atop jeans and biker boots.

"Just doing my job."

Her gaze followed his to Noah. "He's got ink."

"Does he?"

"It needs some work."

"How much work?"

"Re-outlining, coloring." She had to give Noah credit. He stood motionless, not backing down beneath Thomas's stare or their talking about him as if he wasn't in the room. "See for yourself. I need to visit the restroom."

She turned away smiling. At the door leading to the back room, she stopped, sent one last warning to her father. "Be nice."

Silence was his only reply.

With the silence, the siren song in her head played louder, calling to her. Unable to shake it, she checked over her shoulder. Assured they remained locked in some male stand-off, neither paying attention to her, she allowed herself to be drawn past the restroom she'd used to excuse her absence, and to the stairs leading up to her father's apartment.

She paused before going up. Indecision swirled inside her, mixed with the pounding rhythm that grew stronger with each step closer to the staircase. Sweat slicked her palms. Her body began to tremble. She didn't want to take that first step, knew once she did, there was no turning back.

Pressing her fingers against her eyes, she attempted to resist. She dragged in a deep breath, then another hoping the act would help to clear her mind. Only, without her other senses to distract her, the music strengthened its hold on her.

Releasing her breath on a sigh, she gave in and placed her foot on the stairs. In silence, she climbed. She found what she was looking for in the front room, set against the inside wall, away from damaging sunlight.

Her grand piano.

A gift—from mother to daughter.

Memories pushed in on her, images she didn't want to see. A sudden, unexpected sense of loss filled her, then something deeper, stronger than she'd expected. Something she had no desire or intention of analyzing. Not today. Not anytime soon.

Isabeau took a careful breath to counteract the flipping of her stomach. She shoved her hand through her hair. Unable to ignore the irresistible pull any longer, she crossed the room to lay her hand atop the piano's cabinet.

Her pulse skipped. Her throat knotted. Beneath her fingertips, she swore she could feel the instrument's pulse, its very life. Her whole body trembled.

Don't panic. Breathe.

She was too late. Fear of the inevitable had taken hold. The day was coming when she would no longer be able to ignore the pull of the music.

It was coming. There was nothing she could do to stop it.

She hoped it wouldn't be her undoing.

CHAPTER SIX

Thomas Cahill's smile faded the moment Isabeau stepped from the room. He pinned Noah with a look. "You like my daughter."

Noah nodded and glanced toward the hallway Isabeau had disappeared down. "Very much."

"You the one gave her that bruise?"

"Of course not."

Noah's denial did nothing to soften Thomas's expression. Damn but the man was intimidating. Hard. Cold and furious. He had the build of a linebacker—wide, solidly muscled with a thick neck, his arms covered in tattoos. For a moment, Noah was reminded of the younger Cahill. The two men resembled each other in height and build, but that seemed to be where the similarities between them ended. When Junior looked at Isabeau, his gaze had been filled with resentment. Thomas looked at her with affection.

Thomas's mouth tightened. His hands fisted at his sides. "Do you know who did put that bruise on her?

"Yes."

"Who? Give me the bastard's name."

"I don't think that's a good idea."

Thomas's jaw bunched.

"I think this is something you should hear from Isabeau."

Thomas turned away—but not before Noah caught the flash of emotion in the man's eyes. "Are there any more, or is that the only mark on her? You can tell me that much, can't you?"

"That's it, that's the only one."

"Good." Expelling a slow breath, he turned back to Noah. The rush of angry emotion had disappeared from his face. In its place was quiet assessment. "So where's this tattoo I'm to look at?"

Noah pushed his sleeve up to reveal his right upper arm. He waited as the man looked closely at the tattoo.

"How long ago did you get this?"

"A long time ago." Noah's thoughts drifted to the day he and Danny visited the shady little tattoo parlour. Two scrawny boys on the verge of becoming men—believing a tattoo would get them there quicker. "I was a teenager."

He noted the clean, sterile conditions of this shop, and was grateful shoddy body art had been all he'd taken home with him that day.

Thomas considered him before asking, "This the only ink you have?"

"Yes."

"It's a bit crude, but not bad for its age." He crossed to the glass display case and began to sketch. "My daughter, she can be a bit headstrong at times."

Noah blinked at the abrupt change of subject. "So I've noticed."

"More than once, she's had me beating my head against the wall."

"I know the feeling."

A deep chuckle rumbled from Thomas. "So tell me, do you want something done with this, or are you humoring Izzy?"

"I haven't given it much thought," Noah replied. Curious, he walked to the counter to see what Thomas drew. "She didn't tell me your profession, only that we would meet you for lunch."

"She's never brought anyone to lunch before," Thomas said as Noah stepped to his side.

"No?"

"No. She's never mentioned you, either."

"That doesn't surprise me."

"No?" Thomas gave him a hard, long stare. "But it bothers you."

It did. More than he wanted to admit. Isabeau was a bit too unaffected by him, when he couldn't seem to get through more than a few hours without thinking of her.

Never before had he been so aware of a woman from the moment he saw her—those incredible eyes, that compact body. After holding her in his arms last night—discovering her skin was warmer than he'd ever imagined, her hair softer—he knew it was going to be damn near impossible to keep thoughts of her at bay.

"You live around here?" Thomas asked absently.

"No. I'm here to record."

"With Pete?"

"Yeah."

"Pete's a good guy."

"He seems to be."

Thomas made one last mark on the sketchbook, placed the pencil down and pushed the book in front of Noah. "You're a musician then?"

"I'm a singer." Noah studied the sketch before him and smiled. Thomas had started with the crude, rudimentary skull tattoo from Noah's arm, then added and tweaked the design until it resembled something totally different. Something far more unique and artistic. If the man could do something like that in a matter of minutes, Isabeau's praise had not been exaggerated.

"Where do you call home?"

"California," Noah replied and Thomas's brow knitted. "This is brilliant. You're very talented."

"Thank you. If you weren't interested in

any changes, you could have it re-worked, brought back to its original vibrance."

Noah raised a shoulder. "I'll let you know."

He shifted his gaze as Isabeau stepped into the room, sending a flash fire through his bloodstream. His gut tightened as he studied the intriguing lines of her profile while she closed her eyes and took a deep breath. After a moment her eyes slid back open and she turned, locking her gaze with his.

Noah knitted his brow. She was pale. Her eyes full of something he couldn't name. She pushed her hair away from her face, the impression of fragility fading as she continued to watch him, her mouth curving into a smile.

"Are you two ready?" she asked.

He let his gaze travel slowly over her, taking in her glossy ebony hair, the band insignia that decorated the front of her vintage tee, and the body-hugging jeans that rode so low on her hips that he was amazed they didn't slide right off. He frowned as he zeroed in on her strappy, open-toed stilettos and for one blinding moment imagined her without the clothes—only smooth golden skin and those sexy damn shoes.

"You'll have to go without me today," Thomas stated, pushing away from the counter and crossing to Isabeau.

Noah blinked away the libidinous image.

"What? Why?" Her eyes took on a sudden

awareness. "What are you up to?"

Noah wondered the same thing. Then he watched, intrigued as Thomas raised his hand to touch the bruise on Isabeau's arm, only to lower it without making contact.

"Your friend assures me that this is not his handiwork."

She straightened her shoulders and glanced in his direction. "Noah had nothing to do with it."

"Who did this to you?"

Isabeau paused, letting the question hang in the air.

"Tell me who did this to you," Thomas persisted.

She gazed up at her father, her concern evident. Her hand settled on his arm, where his muscles tightened and flexed. "He didn't mean..." Taking a deep breath, she continued. "He was drunk."

"That's supposed to make me feel better?" Thomas rasped, anger seething in his voice. His hands curled against his sides. "Tell me the bastard's name."

Her eyes slid closed. A tightness settled in Noah's chest as, even from his distance, he noticed the fine tremor that wracked her body. Because he wanted to go to her, to touch her, soothe her, he pushed his hands into his pockets.

"Tommy," she said quietly. "Tommy did

this to me."

One by one, Thomas's muscles tensed. Pain flashed in his eyes.

"I'm sorry," Isabeau whispered.

"You're sorry? What do you have to be sorry about?" A look of confusion crossed Thomas's face before his expression tightened. "What did you do, refuse him a drink?"

Slowly, Isabeau's eyes opened and locked with her father's.

"Sonofabitch!" he exclaimed and took a step back, away from her.

"Dad, don't."

Thomas continued to curse under his breath, his voice pitched so that Noah only caught every other word. Hands tightly fisted, the man's anger was palpable. It pulsed off of him in waves.

"Dad—"

"You need to leave now, Izzy. Take your friend to lunch."

"Dad—"

"Noah. Get her out of here."

Noah crossed to her, settling his hand at the small of her back. "Come on, Isabeau. Your father needs some time to absorb."

Temper flashed in her eyes before she stepped out of his reach. "Don't coddle me," she warned. "Either of you."

Without another word, she turned and walked out the door.

Isabeau was three storefronts down before Noah caught up with her. He walked with her in silence for another block and a half before he spoke. "I didn't tell him, you know."

"I know."

"You could have postponed your lunch plans, given yourself a day or two to heal, allowed the bruises to fade."

"No, he needed to hear it from me."

"Perhaps I shouldn't have come along."

Easing out an audible sigh, Isabeau stopped in the middle of the sidewalk. She tipped her head up and met his gaze from beneath dark lashes. "I knew all along that he would notice the mark on my arm. I just…The sunbathing I did this morning was as much about preparing myself for his disappointment as about disguising the severity of the bruise. Unfortunately I wasn't any more successful at preparing myself than in keeping the truth from him."

She closed her eyes for a moment, opened them. "Your presence doesn't change the facts— that his son got angry when I cut him off last night and decided to tell me what he thought of me in a display that left me bruised and sore."

"Is that what he did, told you what he thought of you?"

"What he said isn't important."

"No?"

"No."

She was lying.

He fisted his hands against his thighs. "What exactly did Tommy say to you?"

"It doesn't matter."

"I think it does. I think it matters a great deal. Otherwise you wouldn't have just gone white as a sheet."

"I don't think that's possible with my coloring," she replied dryly.

He narrowed his eyes.

"I'm fine."

"Another lie," he muttered. He shot his hand out and took hold of her elbow when her color worsened. "Hey."

She stared up at him from eyes that had gone as pale as her face. Her voice wasn't quite steady as she asked, "What do you mean another lie?"

"There's no point in denying it, Isabeau. All I have to do is look at you to know that you're not fine. You're upset."

She stepped back slightly, pulling free from his grasp. A gentle reminder—no touching. "Of course I'm upset. I caused my father pain."

"No, that would be Tommy. He hurt your father, just as he hurt you. Tell me what he said to you."

Her eyes flicked to his face, then away. "I already told you, it—"

"Doesn't matter. Yeah, I got that."

"Good."

Noah clenched his jaw. He scrubbed a weary hand over his face, resisting the urge to reach out and snag her wrist when she started down the sidewalk away from him. What good would spinning her around and hauling her back to him do except give her yet another reason to be wary of him. Isabeau didn't like to be touched. For weeks now, he'd assumed her aversion was only to his touch. If he hadn't witnessed today's interaction with her father, he might have gone on believing that. Now he wondered.

They walked in silence. To the casual observer she looked like every other pedestrian enjoying a walk through the city, her dark hair rustling in the breeze. But he noted the way she held herself erect and alert. How her eyes never strayed from the people closest to her as she countered any move in her direction with a subtle shift that kept her out of reach.

He frowned, recalling her words from the night previous. That she'd had worse bruises than the ones left by Tommy. Every muscle in his back tightened. When questioned, she'd refused to talk about it. She was good at that, at refusing to share anything too personal.

Very good.

"Is this something you do often?"

"Have lunch with my father? I try to make it once a week, but sometimes it's every two weeks."

"Do you always walk to the restaurant?"

"Sure. I spend most of my time indoors so whenever I come into the city, I walk."

"Odd."

"Why is that odd?"

"You don't let people close to you. You don't like people to touch you. I thought it was me, but even Thomas is hesitant to do so."

She came to an abrupt halt and turned sharply. "What?"

His fingers curled around her elbows as someone bumped into her. He shifted her out of the flow of foot traffic and closer to the building they stood before. She took a step back, pulling free from his grasp.

What else did he expect? He dropped his hands. "If not for what you told me last night, I may have believed your father hesitated because of what Tommy did to you. It's more than that, isn't it?"

She lifted her chin a fraction, straightened her shoulders. "I don't know what you're talking about."

"Yes, you do."

"What does this have to do with walking?"

"The amount of people. This many and someone is bound to touch you." He considered her for a moment. "Was it Thomas? Was he the one who hurt you?"

"How dare you! Thomas would never hurt me."

"But someone did."

She turned away from him and stared at the window display, which frustrated the hell out of him. "I refuse to talk about this with you."

Noah shoved his hand through his hair. He'd had such hopes when she invited him to lunch. That she was willing to give him a chance. But it didn't take a genius to figure out that the wall she used to keep him at bay was still firmly in place. Bloody hell, he hated that wall. He wanted past it. Over it, under it, around it, he didn't care.

"Do you let anyone close?"

"Why?"

"Why do I ask, or why would you allow anyone close to you?"

"Why..." Shaking her head, she took a deep breath, then another. "I touch people," she argued.

He moved closer, invading her space. "Do you let them touch you?"

Her body tensed, telling him she wanted to step away. She didn't. "Why are you doing this?"

"No? That must make it difficult to have a relationship."

"Noah, please."

"You do have relationships, don't you?"

"Yes."

"Physical relationships?"

That finally got her attention away from

the window display and back on him. Her brows shot up so far on her forehead they disappeared in her hair. "I don't see how that's any of your business."

"No? Then you haven't been paying attention."

She blinked. Her chin rose. "I have physical relationships."

He couldn't imagine a relationship without touch. Didn't even want to consider what exactly she was qualifying as a relationship. Cold, clinical, get-your-rocks-off sex?

"No one's ever complained," she argued.

"And you?"

"What about me?"

He sighed. "Isabeau," he said softly, leaning in so that every breath he took drew the scent of her into his lungs. A warm, soft scent with a hint of tanning oil. "What kind of lovers are you taking?"

"I—"

He brushed the back of his hand down her arm from shoulder to elbow. That electric current hummed between them. "It's not supposed to be just about the finale. It's about the journey. It's all about touch, Isabeau. Soft caresses. Slow, deep, wet kisses. Why would you settle for anything else?"

Her tongue darted out and wet her lips. He wondered what she'd do if he leaned in right now and showed her what he meant.

"Maybe you haven't taken a good look at me?"

"I'm looking at you now." He cupped her face with one hand, traced his thumb along the curve of her jaw. Her skin was warm and soft as silk beneath his.

"Noah." His name crossed her lips, a husky rasp barely heard over the street noise. She reached up and wrapped her hand around his.

She had a mouth that begged to be kissed. A mouth meant for pleasure. How was it she didn't realize her own appeal? He traced his thumb over the palm of her hand. Satisfaction welled inside him when she trembled. "You don't have to settle, Isabeau."

"I...don't?"

"No." Noah raised her hand and pressed his lips against the center of her palm. The eyes that stared up into his changed color, from gray to blue. Her lips parted, then snapped shut as someone spoke her name.

"Izzy?"

Isabeau dragged in a shallow, ragged breath. Her pulse throbbed, her legs felt like jelly. The press of Noah's mouth against her flesh made her throat ache and her body yearn. She wasn't used to feeling those things, and the fact that she felt them about this man, this one man, scared the hell out of her.

Desperate to regain control, she curled her fingers over her sensitized palm and turned in the direction of the voice.

"Isabeau Montgomery, it is you."

Years of practice kept her grimace from showing as her gaze landed on Gregory Howard. As long as she'd known the pianist, which had to be nearly her entire life, she was uncomfortable around the man. She'd never been able to figure out exactly what it was about him that disturbed her, just that she preferred not to be in his company.

"Gregory," she acknowledged.

"My God, how long's it been?" he asked, his gaze traveling down the length of her. He turned to Noah, apparently not looking for an answer. "Who's your friend?"

Waiting for her nerves to settle, Isabeau slowly turned her gaze. Noah watched the pianist, his expression cool and focused, his eyes impassive. "Noah Clark, this is Gregory Howard."

"Good to meet you," Noah said, shaking the hand Gregory extended.

"Likewise," Gregory replied before turning back to her. "How have you been, Izzy? Jeeze, it's been years since I've seen you. You look good."

"I've been fine."

"Good, good, so what have you been up to?"

"I have my own business in Long Island City."

"Really? How interesting." His tone was flat in the way that let her know he didn't find her answer interesting at all. She stiffened her spine as his eyes moved over her again. It wasn't a suggestive look, but it made her uncomfortable. "Do you still play?"

What was he up to? If anyone knew she didn't play any- more, it was Gregory Howard. After all, he was the one to step forward and take her place after her accident. A move that propelled his career to new heights.

"No. No, I don't."

His gaze shifted to her hands. His thin lips turned down. "I don't know how you do it. I think I'd go out of my head if I lost the ability to play the piano."

She'd found it best not to respond to statements like Gregory's. If she did, it opened the door for the person making them to continue.

Gregory continued anyway.

"Seriously, I think I'd rather die. I can't imagine. You were once something spectacular and now—"

"We were on our way to lunch," Noah interrupted, his palm settling against her lower back. Unlike most times he reached for her, the desire to shift away never surfaced. Instead, she found an odd sense of comfort in his touch. "If you'll excuse us, I'd like to be on our way."

"Yeah," Gregory replied, his frown deepening. "Sure."

"Great." Applying the slightest bit of pressure against her back, Noah steered her around Gregory and down the street.

She waited until they were out of earshot to tell him, "We're going in the wrong direction."

"I've lost my appetite."

She wished she could say the same. Beneath the warm press of his hand, her muscles quivered. As they walked in silence, she studied him out of the corner of her eye. He was tall and lean, and had an air of confidence that drew the eye. She couldn't help but notice the female attention that tracked him—the furtive glances and blatant stares of the women they passed. It caused her to wonder if they felt what she felt when they looked at him—the sharp bite of desire.

The spark that sent her senses humming.

It would be so easy to give in to her attraction. With any other man, she wouldn't hesitate. A relationship with no strings, no commitments was what she needed right now. But she knew Noah wouldn't allow her to maintain her usual distance. He would keep pushing and pushing until she gave more than usual, felt more than usual. And then where would she be?

If she pursued a relationship with him,

she would only end up hurt. He wasn't even going to remain in town long enough to record an album, just a demo. Soon enough he'd be leaving, back to his home, his life.

And she'd be left with her feet knocked out from under her.

Her shoulders stiffened. Sliding sideways, she increased the distance between them, breathing easier as his hand dropped away from her back.

"How do you know that guy?"

His voice was easy, yet she had the sense of coiled frustration beneath the surface. Easing out a sigh, she admitted that she was most likely the cause. "Gregory? He's a well-known pianist."

"He's an ass."

"He's that, too."

They stopped in front of the parking garage where she'd left her Navigator. His stark, green eyes locked with hers. "How old is he?"

What did the man's age have to do with anything? "I don't know. Thirty-seven?"

"That's what I thought—old enough to accept the truth and move on."

"What truth?"

"That you're a much better pianist than he is."

As perverse as it was, a thrill went through her at his words. "You've heard him

104

play?"

"I don't need to. I could tell by the way he looks at you."

She frowned. For reasons she couldn't explain, Gregory always made her uncomfortable. She wondered if Noah had picked up on that. Or if he'd seen what she never had. "How does he look at me?"

"Like you're the better pianist."

"That doesn't make any sense."

A breeze stirred, picking up the ends of her hair and blowing them across her mouth. Her knees went weak as he reached out and brushed his fingers over her cheek, scooping up the strands.

"It makes perfect sense. There are people in this world that hold talent against a person, especially if they can't match that talent. Gregory is one of those people. It was obvious by the way he looks at you."

Isabeau struggled for balance, but knew she wouldn't find it. Not with him standing this close to her. Her gaze took in his black T-shirt, stretched appealingly across his broad chest, the play of muscle in his arm as he toyed with the ends of her hair. He didn't appear to have shaved that morning. Dark stubble covered his jaw, lending him a look more dangerous than normal. It looked good on him, damn good. Her throat tightened and her mouth went dry.

She knew she should step back, away

105

from his heat, away from his touch. Instead, she stood there, staring into his green eyes as she fought the urge to reach for him. Her palms began to itch with the need to test the feel of his stubble, the warmth of his flesh. Deep inside of her, desire pooled.

He shifted, her hair sliding through his fingers as he dropped his hand to his side. She closed her eyes and breathed a sigh.

"Are you ready to head back?"

"I promised you lunch."

"Yes, you did."

"Has your appetite returned?"

His mouth curved in a wide, reckless grin. "You could say that."

"I know this quaint little place in Astoria."

"Sounds good to me." He gestured toward the parking garage at her back. "Lead the way."

He fell into step beside her as they made their way into the parking structure and toward her black SUV, its vanity plate, sporting the name of her bar, visible ahead. Out of the direct sunlight, the temperature dropped about ten degrees. Her heels echoed off the concrete floor.

Circling around the back of the vehicle, she pulled her key out of her pocket and stopped. Irritation crept up her back. She narrowed her eyes and stared at the long, ugly scratch that ran the length of the driver's side of the vehicle.

"Isabeau."

Her stomach churned. An icy cold rage washed over her. She stepped forward, and ran the tips of her fingers over the scratch, measuring its depth. Her anger increased as she realized the scratch was deep enough she would have to call a body shop and schedule a repair. Her SUV was nine months old and someone deliberately damaged it.

"Isa," Noah said again, and this time his tone penetrated.

"What is it?" she asked, circling to the passenger side. "Another scratch?"

A scowl on his face, he turned to her as she stepped to his side. "Someone scratched your vehicle?"

"Yes." She fisted her hand around her key. "Damn it, it's a bad one, too."

"I'm sorry."

"So am I."

"Maybe now would be a good time to tell me what Tommy said to you last night."

His abrupt change of subject made her extremely uncomfortable. "Why?"

Her gaze followed his as it shifted to the front of her SUV. Her eyes narrowed. Then everything inside of her froze as she focused on the knife handle sticking out the side of her very flat tire.

"Someone did more than scratch it, Isa."

****

"So you have no idea who would do this to your vehicle?"

One of New York's finest stood before Isabeau, looking pressed, polished, and in control while her nerves continued to two-step up and down her spine. Behind her, the man from her roadside assistance plan changed her tire, while Noah stood off to her left, engaged in conversation with this officer's partner. "None."

"But you believe this is personal."

"I don't know," she admitted. "I suppose it could be a random act, maybe bored kids." She glanced up at the tall, slim officer with short-cropped brown hair and dark brown eyes. The name tag over the left pocket of his spotless uniform shirt read Grant. "Honestly, if it wasn't for the fact that I need a police report in order to get my insurance company to cover the repairs, I probably wouldn't have reported this."

Officer Grant flashed her a smile. It was a nice smile, even if it didn't have the desired effect on her.

"You did the right thing," he said, his gaze moving over her face. "Not that I can't imagine kids slashing tires for fun, but the knife being left like that feels a bit menacing."

She rubbed at the sudden chill in her arms.

The officer's smile melted into a frown as he focused on her left upper arm. "How long have you known him?"

"Who?"

He tipped his head in the direction of Noah, standing off to the side.

"A few weeks."

Officer Grant kept his gaze on her face, frank and assessing, as he propped his hand on his utility belt. "He responsible for that bruise you're sporting?"

"No."

"Maybe he's got a temper? Objected with a bit more force than necessary over something he perceived you did wrong?"

She shook her head. "You're right about the temper, but you've got the wrong man. Noah didn't do this."

"Noah?"

"Noah Clark."

He shifted his gaze. "As in Noah Clark, from Black Phoenix? I thought I recognized you."

You? She closed her eyes. She didn't need to glance over her shoulder to know Noah had moved. Even knowing, she startled as his hand settled on her lower back.

Nerves and desire mixed, sent her pulse skittering. She could have sworn the temperature in the parking structure shot up ten degrees.

Officer Grant offered his hand. "I've been a fan of yours for years."

"Thank you," Noah replied.

"Are you planning anything new?"

"There's a new album in the works."

"I can't wait."

Keeping his hand firmly against her back, Noah leaned in. "Did you tell him about Tommy?"

She opened her mouth, closed it. She couldn't concentrate. Not when Noah touched her. She needed to step back, get away from this man who made her head spin. But every minute she spent in his company seemed to move them closer. A few hours ago he never would have reached for her as if he had every right to touch her. More importantly, she never would have let him.

She forced herself to meet his unnerving green eyes. She shifted, but Noah didn't remove his hand from her. Instead, her change in position shifted his hand higher on her spine. His fingers slid beneath her shirt and brushed across her bare skin.

Longings sprang through her. She swallowed hard, shook her head and tried to stay on topic. "No."

He gave her a knowing look. "But you were planning to, right?"

"I don't know that he had anything to do with this."

"You don't know that he didn't."

Easing out a breath, she rubbed at the

bruises on her arm. Despite the damage to her car, she wasn't ready to give voice to the happenings of last night. Or to lay blame for the damage to her SUV at Tommy's feet. "I won't accuse him of anything."

"Then don't make any accusations. Give the officer the information and let him take it from there."

Officer Grant looked from her to Noah, then back at her. "Who's Tommy?"

"Tommy Cahill," Noah supplied.

"Junior," she quickly corrected. The last thing she needed was the police knocking on her father's door instead of Tommy's. "Thomas Cahill, Junior."

"Junior, got it. What did Junior do that I need to know about?"

"He roughed her up last night," Noah supplied when she didn't respond quickly enough.

Isabeau frowned at him.

"He had a few words with her, too. She won't share with me what he said, but I get the feeling it's something you should hear."

"Ma'am?"

She looked away. She hugged her arms around herself and shivered. Because suddenly, she was very, very cold.

She'd looked Noah in the eye and denied Tommy's words held any importance, because they'd been so painful she didn't want to repeat them. Didn't want him to know what Tommy said to her hurt more than his hand vised around her arm. That as an only child who'd lost her mother at twelve, she'd always hoped to form a bond with the son of the man she thought of as her father. Or that during those few minutes he'd had her pinned against the wall, Tommy shattered that optimism with more than cruel words.

Tears welled up and she blinked them furiously away. His words didn't matter. None of it did. From now on, she'd be more careful whenever Tommy was around—careful not to find herself in a position where he could get his hands on her.

Or any other part of his anatomy.

A wave of dizziness washed over her.

"Whoa." Noah shifted his hand from her back to snag her elbow. "That's the second time today all the color has drained from your face at the mention of Tommy's comments to you."

"It's just..."

"Ma'am, I think you should tell me what he said."

Her stomach cramped abruptly, bile climbed up the back of her throat. In her mind she replayed not just the hate-filled words, but the press of his erection against her abdomen as he snarled them.

Shifting sideways, she made sure Noah no longer touched her as she repeated Tommy's words verbatim. "'You think you're something special, don't you, half-breed? You think you're better than me? Because you've got my father's affection? Let me tell you, you're nothin'. Just the daughter of his dead whore girlfriend. A little half-breed nothin'.' "

Noah's body went tight as a bowstring. "Bastard."

"No, technically, that would be me."

"Isabeau," he warned.

"My parents weren't married," she explained, her focus now on Officer Grant. "I was a toddler when my mother moved in with Tommy's father."

"Who is also your father?" the officer questioned.

"Biologically, no. My father and Tommy's are two different men, hence Tommy's referring to my mother as...It doesn't matter."

"It matters," Noah argued.

"No." She closed her eyes, opened them. "They're just angry words, spoken by a man who'd had too much to drink."

Noah reached out, tucked an errant strand of hair behind her ear. "Which is why you shouldn't take them to heart."

"What he said is—"

"Not true. Nothing he said is true, Isabeau."

"But it does tell me that Tommy Cahill, Junior, is someone I need to speak with," Officer

Grant stated. "A man with that kind of anger toward you wouldn't hesitate to vandalize your vehicle." He tipped his head toward his partner, who stood next to their cruiser. "My partner and I will check it out. When we find out anything, we'll be in touch. In the meantime, a copy of the report will be available to you tomorrow."

"Thank you." Her gaze tracked Officer Grant until he slid behind the wheel of his police cruiser and maneuvered out of the parking garage. She looked back at Noah.

He'd narrowed the distance between them and now stood dangerously close to her. The fact that every nerve in her body scrambled had her desperate to step away. Then her lungs drew in the inviting scent of him, and she couldn't bring herself to move.

"He's wrong," he said, drawing the back of his fingers down her cheek.

How did he do that? Take her from cold to hot with one touch? "Who's wrong?"

"Tommy. You are special."

Emotion clogging her throat, she stared at him.

"You're special to me."

CHAPTER SEVEN

Isabeau stood at her kitchen sink, staring at the swirl of red as it washed down the drain. It was Thursday, her night off, and because she found it impossible to relax, she'd painted her bathroom. Every time she sat still for more than five minutes, her thoughts would drift to Noah, always to Noah. Even now, as she worked to rinse paint from the brush, his face slipped to the forefront of her mind. She saw his eyes, those striking green orbs that seemed to see right into her. She felt his hands on her back, the shock of electricity his touch sparked, and something inside of her quickened to a gallop.

Even as her brain tried to warn her away.

Thoughts of him kept stirring up feelings she didn't want to examine too closely. Staring blankly while her mind raced, she worked to clear her thoughts of him. She focused on the music that drifted softly from the speakers around her apartment. But as the whiskey-smooth tenor crooned about being ready for love, sighed in defeat.

She'd been happy with her life, content to mind her business when Noah walked through her door and smacked her between the eyes. He knocked her off kilter, made her feel unsettled and edgy. Made her think about things she hadn't thought about in years, wish for things she couldn't have. Not with him.

Not with any man.

Isabeau sighed. She flicked off the water. Turning, she leaned back against the counter and studied her surroundings. Thanks to her restlessness, her apartment was spotless. Everywhere she looked surfaces gleamed and sparkled beneath the glow of recessed lighting. There was nothing left to dust or vacuum. Nothing left to keep her mind occupied, away from thoughts of the too-sexy singer.

A knock sounded at the door. She frowned. Suddenly the music sounded louder, her body more sensitized. She knew before opening the door, the identity of her visitor. "Noah."

He stood with his shoulder against the doorjamb, legs crossed at the ankles, as he skimmed his gaze from her toes up her bare legs. His attention paused on her paint-splattered tank top and cut-off jean shorts before continuing to her eyes. "Hello."

She dragged in a breath as her nerves scrambled. Dark need stirred her blood. "Hi."

How could he look even sexier than the last time she'd seen him? It wasn't possible. But he did. From the worn, comfortable jeans that hugged him in all the right places, to the green T-shirt that matched his eyes, the man looked sinfully good. She was still trying to absorb the effect he had on her nerves when he smiled. Damn him. His smile was wicked and cocksure.

It took her breath away.

"Should I have rung you first?"

"What? No." She stepped back and gestured with her hand. "Come on in."

He stepped inside, and she shut the door behind him. His gaze swept around the room before coming back to her. "Have you been painting?"

Maybe she should have left the door open. Was it hot in here? "I painted the bathroom. How'd you know?"

"I can smell it," he replied. "Plus, you have a bit of red paint right..." He reached for her, the pad of his thumb brushing slowly across her collarbone. "Here."

Heat sizzled to life between them. Every cell in her body tingled. Her breath froze in her lungs. She felt herself leaning toward him. For her own peace of mind, she eased back.

His hand dropped away. He frowned. "I didn't get all of it."

She absently scrubbed at the spot. "It doesn't matter. It's latex paint, it will come off in the shower."

"Okay." He rocked back on his heels and continued to watch her in a disconcerting way.

She was unable to read his expression until the music on her stereo changed to the next CD. As the first few beats played, his smile returned. "Aren't you a little too young to be a fan of Thin Lizzy?"

"You can never be too young or too old for great music."

"How do you decide what is great and what isn't?"

"You expect me to say by the artist's skill, don't you? But that's only part of it. Personally, I judge music by the way it makes me feel."

"And how does Thin Lizzy make you feel?" he asked, as he crossed the room to her fireplace and the racks of compact discs that littered the mantel top. The fact that he appeared totally comfortable in her home, while she was a mass of nerves, filled her with dismay.

"Energized," she replied. "Happy."

His fingers traced over the spine of each disc until he located and removed one. "What about this one? How does it make you feel?"

She shifted her gaze, then wrinkled her nose. "You can have that one if you'd like. It gave me a headache."

Amusement slid into his eyes. "No, thanks. It had the same effect on me."

Her lips curved.

"You have an extensive collection," he commented, his attention back on the collection he spoke of.

"It's a passion," she admitted, then crossed the room to stand next to him. "Some might call it a compulsion, but I love all kinds of music."

"Do you ever listen to your own music?"

"No. Do you?"

"Sometimes." He faced her. In his hand, he held one of his own CDs. "I'm surprised you have this one. It didn't sell very well."

"No?"

He opened the case and discovered it was empty.

"In the CD player." She had one of those players that held over three hundred CDs. She kept it full. "Number thirty-two."

He shifted to stand before the player, studied it for a minute, then turned the dial. The machine responded immediately, shuffling through the discs until it reached the correct slot. An electric guitar riff filled the room, immediately followed by his voice.

Tempted; her favorite song.

He shook his head.

"You didn't believe me?"

"I thought perhaps you were being kind."

"Why would I be kind?" She winced the moment the words left her mouth. "I didn't mean that the way it sounded."

He gave her a slow, alluring smile that turned into laughter. "I'm not certain if you're

119

good or bad for my ego, Isa."

She couldn't breathe. For a split second, she forgot how. The man's smile was powerful enough, but when he laughed? Nothing had prepared her for the power of his laughter. Her knees turned to jelly. Her blood heated.

"I think your ego will survive," she managed around the knot in her throat.

His gaze moved over her with a touch as sure as his fingertips had been a few moments ago. "You think your opinion of me doesn't matter?"

"In the grand scheme of things, I don't see how it would, but you don't need to worry, I like you just fine."

More than fine. His nearness put knots of tension in her stomach. The way he continued to look at her made the tightness she'd felt in her chest since he told her she was special, intensify. Desperate to put a bit of space between them, she asked, "Would you like to sit down?"

He sprawled—there was no other word for it—on the couch closest to him. Resting his arms across the back, he placed one booted foot atop the opposite knee. The position of his arms pushed the sleeves of his shirt up higher than normal and revealed a wrapping around his right upper arm. The light reflected off of it in a way that told her exactly what it was. "You've seen my father today?"

"I have."

"How's he doing?"

"Haven't you spoken with him?"

She sank onto the second couch across from him and shook her head. "No. I didn't know what to say to him. I hoped to hear back from Officer Grant before I told him about what happened to my vehicle."

"What if I told you he already knows?"

"How? Did you tell him?"

"I didn't have to."

Removing the clip that held all her hair atop her head, she tossed it on the coffee table between them, then raked her fingers through her hair. "What did he say?"

"That he'd heard you had a bit of trouble. He asked how bad it was, and how well you were taking it. He also asked whether I believed Tommy was to blame."

"And you told him what?"

He eyed her for a long moment. "That Tommy was the first person to come to mind when I saw the knife sticking out of your tire."

Everything inside of her went still. She closed her eyes and took a deep breath. "I should call him."

"I'm sure he'd love to hear from you. He's an interesting man, your father. He cares about you a great deal."

She gave him a cool look. "Yesterday you questioned his integrity. You accused him of hurting me."

"I didn't accuse him of anything. I asked if he was the one who hurt you."

"Who said anyone hurt me?"

He returned his foot to the floor and leaned forward, his elbows on his knees. "You did. I simply questioned whether your father was that someone."

Her heart skipped a beat or two. He had no idea how close to the truth he was. Too close. She wasn't going to talk to him about this. Her past was exactly where it belonged, in the past. She wouldn't revisit it for anyone.

"Thomas isn't my..." Her voice wavered, and she dragged in a breath to steady it. "I'm not actually his daughter."

"According to biology. If I asked him, I bet he feels differently. Otherwise, he never would have fought so hard to keep you."

She went still for a long moment, her eyes closed, wishing he hadn't just said that. There was only one way he knew of Thomas's fight to win custody of her. "You've been on the Internet."

"Only after you made your accusations that day in the bar. At the time, I had no idea what you were talking about. How much of what's there is true?"

She hated this part. Telling people about her past.

Who was she kidding? She didn't share

her past with anyone. Ever.

"They got the major points right. There was an accident—my mother died, I nearly died. My biological father took Thomas to court to get custody of me and won."

"Yet quite a bit is incorrect. You're not horribly disfigured, or dead. And having met Thomas for myself, I do not believe he had anything but the truest of paternal love for you."

"God, what the press made him out to be." She dragged the heel of her palm across her forehead as tears welled in her eyes.

Noah rose off the couch, stepped around the coffee table and sank down next to her. He laid a hand over hers. "The press can be brutal."

The touch of his hand atop hers warmed her blood. The understanding in his voice soothed the sharp edges of her memory.

"How did Thomas and Nicole meet?" he asked, surprising her by remembering her mother's name.

"Through a mutual friend."

"You were two?"

"Yes. They had two years together before that day at the symphony hall."

"The day you first played the piano?"

"Yes." The day she walked onstage after her mother's rehearsal and sat at the piano. Pressed her fingers to the keys and turned the music world on its ear by playing the last number the guest soloist had practiced.

Perfectly.

It was the first time she'd ever touched a piano, but far from the last.

"After that day, things got pretty out of hand. Instantly, I was an international sensation. A child with an ear for music; a raw talent that rivaled the masters of the time." Her breath became shallow. She lowered her voice. "A child who'd only been doing what she loved and didn't understand the fascination."

"I can't imagine."

"At first, I was too young to realize how different I was. It was only after the fallout of my first television interview, the one where with the innocence of youth I told the reporter, 'There's music all around us. Only certain people hear it and even fewer take the time to listen,' that I learned to keep my mouth shut about exactly how I played music after hearing it only once."

"I never saw that interview."

"Lucky you." Nerves humming, she pushed off the couch and walked a few paces away. She never talked about it, never gave so much of her soul away. Noah needed to understand. He needed to know why she was not what he wanted.

"As I got older I began performing as a guest soloist throughout the world with well-known symphony orchestras. Between the tours, the appearances and the interviews, Mom and I were on the road more than we were home with Thomas. I always felt bad about that, that because of me, their time together was cut short."

"Cut short? She was your mother, she wasn't forced to tour with you, she chose to. She could have taken you back home after that first day, never to let the world find out about you."

Isabeau closed her eyes and shook her head.

"Certainly you don't believe you are the reason for her death?"

Her chest ached. It was her fault. The injury to her hand. Her mother's death. All of it.

"Isabeau?" His warm hand settled on her shoulder and she startled, snapped her eyes open and came face to face with him. "You can't hold yourself responsible for her death."

"We had been on the road for ten weeks," she explained, her voice barely above a whisper. "It was the last performance before returning home for the Thanksgiving holiday. I couldn't wait. I was tired of touring. Tired of being put...I didn't want to perform any more. I wanted to go home and see Thomas. I missed him."

Her voice hitched. She attempted to level it. "The performance went well. We were scheduled to fly home the next morning, but I convinced my mother to catch the red-eye instead. I hate to fly. Normally I would never do it sooner than necessary, but I was exhausted. I wanted it behind me." She paused as it all came back to her with perfect clarity. "It was late. I remember asking if I could lie down in the back seat and mom insisting I couldn't. She buckled my lap belt, and we were off. We were only two blocks from home when the accident happened. It was snowing, and the roads were icy. I remember taillights, a car swerving in front of us then..."

She closed her eyes against the painful memory. "My mother screamed. I'll never forget that. She reached for me. Then there was this sound—metal bending—and this blur that must have been the car tumbling. Then, silence."

His hand atop her shoulder flexed.

"Mom hadn't buckled her own belt. She'd secured me in, but not herself. Her body was tossed around like a rag doll as we rolled over and over. She bled to death while I watched, while the wail of sirens echoed off the buildings." Her stomach clenched painfully, her body trembled as, in her mind, she revisited the accident. "They were too late. Too late to save her."

"I'm so sorry, Isa."

"She was smart and funny, then in the blink of an eye, she was gone. I couldn't get to her. I tried. I struggled and I tried to get across that backseat so I could hold her. I thought if I could hold her, I could save her. Of course what I had yet to realize was that my hand was pinned, crushed between the seat and the side of the car. I couldn't possibly get to her."

The palm he placed against her cheek was gentle. She reached up and pulled his hand from her face. But instead of letting go, she curled her fingers around his. "If only I hadn't pushed her to come home early."

"You're not responsible for her death."

"Aren't I?"

"It was an accident, Isabeau, a tragic accident."

She stared down at their joined hands, hers so small and tanned and scarred, his so much larger and paler. She had allowed him to cross a barrier, and suddenly he could touch her. If he could touch her, he could pull her toward him—literally and figuratively. She told herself she didn't want that.

Liar.

"I miss her so much." The words kept coming. Intimate. Revealing. "My mother would hold me. She was the sort who touched people often, not just to comfort or soothe. Every day, at least once a day she would stroke my hair and tell me how much she loved me. Every night she held me as I drifted to sleep. I miss that."

He gazed at her intently. Without judgment, without that look of fear men tended to wear when emotion came into a conversation. Looking back at him, she felt it again—that thing that had been between them from the start. Stronger now. Not as easy to ignore.

"Tell me about her."

"My mother was beautiful—blonde hair, blue eyes, about my height and build. She was friendly, a bit naive. My biological father was eight years older than she, twenty-six to her eighteen when they first met. She was twenty when she left him, pregnant with me. She struggled for a couple of years before being picked up by the New York Philharmonic, but she got by. Six months later, Mom met Thomas."

"Whom she moved in with."

"She wasn't...a loose woman. No matter what Tommy said."

"I'm not judging her, Isa, believe me."

She eased away from him, wrapped her arms around her middle. "You're right, I'm sorry."

He stared down at her. "You didn't say, was your mother French?"

"No, but her great-grandmother was."

"Is that where you got your name?"

She nodded. "Mom loved her dearly. When she died the year I was born, Mom gave me her name."

"It's a beautiful name."

His soft statement jump-started her pulse. But it was nothing compared to the effect his next question had on her.

"What about your biological father? That's how you always refer to him. Does the man have a name?"

"The devil incarnate," she thought with a shudder of revulsion. *Oh God, had she said that out loud?*

She waited for him to comment. His expression was serious, but he remained silent. Thank God. No way would he let a statement like that pass. "His name was John Whitehorse."

"Was he the man in the picture taken in front of the court house?"

Her spine went rigid. She didn't have to ask him to know which picture he was speaking of. He meant the one taken at the end of the trial, when she'd literally been ripped from the arms of the only father she'd ever known and given to a man who didn't want her, just her bank account. The media loved the drama of it, and had splashed that picture on the front page of newspapers nationwide.

"He was the man pulling me away from Thomas, yes."

Eyes eloquent, he reached up and cupped his hand against the side of her face. His thumb swept back and forth across her cheek. She closed her eyes. It would be so easy to fall for him, to forget that he wasn't the guy for her. There was something about him that made her want. More than she'd ever wanted before.

A lot more.

Shifting away from him before she did

something she would regret later, she circled the couch and reclaimed her spot on the end. "Enough about me. Tell me something about you."

He leaned his hip against the back of the couch. "What do you want to know?"

"What did you do after you stopped singing? You said you went back to London?"

"Yes, for about six years. The first few months of which I did nothing but wallow in grief. I drank too much, didn't sleep enough, and was very unpleasant to be around. Then my grandfather decided he'd had enough. He came over and dragged me back to life, literally. Right out the front door and into the rain. Left me out there until I sobered up, after which he hauled me back inside, sat me down, and explained to me how things were going to change. He made certain I understood that my behavior would no longer be tolerated."

"An intervention."

His mouth curved. "I guess it was."

"He loves you, he didn't want to see you waste away."

His smile faded as he gazed at her. She curled her left hand around his wrist. "What's the matter?"

"Henry's not a young man any more. I'm worried about him. I could see the last time I spoke with him that his health is failing."

Without thinking, she slid her hand down

and linked her fingers with his. She ached for him, knowing how difficult it was to lose a loved one. "When is the last time you saw him?"

"Right before I moved to the new house. About six months ago."

"You should go see him again, once your demo is done."

"I plan to." He shifted their joined hands, used his free hand to trace the length of her pinky and ring finger. "Your fingers are cold."

"They always are. They sustained too much damage in the accident."

"Any nerve damage?"

"Yes. Not the way you'd think though. They're actually more sensitive than the other fingers." Overly sensitive. The brush of his fingertips sent a shock of electricity up her arm, jolting her already raw nerves. Her body hummed as his warmth began to seep into her hand, then into her bloodstream.

"It's a miracle you can still play at all," he commented softly.

Her stomach crawled into her throat.

At one point in her life she would have agreed with him, but that time was long past. "I don't play anymore."

His hand tightened on hers as she tried to pull away. "Because you choose not to."

"Yes."

"But you regained the ability, should you ever change your mind."

"I won't change my mind."

His lips curved, but his smile was not reflected in his eyes. "After Henry's intervention, I straightened up my act. I was happy—I had a job, a woman—I never thought I'd go back to performing."

She didn't miss performing. She would never admit it to him, but there were times she did miss playing. Like the night they'd met, when she longed to relive the joy only the piano brought her. But performing, sitting in a hushed symphony hall, with all those eyes focused on her...

She would never go back to that. "We're two different people, Noah."

"I'm just saying that you can only pretend for so long. When you live music, the way we do, you can't push it aside. Eventually, it comes back into your life and when it does...it's not always pretty."

They were two different people, she silently repeated. Just because she could no longer silence the music in her head, didn't mean that she had to give in to it. She wouldn't let it rule her life.

Or ruin it.

Wondering how ugly his return to music had been, she asked, "What happened?"

"Beth and I had been living together for about two years, when I quit my job. I remember the night I told her I wanted us to move across the pond, so I could get the band back together. She laughed. I guess she thought I was joking. When she realized I had never been more serious, she accused me of deceiving her."

"Deceiving her?"

"I never talked about singing, not once while we were together, not even to reminisce. She was blindsided by my sudden change of heart."

"What did she do?"

"She yelled and she cried, then she left me. I was no longer what she wanted. She wanted marriage and family—a husband who worked nine-to-five and could be home with her in the evenings. I wasn't willing to give her that last bit."

"There's nothing nine-to-five about the music industry."

"No, there isn't."

She noted he didn't say he hadn't been willing to give her marriage and family. Family. Her free hand shifted to rest on her abdomen, as her eyes slid closed. It wasn't difficult to picture his child, a child with his striking green eyes and incredible smile. There was no doubt about it, he would have beautiful children. Just not with her. Never with her.

Her chest ached. Her throat tightened.

"Is something wrong, Isabeau?"

Her eyelids snapped open. He waited,

eyes warm as she struggled with control. A sharp rap on her door stopped her from having to explain.

Isabeau slid off the couch and crossed the room. She swung the door open. "Dad. You're out late."

"We need to talk to you."

"We?" That's when she noticed Tommy standing to his right, eyes bloodshot, the left one bruised and swollen.

Cold seeped into her bones. Her father couldn't have done that to him. He wouldn't.

Her gaze lowered to Thomas's hands.

"Izzy?" he questioned.

"Come on in."

Her father acknowledged Noah with a tip of his head, then looked back at her. "Tommy has something to say to you."

"I'm not a kid anymore, Dad," Tommy replied caustically. "I can manage my own apology."

"You wouldn't know it by the way you act."

Tommy narrowed his eyes. He let out an audible breath and skimmed his gaze over her arm. "You were right to cut me off the other night."

"Tommy, I—"

"I'm not done!" he hissed, his hands fisted.

She took an automatic step in retreat.

Tommy frowned. He swore under his breath and shoved a trembling hand through his hair, which only left it more disheveled.

Bloodshot eyes. The shakes. He was suffering from alcohol withdrawal. She'd witnessed the effects enough times to recognize them. More than once, a patron came into the bar in much the same condition as Tommy, desperately in need of a drink to ease the discomfort. Despite everything, it pained her to witness Tommy's suffering.

"I have a problem," he admitted. "A problem with alcohol. It's my problem. I shouldn't have taken it out on you."

She waited, making sure he was done before she responded. "I appreciate you coming here, Tommy."

"Yeah. Listen, the cops came to my place yesterday. They said your car was vandalized. I want you to know I didn't do it. Damn cops. Woke me up, pounding on my door."

"Okay."

"That's it. That's what I had to say." And with that, he turned and walked out the door.

Relief flooded her. She knew Tommy wouldn't—couldn't—hurt her with both Noah and her father standing right there. Still, his presence unsettled her.

"Lock your door tonight."

At the firm command in her father's voice, her muscles tightened all over again.

135

"If Tommy isn't responsible for the damage to your SUV, then there's still someone out there who has a problem with you." Thomas scrubbed his hand over the back of his neck. "Next time, Izzy, tell me yourself when something like this happens. I don't appreciate having to hear about it from the cops."

"They questioned you, too?"

"Yes, they did."

"I'm sorry." More sorry than he knew. Thomas Cahill and the New York City police had a long history because of her. One he didn't deserve. "I didn't know."

"I know you didn't."

"Dad."

He sighed and shook his head. "Noah, watch out for her."

"I will."

"And get that wrap off. It's been on there long enough."

"Straight away."

Thomas left, pulling the door closed behind him.

"He's right, you know, you need to be careful."

Her stomach clenched painfully. She didn't see the damage to her vehicle as a threat. Maybe because in the back of her mind she agreed with Noah that Tommy was the most likely suspect. But Tommy denied the vandalism, and Isabeau believed him. If not

Tommy, who?

She needed a distraction. "Take the wrap off. I think I have some triple antibiotic ointment in the medicine cabinet."

She did, and she returned to the kitchen with it, along with a two clean washcloths.

Noah held the wrap from his arm in his hand. "Where's your trash?"

"Under the sink."

She ran a washcloth under warm water. Ringing out the excess, she turned to him and pushed his sleeve out of the way. The area was a bit swollen and had scabbed in a few places. It was because of this totally natural reaction to getting a tattoo that her father had wrapped his arm in plastic wrap. Had he used something like gauze, it would have stuck to the area, and removing the gauze would pull the scabs loose, bringing the ink with it. As a result, scarring of the area, and blotching of the color could occur.

His shirt sleeve slipped down as she pressed the warm cloth to his skin. She shoved it back out of the way.

"Wait," he said as it slipped a second time. He reached his arm over his head. Fisting his hand in his shirt, he pulled it off.

There was something so inherently male about the move that she didn't look away. Then, once he stood before her wearing nothing but his jeans, she couldn't look away. He was built. His body was sleek, smooth, and leanly muscled.

Lightly tanned, with hard six-pack abs and a dark blonde line of hair that started below his navel and trailed down to disappear beneath the waistband of his jeans.

Not that she was looking.

Or drooling.

There was no doubt about it, he looked better than most men half his age.

"Is something wrong, Isa?"

Arousal clouded her mind. Her body thrummed with it. "What? No."

But as she pressed the cloth against his skin, her hand shook.

She tried to keep her focus on her task and off his chest, but it was right there. Suddenly she was hyperaware of the heat coming off him, of the scent of musk and man that swam through her senses.

"So what do you think?" His breath whispered across her temple.

She thought she wanted to reach out and see if his skin was as soft as it looked, his body as hard. She swallowed. Her dry throat stuck together. "What do I think?"

"About the tattoo."

"The tattoo?" Perfect. She sounded like an idiot.

Heat flooded her cheeks. She could feel his eyes on her and knew he noticed. He had a habit of watching her in a way that made her toes curl, her stomach turn over. She'd caught him doing it on more than one occasion and knew if she tipped her head up, she'd catch him doing it now.

So she focused on his tattoo, and smiled. Thomas had given him a small skeletal body, wings and a halo above the over-sized and even more animated skull. "It's perfect."

Trading the wet washcloth for a clean, dry one, she patted his arm dry, then applied a thin layer of ointment. "There you go."

"Thank you." Reaching up, he tucked a stray wisp of hair behind her ear.

Her breathing shallowed when his fingers grazed the side of her throat, caught as his other hand settled on her hip. Slowly her eyes raised, moved up his throat, past his dangerously tempting mouth, before she met his gaze and felt a punch of awareness.

"You have the most beautiful eyes," he said, and shifted just a little closer.

Never had her eyes been called beautiful. Strange? Yes. Beautiful? Never.

"They change color depending on what you're feeling, did you know that?"

"I...no."

"Right now they're blue—a very pale blue. What does that mean, Isa? Tell me what you're feeling right now."

Desire. Need, unlike she'd ever felt before. She'd had no idea how much she'd craved a physical touch, his touch. Her stomach fluttered. Her heart skipped a few beats. She slicked her tongue over her lips, and his hand flexed against her hip.

"I have to know," he murmured.

"What?"

"Your taste."

He slipped his hand from her hip to the small of her back, pulling her against him. Their bodies molded, soft to hard. His thigh slid between hers and desire curled her toes, tightened her nipples into hard, aching points. And still, he didn't kiss her. Why didn't he kiss her? Then he did. *Finally*, he did. He teased her lips with his tongue, and she opened to him, drank in his dark seductive flavor.

She settled her hand against his chest, reveling in the feel of hard muscle and hot male. Good God the man could kiss. His body surrounded her, engulfed her as his mouth continued to seduce. She arched into him, and as his erection pressed against her stomach, she couldn't hold back a moan.

The tube of ointment dropped to the floor. Her fingers tangled in his hair. Her heart raced and she realized his was pounding a matching rhythm against her breasts. Deep inside her, something quivered.

He pulled his head back, easing out of the kiss. His left hand still cupped her throat, his thumb slowly brushing back and forth. His skin was flushed, his eyes full of longing. He leaned down and kissed her softly one more time before releasing her and stepping back.

"Noah?"

His gaze ran the length of her, his attention paused on her erect nipples before returning to her face. He let out a slow breath as if struggling for control. "I think I'd better leave," he said, his voice all low and husky.

Sexy.

Arousing.

She squeezed her thighs together. He must have caught the action because his pupils dilated.

"Oh, yeah, it's time to go," he said softly as he scooped his shirt off the floor and pulled it on.

He walked to the door, opened it and started outside as if desperate to get away from her. Then he stopped, half in and half out the door and looked back over his shoulder. "Don't forget to lock your door."

"Right."

"Isabeau?" He waited until her gaze returned to his. "Pleasant dreams," he said, and then he was gone.

CHAPTER EIGHT

"You should join us."

Isabeau placed the studio's lunch order next to Dominic's elbow, then slipped through the pass thru and took her place behind the bar. It was still about forty-five minutes before any of her employees arrived, so she had the time for a friendly chat. "Join you and do what?"

"Play, of course."

"You want me to play soccer with the four of you?" she asked, not bothering to hide her skepticism. "Have you looked at the size of me compared to the rest of you?"

Dominic placed his elbows atop the bar and leaned forward. He gave her an engaging smile. "Your build will work to your advantage, trust me. We're not talking about your American football, Isabeau, but soccer. In soccer it's about speed and agility."

"And fancy footwork."

"There's a bit of that, too."

She thought about all the photos of the professional soccer players she'd seen in her lifetime. They always depicted a player hanging in mid-air, feet out to the side as they kicked the

142

ball, or worse, chasing down the field, ball between their feet while a slew of the other team's players attempted to steal it. She looked up at Dominic, who stood around the same height as Noah, then she pictured four guys that size swarming her on the soccer field. It may not be American football he was talking about, and tackling might not be a part of the game, but the thought of being the tiny girl in the middle of that much testosterone and competitive spirit didn't thrill her.

"How often is one of you injured during one of these games?"

The corners of his mouth turned down.

"That's what I thought."

"We'd take it easy on you."

"Don't do me any favors," she replied dryly, turning his frown into a wide grin.

"Come on, luv," he challenged. "I've seen you run. Combine that with your size, and I bet you're a bleedin' dynamo on the field."

She was crazy to even consider it.

"You can be on my team."

"Is that supposed to convince me?"

"I'm a good player," he said modestly.

"I'll think about it."

"Brilliant!"

She glanced at the clock on the wall behind her, and frowned. Her fingers danced atop the bar, unconsciously playing along with the song on the stereo. Where was her father?

When she'd called him up this morning, and asked him to come by because she needed to speak with him, he'd assured her that he would arrive before her lunch rush.

"What's with you today, Isabeau?"

"What do you mean?"

"Do you have somewhere you need to be?"

"No."

"Something's up with you. You keep looking at the clock, and you're fidgeting."

Her hand stopped moving. She curled her fingers against her palms. "I've got a lot on my mind this morning."

"I see. That would explain why you forgot to turn on the stereo."

"I didn't..." she began to argue, but then stopped as she realized that he was right, the only music in the bar was what was playing in her head. Dread settled in. It was getting worse.

She was losing her mind.

Without comment, she turned and flicked on the stereo. She tucked the remote into her back pocket, then turned back to Dominic only to find him looking at her, an odd look in his eyes. "What?"

His gaze drifted down the front of her and stopped on her lower half. "I like your trousers."

She glanced down at her airbrushed jeans. "My pants? A friend made them for me."

"A friend made your pants?"

"Yes."

He didn't comment for a full minute. Just stood there, his mouth hitched up on one side, blue eyes twinkling. "Can I see them? I've never seen custom-made pants before."

"You're looking at them."

"No, I'm looking at your trousers," he replied with a devilish grin. "If you removed your trousers, then I'd be looking at your pants."

Surprise jolted through her and her mouth dropped open. "You mean my panties? You're talking about my panties, aren't you?"

He raised a palm and said with complete innocence, "I complimented you on your trousers. You're the one who brought your knickers into the conversation."

She laughed; she couldn't help it. He'd done it on purpose, of course, managed to twist the conversation in a way that made her head spin. "How long have you lived in the States and you still don't know the difference between women's underwear and jeans?"

"It seems to me, you were the one confused."

"You're incorrigible, you know that?"

"So I've been told. But to answer your question, I don't live here. I live in London."

She leaned against the bar. "That explains a lot."

"Meaning what?"

"For one thing, it explains why your accent is stronger than Noah's."

"Yes. He's been in California almost three years now." He arched an eyebrow, his gaze slowly sliding down the length of her. "Is that what's got you all twitchy this morning? You finally gave that sorry bloke a chance, did you?"

"A chance at what?"

"A chance at you."

She was still searching for the right response when the inner door swung open and Thomas walked in, stiff-necked and forbidding in his black leather vest and matching skull cap. His narrowed gaze drifted over Dom and settled on her.

"You wanted to see me," he stated acridly.

She glanced pointedly over her shoulder. Over two hours had passed since she'd called him.

He followed her gaze to the clock. "I was with a customer," he supplied, daring her to argue.

She knew his moods, knew his intimidation tactics. They didn't work on her. "Now I am. Have a seat, I'll be right with you."

Thomas harrumphed and crossed to the nearest table, where he chose a chair facing the bar. He openly scrutinized Dom as he said, "Do your old dad a favor and bring something for me to drink, will you?"

Although he was purposely trying to rile her, it wasn't going to work. She understood why he was short with her. After all, she hadn't given him an explanation that morning when she'd called and asked him to come. He hadn't been happy about it at the time, and apparently he still wasn't. That couldn't be helped. She couldn't have this conversation over the telephone. It had to be in person.

"Is that Thomas?" Dominic asked, drawing her gaze away from her father and back to him.

"Yes."

"He's one big guy."

She grinned at him. "You're not falling for his intimidation tactics are you?"

"I'm wondering if his son has the same build."

She took in her father's broad shoulders, bulging biceps, and overall size. "He does."

"That would explain it then."

"Explain what?"

"Why Noah was concerned enough to take the next day to check on you. You were lucky, you know."

"I know."

Dominic grabbed the handle on the bag containing lunch and lifted it off the bar. "I'd better get going and let you talk to your dad. I'll ring you when we head to the field for soccer."

"Sure."

Her gaze tracked him until he pushed open the door and slipped outside. "What can I get you to drink, Dad?"

147

"I'll take a beer."

Grabbing a bottle out of the cooler, she slipped out from behind the bar and carried it to the table with her. She placed the beer before him as she slid into the seat opposite his.

Thomas gave her a long, silent inspection. He reached out and curled his hand around the bottle. "I thought you liked the other one, the singer."

"Noah."

"I know his name," he growled.

She grinned.

"Who's the guy that just left?"

"His name is Dominic."

"I don't like the look of that one."

"What's wrong with the way he looks?"

"He's a pretty boy. He's good looking and he knows it. Men like that don't stay with one woman for long."

She studied him across the span of the table. His Fu Manchu mustache and bulging biceps, the shirts that always appeared one size too small because of the way they hugged his brawn. If not for the tattooed arms, he looked a little like the bald guy on the cleaning product ads. She wondered what he'd say if she told him so.

Better not.

Most people took one look at Thomas and made assumptions about him. The wrong assumptions. They never took the time to get to know him. The time to discover that beneath his daunting exterior beat the heart of a teddy bear.

"I like the other one," he said, interrupting her thoughts. "The singer."

"So do I."

He cocked his head. "You don't sound happy about it."

She rested her arms on the table and leaned forward, locking her gaze with his. "Dad, why did you bring Tommy by last night?"

"He wanted to apologize to you."

"But why last night? Why not tonight, or tomorrow?"

"Thursdays are your nights off."

She shifted her gaze to the piano set against the wall. His answer sounded reasonable enough. Still, she had to wonder at the timing. "It didn't have anything to do with Noah being there?"

"How was I supposed to know he would be there?"

"Maybe you two planned it. He was with you yesterday afternoon."

He took a drink from his beer for the first time since she'd brought it to him. "Yes, he was."

"Did you?"

"Did I what?"

"Dad," she said with a sigh. She'd spent half the night reliving the kiss she and Noah shared. The hot press of his body against hers, the exquisite male taste of him. The second half wondering whether his arrival at her place had been an elaborate set-up orchestrated by the man sitting across from her right now.

If it had...Oh, God, she didn't want it to be true. She pushed both hands over her face and through her hair.

"Is he who all this is for?"

"This?"

"The flash of skin, the perfume you're wearing."

She looked down at herself and frowned. She couldn't deny it. She'd dressed with a certain singer in mind. Sitting here now, she didn't know why she'd gone to so much trouble. "I thought he might stop by."

"And when he didn't, you started to wonder about last night?"

"No. I wondered last night after you and Tommy left. Today just..." She placed her elbows on the table and dropped her face into her hands. "I don't know what I'm doing."

"Would it help if I told you I had nothing to do with Noah showing up at your apartment last night?"

Although his admission came as a relief, her confusion about Noah and the feelings he brought out in her remained a tangled mess. "Not really."

"You don't need it, you know."

Her hands fell away from her face as she

focused on him again. "What don't I need?"

"The flash of skin or the perfume. I've seen the way he looks at you, Izzy. Noah likes you fine, without the extra fuss. Be yourself. The rest will come."

It was "the rest" that had her tied in knots. From the beginning, she recognized that Noah was different from any other man she'd been attracted to. Different in the way he saw her, and in the way he made her feel. It was unsettling enough that she couldn't decide whether she wanted him to go back to California and leave her to her life, or kiss her again so that she could make sure she wasn't mistaken about last night. That she hadn't imagined the shock of desire that shot through her at his touch, or exaggerated the way his kiss made her feel.

She let out a weighty sigh. "He doesn't plan to be in town long. As soon as his studio is completed, he'll go back to California."

"Are you asking me what you should do?"

She reached out and took hold of his hand. "Would you? If I asked you, would you tell me?"

"I won't tell you how to live your life. I will tell you that you've changed since he's come into it."

"I have? How?"

"For one thing, you never used to hold my hand."

At the emotion in his voice she glanced down to find her hand engulfed in both of his. It had been years since she'd accepted even the most casual of touches from anyone, including him. The times she did were only when she initiated the contact, and even then she was always quick to shift away.

She didn't know what to say.

"So do you let just any guy hold your hand anymore?" he asked lightly.

"Only the good-looking ones."

He cleared his throat and looked away. It was a moment before he commented. "You invited me here to talk, aren't you going to talk?"

"I thought that's what we were doing?"

He looked back, the expression on his face serious. "You and I both know what you want to ask me."

Isabeau turned her attention back to his hands. She needed to know, to hear it from him. At the same time, she didn't know how she would handle it, depending on his answer. She couldn't have him hurting Tommy in her name. Violence, in any circumstance, made her blood run cold.

She looked up at him again. He endured her long scrutiny with quiet patience. "Did you do it?"

"You'll have to be more specific."

"Did you hit Tommy? Are you the one

responsible for giving him the black eye?"

"And if I did?"

Her stomach knotted tightly. She knew the sound a fist made as it made contact with flesh—felt the shock of pain herself, a time or two. A tremor worked through her.

"Would you pull away from me, again?"

"No." She knew he'd never hurt her. He wasn't that type of man. "Just tell me, please."

"Would it be so bad?"

"He's your son."

"You're my daughter."

"Not—"

"Don't say it," he warned. The hand resting atop hers flexed. "You are my daughter."

"I'm not. Not by blood, the way Tommy is."

"Do you think that matters to me? Do you think that has ever mattered to me?"

Emotion tightened her throat as his voice cracked.

"Tommy is my son by blood, yes, but his mother did such a bang-up job filling him with hatred for me that he can't see past it. He doesn't need or want me in his life. But you, Izzy, you do. From the day I first met you, you welcomed me as your father. You mustn't feel bad about that, because I've needed you, too. All these years I've needed you as much as you've needed me."

"I do need you, and I love you, but..."

"There were years I couldn't be there for you," he stated abruptly.

No.

She tried to withdraw, but he stopped her by tightening his hand around hers. She held her breath, afraid of the direction this conversation seemed to be heading.

"I'd give anything to be able to go back and change things. To save you from the years we were apart. I know how you feel about violence, Izzy. I would never do anything to hurt you."

"I know you wouldn't, I do."

"It wasn't me."

It wasn't him. Her fears were unsubstantiated.

He hadn't decided to teach Tommy a lesson or hurt him in her name. She'd been wrong to even consider it, she knew that now. Her eyes slid closed as she worked to pull her emotions back under control.

The one thing that still unsettled her was the timing. Tommy's black eye appeared fresh, as if he'd gotten it not long before he'd showed up at her apartment to apologize. And his apology, that didn't fit with the Tommy she knew. Which is what led her to question her father in the first place. After all, he was the one to deliver Tommy to her door.

Her father wasn't the only person who knew how traumatic Tommy's attack had been for her. There was another who witnessed the event firsthand. Who then saw the damage to her SUV and immediately suspected Tommy for that second attack as well.

Her eyes snapped open. "You don't think Noah…" her words trailed off as a knot formed in her throat. He wouldn't, would he? She pushed out of the chair and to her feet. "I'll be right back."

"Isabeau." His tone and use of her birth name over her nickname stopped her dead in her tracks, only a few feet from their table. "You know Tommy's temper. If he upset the wrong person…His assailant could be anyone."

She took a deep breath. "I have to know, Dad. I have to know if Noah is capable of—"

"If he's capable of protecting you?"

"I don't see it that way, you know I don't."

He sighed wearily. "What if he is responsible? What are you going to do?"

Her stomach cramped abruptly. She could tell that he didn't want her to go. It only made her that much more determined.

"You can't leave the bar unattended," he argued, shifting her anxiety up a notch.

"You're here."

"I don't know enough to be here alone. It's almost lunch."

She turned and started for the door. "Betty will be here soon."

"I don't much like Betty," he mumbled.

155

"Don't worry. I'll be back before the first customer walks through the door."

****

"We need to talk."

Noah looked up from his seat in the studio lounge and came face-to-face with a fiery-eyed, ebony-haired bartender, sporting stiletto heels and a frown. His entire body reacted.

"Noah?"

His breath caught in his throat. Words failed. Setting his guitar aside, he savored the sight of her. Subtle hues of smoke emphasized her incredible gray eyes. Her black-lace-over-blue top molded her torso, hugging curves and showing off her breasts. The top's scalloped edge ended one inch above the waistband of her jeans, leaving a strip of smooth, golden skin exposed.

He dragged in a ragged breath. Then another.

Last night when her hand settled against his chest, while her mouth opened beneath his, he had wanted her badly. Wanted to peel her clothes from her body. Lose himself between her legs. Today, as the subtle scent of her perfume breached the space between them, the desire returned with enough force to blot out everything else.

"Dom was right," he managed, then swallowed past the tightness that had settled in his throat. "You look great today."

"Yeah, I smell good, too," she replied sardonically.

"You do."

"Did you hit him?"

His gaze slid to her overfull lips. Was she wearing lipstick? Something subtle, like her beauty, yet effective. "Who?"

"Tommy."

He grinned. "You mean the shiner? Nice handiwork. I did enjoy that."

She kept her eyes on him, saying nothing. Then she spun on her heel and headed out the way she came.

Noah opened his mouth. Closed it. He blinked once, twice. It didn't help.

Was she trying to drive him out of his mind? Her jeans were air-brushed with climbing roses that worked up her leg, around her thigh, and culminated in a vibrant blue blossom on her ass. It was enough to make a dead man salivate.

"Suck it up," Dominic warned, as the door closed behind her with a snap. "She's moving fast."

Noah managed to pull himself back together. Barely. Had he ever felt this clawing hunger for a woman before? He couldn't remember. "You failed to mention those jeans."

Dom's only reply was an unapologetic smile.

Chuckling, Noah stepped into the hall in

time to watch the back door close. He turned to the right and followed the path she'd taken, pushing out into a small garden area he hadn't known existed.

Neatly trimmed green grass covered the ground, bisected by a flagstone path that led to a rectangular wooden dining table. The table was topped with an oversized cloth umbrella, unnecessary since the area was shaded by a large red maple that stood off to his right. He spotted Isabeau near the maple, her back to the studio.

The door clicked shut behind him as he stepped onto the grass and headed in her direction. Before he was more than halfway to her, she turned.

"I abhor violence," she stated, her voice full of emotion.

Standing beneath the shadow of the tree, he couldn't see her face, but her arms were crossed in front of her, her hands cupping her elbows in a white-knuckled grip. "Sometimes it's—"

"No, it's not. It's never excusable."

He continued in her direction, stopping inches from her. "I understand how you feel."

She stared up at him from eyes a little too bright. "How could you?"

He smoothed his hand over her hair. Silk. "What happened to you? You can talk to me. You know that, don't you?"

Shaking her head, she took a step in retreat.

Secrets, she seemed to be full of them. Would she ever share them with him? "Isabeau?"

"I didn't think it would matter. I was wrong."

Confusion filled him, warred with the desire still burning in his gut. "What are you talking about?"

As he took a step forward, she took one in retreat. "This isn't easy for me. I care about you."

"That's good, because I care about you, too."

Showing no outward sign of having heard him, she kept talking as if he hadn't spoken at all. "I dressed up for you. I chose this outfit, the perfume, all with you in mind. I was looking forward to seeing you this morning, but you didn't come by. So you didn't come by, who cares?"

"I'm guessing you do."

"Maybe this is normal for you, I don't know. I have no idea how women are with you. I only know how to be myself, and this isn't me. I don't watch the door looking for that one face, yours. And I don't fret over my appearance."

"You don't have to fret, you're beautiful."

"Don't say that," she whispered, her eyes drifting shut. "We both know it's not true."

She took his breath away. Didn't she realize that? Not just today, but every day, every time he saw her. It wasn't her clothes or the addition of makeup that had his blood up, it was the woman beneath it all. Now that he knew her taste, the feel of her body pressed against his and the fit of her in his arms, he wanted nothing more than to experience it again.

Settling his hands on her waist, he eased her closer to his body. "It is true."

She stiffened in surprise. Her hand came up and settled in the center of his chest. Not a caress, but a barrier between them. "Noah, don't. I can't do this." Her eyes slid closed again, then opened as she pushed out of his arms. "I'd appreciate it if you didn't come by for a while."

"Isabeau?"

Without further explanation, she turned and started to walk away. Not back into the studio, but around the outside of the building.

"What? Wait a minute." Catching up with her, he snagged her wrist and spun her to face him. "Damn it, give me a minute will you?"

"I have to get back to the bar."

"The hell with the bar." His jaw bunched. "Is that what you needed to talk to me about? You wanted to ask me to stop coming by? At least tell me why."

She pulled her wrist free of his grasp, regret creeping into her expression. "I already

160

asked you what I needed to ask you."

She had? He was missing something, something big. But damn if he could figure out what it was. He took a step forward as she took one back. She wasn't walking away from him. Not today, or anytime in the near future. Not before he had a chance to better explore his feelings for her.

He furrowed his forehead, running the past few minutes through his mind. "You asked me about Tommy."

"Yes," she replied with a nod.

"Then you left the room before I answered."

"You answered me."

"No, I didn't."

She blinked. "I asked if you hit him and you said you enjoyed doing it."

"No."

"Yes. You—"

He put his finger on her lips. "I said I enjoyed the fact that he was sporting a shiner. I never said I was the one that gave it to him."

She studied him for a moment, then pushed his hand away. "The fact that he was hurt pleases you?"

"It does."

"Why?"

"Sometimes all a bully needs is someone to turn the tables on him, someone to show him what it feels like to be on the receiving end."

161

"But you weren't that someone?"

"No. I never touched him, Isa."

"Okay. Good." She dragged the heel of her palm across her forehead, then pressed it against her temple.

"Headache?"

"You...make my head hurt."

"Do I?" He stepped closer, and because he needed to touch her again, lifted his hands and took over for her. Sliding his fingers into the dark silk of her hair, he pressed his thumbs against her temples. "Better?"

A soft sigh escaped her lips. "Thanks."

"It's the least I can do. After all, I am the cause of your discomfort."

She stared at him for a long moment. "You and me..."

"Yes?"

"It's not smart."

"Do you always do what's smart?"

"Yes."

"Then maybe it's time you didn't," he reasoned.

Slowly, the stiffness went out of her spine. She reached up and cupped her right hand against his jaw. Her fingers brushed across the stubble he hadn't had time to shave off after sleeping through the alarm. "It's softer than it looks."

"Yeah?" he managed, as desire returned so quickly it made his head spin. Her hot, incredible scent enveloped him. "I overslept."

Which was why he hadn't stopped by the bar on his way to the studio. He might have anyway, taken the time for a quick hello, if he didn't already feel the heat of the record company's breath on the back of his neck. He needed to concentrate on pulling together the demo—getting it right. New and fresh. And he couldn't do that when thoughts of her kept creeping in like fog.

It didn't work. She snuck into his mind anyway. Then, as if she knew how much he'd regretted not going to see her, she walked through his door instead.

"I like it. It looks good on you."

He tightened his fingers in her hair and tipped her head back. "As good as those jeans look on you?"

Her slow smile heated his blood. Her left hand settled on his shoulder, then slid up to curve around his neck. "Much better."

Impossible.

Her eyes had changed color again, from gray to blue. They'd done that last night. Right before she melted into his arms.

He leaned into her. "If you still want me to stay away from you, you'd better tell me now."

"Noah?"

"Yeah?"

"Kiss me."

163

She didn't have to ask twice. He dipped his head, settled his lips on hers and plundered. He dragged her against him, and drank in the hot, potent taste of her as he fed on her mouth like a starving man.

She softened, a tiny sound of passion slipping up her throat—an urgent invitation. His pulse leaped. So did other parts of his anatomy. Her fingers burrowed through his hair.

He deepened the kiss, stroking his hands down the sides of her body to settle on her hips. He used them to guide her as he stepped forward once, twice, until her back settled against the trunk of the maple. Awash in the smell of her, the feel of her, he pressed closer, until no space existed between them. Her breasts flattened against his chest, her hips arched into him. Heat from her body flowed into his, sparking a fire. His heartbeat echoed in his head.

"Isabeau..." He kissed her again. His lips trailed over her jaw to her throat, pressed against the sensitive spot beneath her ear. Her fingers dug into his shoulders.

Lost in her, he slid one hand up her body and settled it on the soft swell of her breast. Her nipple beaded, pressed against the center of his palm. Her breath left her in an audible rush.

"What are you doing to me?" she gasped.

"Isn't it obvious?"

164

"I…need to go back."

"Stay," he coaxed, tracing light kisses along her jaw, before returning to her mouth for a long, hard, wet kiss. Beneath his hands, her body shuddered.

"Noah." She shifted so that their lips no longer touched, but remained a scant inch apart. "You have work to do. So do I."

Her breasts rose and fell against his chest as she struggled for breath. Her cheeks were flushed, her lips swollen. The last thing he wanted to do was let her go. "Work can wait. I'm not sure I can."

"We can't do this. Not here."

Reason resurfaced from his desire-clouded mind. No matter how much he wanted to strip away her clothes and lose himself inside of her, finally sating the ache that filled him whenever she was near, she was right. Now was not the time. This was not the place.

The hand still holding her breast flexed. He dropped his forehead to rest against the rough bark above her head. "You're right."

She took a step sideways, out of his arms. He steadied her with a hand on her elbow when she wobbled. "Easy."

"I'm okay."

He kept his gaze on hers as he brushed his free hand down her cheek. "I'm glad one of us is."

Her eyes drifted shut, her body swayed

closer. While the urge to pull her back into his arms screamed through him, he held her away. "Isabeau, you need to go." If she didn't, he was going to lay her in the grass and crawl on top.

She must have read his intention for she took a hurried step back, then another. "Uh...right. I have to...go." She took three steps in the wrong direction before she turned, and disappeared around the corner of the building.

Once she was out of sight, he reached down and adjusted his straining erection.

CHAPTER NINE

Noah walked out the front door of the studio and hung a left. The sky had darkened to an ominous shade of gray. The wind swirled, rustling the leaves on the trees along the street. He could pretend his walk was nothing more than a way to clear his thoughts, the result of his intense need to get out of the studio for a breath of fresh air. But he wasn't into self-deception. No, his feet moved with purpose toward a single destination. The two-story brick that sat on the corner two blocks ahead.

A bolt of lightning split the sky, followed a few strides later by the rumble of thunder. He kept walking. No chance he'd get struck by lightning twice in one day.

Hours, six ruthlessly long hours had passed since he'd kissed Isabeau beneath that red maple. Six hours of struggle to put her out of his mind and concentrate on the demo. The record contract. But every time he breathed deeply, he smelled her. Her scent clung to him like a burr, slowly driving him out of his mind. He couldn't take it anymore, so he mumbled an excuse about needing air, pushed to his feet and stalked out.

Like the night three months before, the red glow from the neon sign drew him. As he reached the parking lot, he stopped. The place was packed. Even for a Friday night.

No chance of a minute alone with Isabeau.

Noah pushed his hand through his hair and stared at the closed door. The pounding rhythm of the stereo washed over him. A tempo that matched the flow of blood through his veins. He let out a long breath, then reached for the handle.

Adam looked up as he stepped inside and nodded in greeting. Noah swept his gaze around the dim interior, noting Clint standing behind the bar as usual. Two waitresses he knew only by sight drifted around the room, scratching orders onto their pads and dodging too-friendly advances. But no Isabeau. His eyes narrowed. He scanned the room again, stopping as a bottle blonde stepped in front of him.

She flashed him a predatory smile. "Hello there, handsome."

He wondered how many men she reeled in with her plunging neckline and generous breasts. Breasts that defied gravity. A plastic surgeon's masterpiece.

Her eyes performed a slow intimate examination of his body before returning to his face. Her smile widened. "Looking for someone?

Someone like me?"

Unlike Isa's smile, which was always warm and genuine, this one's smile said "I know who you are and here's what you can do for me." He wasn't the least bit tempted. "I'm looking for Isabeau. Have you seen her?"

"Now what would you want with her?" Her breast brushed his arm as she leaned in and trailed a long, blood-red fingernail down his chest.

"Betty!" Clint bellowed from behind the bar. "Get back to work."

Noah caught the bartender's scowl. It was a moment before he realized the man was hollering at the blonde now hanging from his arm. He extracted himself from her roaming hands. "Your boss is trying to get your attention."

Her mouth settled into an unflattering pout. "He is not my boss. And Izzy is not here."

Although more than one pair of male eyes tracked her as she sauntered away, Noah's didn't. He hadn't been pawed that completely in years. Instead of wanting more of her, as he knew had been the blonde's intention, he wanted a shower. He crossed to the bar and waited while Clint finished up with a customer.

"What's up?" the bartender asked as a waitress carried away the pitcher he'd filled from the tap.

"I'm looking for Isabeau. Isn't she

normally behind the bar with you on Friday nights?"

"Ah...yeah." Clint signaled the person at the opposite end of the bar that he'd be there in a minute. "Normally she is."

Noah waited. When it became apparent Clint wasn't going to explain, he asked, "Do you know where she is?"

"Look, I don't normally tell a man how to spend his time, but you need to watch out for Betty."

"The blonde? I have no interest in her."

Clint nodded, then scanned the customers sitting at the bar. He signaled to one other person to wait before leaning in, the pitch of his voice indicating he meant for only Noah to hear his words. "Izzy was here, but she decided to...ah...she's taking a break."

Noah followed the bartender's lead and looked to the ceiling before the man's meaning clicked. Isabeau was upstairs in her apartment. He started to turn away.

"She won't answer the door."

"Why not?"

"Can't you hear it? She's a little pissed at me right now."

Hear what? Then he did—the rhythmic thumping of her subwoofer, clashing with the song on the bar stereo.

"Actually, ah...she's more than pissed. I was angry and I said some things that hurt her."

"What happened?"

"The music will change," Clint continued, as if he hadn't spoken. "She always starts with that." He pointed at the ceiling. "Eventually it will transition into quieter, less angry music. She won't come out before then."

Noah studied the man behind the bar. He appeared to be in his early thirties, tall and slender. He had brown hair and brown eyes that at the moment revealed more than the man probably meant to reveal. "How long have you been in love with her?"

Clint expelled a breath. "When haven't I? The thing is she doesn't want me, she wants you. I told her she was wasting her time, that she was nothing more to you than convenient."

Tension crept out of nowhere and tightened his shoulders. "I see."

"I can tell I pissed you off, too. That's good." He leaned over the bar to better hear an order from one of the waitresses, then pulled down three martini glasses. "Go through the kitchen."

"Pardon?"

"There's a set of stairs in the kitchen with a door at the top that leads to her apartment. I'd bet she hasn't locked that door. She wouldn't think to. No one ever uses those stairs but her."

Without hesitation, Noah slipped through the swinging door into the kitchen. His gaze moved around the room, located the set of stairs on his left. The door at the top of the stairs was unlocked, as Clint suggested. Only when he swung it open, it wasn't her apartment he discovered, but a laundry room. Complete with a stacking washer/dryer combination and a hamper overflowing with towels.

He stepped into the room. Music slammed into him like a force at near ear-splitting decibels. Christ, standing onstage in front of a packed stadium, speakers at his back wasn't this loud. The floor beneath his boots trembled and pulsed. The wall in front of him shook.

Wait a minute. Not another door, a wall. He swore aloud. In the dim light, he scanned the room twice before he spotted the door. Braced for the assault his ears were about to take, he stepped into her apartment.

For the space of a heartbeat, he forgot everything, the reason he'd had to sneak up the back stairs, the onslaught of music, and savored. Isabeau stood at the end of the room, before the window that looked out onto the street. Gone was the makeup and the sexy outfit from a few hours ago. What she wore in its place—what little she wore—was enough to make his teeth sweat.

She'd piled her hair atop her head, the long ebony strands held in place by a silver clip. His rumpled chambray shirt hung off her right shoulder, her breasts and the few buttons she'd fastened just enough to keep it from sliding the rest of the way off. Her toned thighs and perfect, golden legs peeked out beneath the hem.

He'd seen her in less, that barely-there bikini, but…damn. He liked the look of his shirt on her. A lot.

The need to close the distance between them and peel his shirt off her body slammed into him and he started across the room. He stopped in front of her CD player and hit the power button, flooding the room in silence.

She jolted and turned, her hand pressed against her chest. "Noah? You scared me to death!"

Heart in her throat, Isabeau stared at Noah. Hands in his pockets, shoulder resting against the wood mantel, he was the picture of relaxation. Except for the heat in his gaze.

Matching heat flared to life in her belly.

And between her thighs.

Suddenly conscious of the fact that she wore nothing but his shirt and a pair of lacy boy shorts, she straightened the drooping shirt and wrapped her arms around her waist. "I didn't hear you come in."

"That's not surprising as loud as you had the stereo."

"How did you get in? I locked the door."

His eyes left her to focus on, not the outer door that came up the back of the building, but the inner door that led to the bar.

173

"Clint," she muttered, her jaw tight. Of course. Lightning flashed through the window at her back, immediately followed by a crack of thunder close enough to rattle the panes of glass. The room filled with the sound of the driving rain against her roof.

"Interesting man, Clint. I don't think he cares for me much."

"Don't worry about him, he's—"

"In love with you?"

"What? Don't be silly."

His eyebrow slid up his forehead and disappeared beneath a lock of hair. His eyes fixed on her. "He's in love with you, Isabeau."

"That's absurd." Her pulse was thrumming. She couldn't help it. He had to be imagining things. "That's not possible."

"Why not?"

"Because." She moved away from the window and began prowling the room. "Because I'm not..."

"You're not what?"

She stopped roaming and faced him. Her fingers curled into the cushions on the back of the couch. "I'm not the type of woman men fall for."

"I've fallen for you."

Heat flooded her system. She forced herself to breathe, to keep her eyes locked with his. "No you haven't. You ..."

He pushed off the mantel and stepped in

her direction. "I, what?"

"Never mind."

"Finish the sentence, Isabeau."

"I don't think so."

"Then let me." He closed the distance between them. "You were going to say I haven't fallen for you, weren't you? You actually believe him? That you're nothing more to me than convenient?"

Her pulse throbbed thick and hard. Heat radiated off his body. The scent of him filled her head. She wanted, more than anything, to press herself against him and relive the pleasure of his mouth against hers. Instead, she lifted her chin. "Maybe."

He leaned in close. So close his breath brushed across her lips. "You believe him, but not me?"

"You are here only temporarily."

"Yes."

"And I am just down the street."

"I suppose."

She ran her tongue over her dry lips. "So the whole thing does seem rather—"

"Don't say it."

"—convenient."

Something dangerous came and went in his eyes. "Now I'm getting angry."

His hands skimmed down her sides, slipped under her shirt and settled on her lace-covered bottom. Her breath went uneven.

175

Searing need swarmed her.

"You want something to believe, believe this." He pulled her into the solid ridge of his erection. She lost her concentration. "There is nothing convenient about the way I feel about you."

"I...no?"

"You think you're not the type to draw a man's attention, think again. I can't stand in the same room as you without wanting to taste you. I can't taste you without wanting to taste all of you."

Oh, God. Her knees turned to jelly. A hot, wet pulse came to life between her legs.

"If you can't see in yourself what it is that I see, feel what you do to me." Taking hold of her wrist, he placed her hand in the center of his chest.

His heart was racing. She tipped her head back and looked into his eyes. Her bones began to liquefy.

"The way you're looking at me," she whispered.

"How am I looking at you?"

"Like I'm important."

"You are."

She swallowed hard, wanting to believe him. "Like I'm beautiful."

His lips brushed across her temple and her eyes drifted shut. "I wish you could see yourself the way I see you. Then you would

176

know how beautiful you are."

Her eyes snapped open as he spun her in his arms. His hands settled on her shoulders, drawing her back against his chest. She gasped at their image reflected in the trio of mirrors that hung on her wall. When had this become a seduction?

He leaned in and put his mouth to her ear. "You have eyes like fog." The lilting baritone of his voice washed over her, and she let out a little helpless moan. "Truly amazing eyes that change color with your mood. Right now they are blue. Can you see that?"

He skimmed his hands down her arms, trailed his fingers over the backs of her hands. The shock of pleasure stole her breath. Every nerve ending in her body quivered.

"Your mouth is so sexy." The sound that rumbled in his throat had something curling hard in her stomach. "I imagine the things you could do with that mouth."

The mouth he spoke of dropped open as he nipped the back of her neck.

"The first time you smiled at me you stole my breath. I spent weeks trying to get you to do it again, struggling to understand what I'd done to stop you from gifting me with your smile. What was it, Isa?"

"You...noticed me."

"I noticed you? How couldn't I? Your hair, your skin." Nimble fingers worked down the front of her shirt, revealing a little more of her skin with every button that slipped free. "I can't stop touching you. Reaching for you. I imagine my hands on you, light against your dark. Here, on your stomach."

Isabeau sucked air greedily into her lungs when his hand pressed against her stomach. She stared, mesmerized by the contrast of his pale hand against her darker, golden tones.

"Look at my hands on you."

His growl was nearly as exciting as those long-fingered hands caressing her skin. The trembling started in her knees and crept up her body. She leaned back into his arms, using his body for support. Against her lower back, his erection pulsed.

She quivered. His name tumbled from her lips as his left hand joined his right on her stomach. Her blood hummed, her body jolted in anticipation. She didn't realize she'd moved her own hands until denim scraped across her palms. Her fingers dug into his hips, pulled him solidly against her.

"Isabeau." His mouth skimmed her cheek, her jaw, all while his hands kept moving, caressing. He brushed his thumb along the underside of her nipple once, twice, before his hand closed possessively over her breast. The pulse between her legs became a throbbing ache. "You're beautiful, Isabeau."

This time she believed him.

His breathing grew ragged as his mouth moved over her temple. Sensations washed over her, paralyzing her.

Seducing her.

The fingers of his left hand rolled, kneaded her nipple into a tight aching bud. Her fingernails dug into his hips. His free hand slid down the pale line of her scar, lower and lower until it slipped into her panties and cupped her heat. She moaned softly and pressed herself into his palm.

"Look at yourself, Isa. Do you see what I see?"

She saw him, only him. What he was doing to her body became second to what the experience did for him. His whole being seemed to be focused on her and he was lost. Lost in her.

Unbelievable.

She looked at his reflection, gasping as he slid his hand lower, slipping first one finger and then another into her hot slick depths.

She went off like a rocket. Her orgasm ripped through her with the strength of never before. Her body convulsed—a symphony exploded behind her eyes. His name slipped from her on a moan that he caught with his mouth as she tipped her head up to meet his kiss.

A sudden ringing sliced the room's stillness like a knife. Noah went utterly still, then pressed his forehead to hers. "Bloody hell."

She turned in his arms, pressed her hand in the center of his chest. "What is that?"

"My mobile."

Ignoring the phone, he took her face in his hands as he dipped his head and plundered her mouth once more.

She loved it. Loved everything about it; the heat, the little bit of desperation. Closing her eyes, she kissed him back. Her hand moved, slid down his chest, over his abdominals, and then lower still.

His fingers wrapped around her wrist like a manacle. "I have to go."

What?

His hot gaze moved across her exposed flesh like a physical touch. "The guys are looking for me."

"Noah."

"I've been gone too long already." A mix of regret and need colored his features as he released her and stepped back.

Her legs were weak. Her hands shook as she worked the buttons of the shirt back through their corresponding holes. "Will you come back?"

"Tomorrow," he replied, his voice full of raw hunger. "Plan on me staying the night."

****

Although she slept better than she had in ages, Isabeau awoke the next morning with a pounding headache. She rolled over, brushed the hair out of her eyes and focused on the ceiling. For a moment, she thought about crawling out of bed, choking down an aspirin and going for her morning run. That moment lasted about two point eight seconds.

The aspirin she needed. The jarring pain her daily run would cause her was a different story.

God, her head hurt. Hurt so bad she couldn't think straight. What day was it? Was it her turn to open the bar, or Clint's?

Saturday. Clint's day to open.

She sighed with relief.

Wait a minute. Saturday was the day she'd agreed to join the guys for soccer.

She groaned.

Ignoring the rich, heady scent that emanated from her programmable coffeemaker, Isabeau closed her eyes against the throbbing ache. She utilized the same techniques she'd used so many times as a young girl to distance herself from the pain. She closed her mind to the sounds around her, her worries and her discomfort. She shut out everything that caused her stress and pictured instead something that brought her peace.

Immediately Noah's image jumped to the forefront of her mind. Without any effort at all, she recalled the sight of him leaning against her mantel, his green eyes displaying a mix of irritation and arousal. Pressing her fingertips against her forehead, she remembered the feel of his hands in her hair as his thumbs massaged her temples. But that memory was quickly exchanged for another, the one where his hands moved over her body—cupping and caressing—setting every nerve ending on fire.

She settled her hand against her stomach as her body recalled the moment with a bit more enthusiasm than expected. Her limbs began to tingle. A warm sensation pulsed through her blood. A tiny shiver skittered down her spine.

The relentless rhythm returned to join the throbbing behind her eyes.

Isabeau threw back the covers with another groan. She eased to a seated position and slipped her arms into the shirt she'd left at the foot of the bed—Noah's shirt. His scent enveloped her. The pain behind her eyes intensified.

With a sigh of acceptance, she walked to the coffeemaker and poured herself a mug of coffee. Pulling the bottle of aspirin out of the cabinet above the sink, she choked down two, then carried the mug with her across the room.

When she stepped into the bathroom, she switched on the faucet in her antique claw-foot bathtub and waited for the water to heat up. She had enough time, before she met the guys, for a shower and a trip across town. There was no use denying it any longer. Not if she wanted to avoid debilitating pain. She had no other choice.

The music had taken over.

****

An hour later, Isabeau took a deep breath and pushed through the door of Brown's Music Emporium. For a moment, no more than a few seconds, the sights and smells once so familiar washed over her, sending her back in time. The moment faded, replaced by the cold reality that her life wasn't what it used to be. She was no longer a happy child that looked forward to visiting the store, but an adult who wished more than anything that she could have gone the rest of her life without returning.

No matter how many memories assaulted her, she pushed them aside. She didn't want to recall how much pleasure she'd once derived from the music that flowed so effortlessly from her brain to her fingers. Today wasn't about pleasure, it was about survival. She couldn't continue the way she had. The act of blocking her thoughts and the melodies that moved through her mind was getting to be too much for her. She wasn't sleeping well, lost her appetite, and no amount of aspirin seemed to combat the ache in her skull.

Curling her right hand around the strap of her black leather tote, she turned right. She kept her eyes averted as she moved with purpose to the spot where her purchase used to be stocked. As each step took her deeper into the store, and farther into her past, she prayed they hadn't reorganized over the years. The last thing she wanted was to run into anyone. She couldn't spend any more time in the store than was absolutely necessary.

At the end of the aisle, she turned left.

"Can I help you find something?"

Today was not a good day.

Grimacing, she shifted her gaze from the floor to the middle-aged man blocking the aisle. Frank. She recognized him immediately. He'd been working here as long as she could remember.

"I need some composition paper."

"You're in the right aisle. It's down here."

She had no other choice but to follow his lead to a spot a few feet ahead of her. "Thank you."

When she didn't automatically reach for the paper, the overly helpful man pointed. "Right there, on that shelf."

The music coming from the recessed speakers above her head was hauntingly familiar. Her fingers moved along the strap of her oversized tote. "Yes, thank you."

Frank remained rooted in place, openly studying her. "You look awfully familiar. Have we met before?"

"I don't think so."

184

"Are you sure? I'm usually good with faces."

Please go away. *Please* go away.

"I'm sure," she lied. Her stomach was in knots. The music in her head swelled to a near unbearable level. Desperate to make her purchase and leave, she grabbed a stack of composition paper off the shelf and turned in the direction of the cash register.

She'd been raised to be polite. It was one of the many lessons her mother instilled in her before her death. But at the moment, Isabeau didn't think she could handle polite. She was coming apart from the inside. She needed fresh air, needed to get away from the memories and the music. Before Frank realized why she looked so familiar to him.

"Well, okay, is that all you need?" His step quickened so that he arrived at the register before she did.

"That's it."

She kept her gaze averted while he rang up her purchase. The music reverberating throughout the store came to an end. There was a moment of silence, then the piano solo started. Isabeau stared at her outstretched hand and wondered how she kept it steady as she waited for her change.

"Izzy?"

Just like that, her day got even worse.

She glanced over her shoulder and

185

wondered what terrible thing she'd done to deserve this. Two run-ins with Gregory Howard in a matter of days? She reached out and grabbed the composition paper, attempting to stuff it into her tote and make a quick exit.

His gaze followed her hand. "Planning on doing a bit of composing, are you?"

She had no idea what he was thinking, but she caught the instant straightening of his spine. Suddenly she realized why she'd never felt comfortable talking to Gregory. He was jealous of her, he always had been. Every conversation she'd ever shared with him turned into a competition. A competition he always made sure to win.

"Izzy?" the man behind the cash register repeated. "That's it! You're little Isabeau Montgomery."

She closed her eyes for a moment and turned back to Frank. "Yes, I am."

"I thought I recognized you. You used to come in here all the time with your mother. You're...not so little any more. But I suppose that happens with the passing of time, doesn't it?"

"I suppose it does."

A crease formed between Frank's bushy black eyebrows. He got that look on his face that she hadn't seen in years. The look that said he knew exactly what happened to her life and felt sorry for her. She didn't like that look now any more than she had thirteen years ago.

"How are you doing?" he asked. "You're doing well, I hope."

"I'm fine, Mr. Marconi. Thank you for asking."

"You know, your music is still very popular."

The walls were closing in on her. "That's good to hear."

"The music playing right now is yours."

She knew that. She'd recognized it the moment she stepped through the door. Memories assaulted her, memories she didn't like to revisit in the privacy of her own home, let alone in public. Forget the pain in her head, the pain in her heart was much worse.

"I...need to get out of here. If you'll excuse me, Mr. Marconi?"

"Of course."

She turned for the door only to find Gregory remained behind her, blocking her escape.

"It's funny, isn't it?" Gregory asked.

Nothing about her day so far was funny. "What?"

"We haven't seen each other in years and then, wham, we run into each other twice now in a matter of days."

"That's funny, all right." Her gaze flicked over his shoulder to the door a few feet behind him.

187

SARAH GRIMM

"I can't believe you're going to compose again." Gregory looked down at her with grim assessment. "I hope you'll keep me in mind. You know I am the one person who can do your music justice."

"Sure." She forced a smile. She was more than willing to play his game if it meant she could get out of there. The knots in her stomach tightened. Her right hand clenched the strap of her tote so tightly, her nails bit into her palm. "Look, Gregory, I have to go, or I'm going to be late."

He turned as she started past him. "Got someplace you need to be, huh?"

Her unease heightening with every second she remained in the store, she answered without thinking. "Yes. I'm meeting some friends at Pete's."

He stepped closer. "Not Pete Knowles, from the recording studio?"

"As a matter of fact, he's exactly who I mean."

Isabeau walked out of the music store, every muscle in her body tight. Her hands weren't quite steady as she slipped her sunglasses into place and started down the street to where she'd parked. By the time she reached her Navigator her breathing had regulated, her memories returned to the box in her mind she kept them locked in. By the time she reached her apartment, she'd forgotten all about Gregory Howard and the look he'd given her as she left the music store.

****

"What happened to you?"

Isabeau smiled broadly, the last few hours just what she had needed to forget her troubles. She joined Clint behind the bar as Noah and the guys eased onto stools.

"Soccer."

Clint arched an eyebrow. His gaze moved over her from head to toe as she washed her hands in the sink. "Last I knew soccer was not a contact sport. You're covered in dirt and..." He shifted closer, peering at her face. A frown line appeared between his eyes. "Is that a bruise?"

A bruise? She turned to the cooler and checked out her reflection in the mirror as she pulled out three bottles of beer. Sure enough, she had a red mark beneath her right eye. "I ran into an immovable object."

"With your face?"

Her gaze took in the ragged bunch on the other side of the bar. They all looked a little the worse for wear, sweaty and smudged with mud from the field that had yet to dry after last night's rain. They all also wore the same broad smile on their faces as she did.

"I think it was Dom," she stated, as she placed a bottle before Nick Saunders, the band's guitarist, and Alex Morgan, the drummer. The third she placed before Dominic.

Noah's grin kicked up a notch. Immediately the fire in her belly burned hotter, her palms began to itch. She'd been fighting the need to touch him ever since she got her first good look at him at the park, wearing nothing but a pair of low-slung shorts and running shoes, his broad shoulders and hard muscles rippling in the sunlight. He'd pulled on a shirt after the game, but the need remained.

Isabeau took a slow, deep breath to control her racing heart and reached into the refrigerator near her knee. She placed a bottle of water atop the bar in front of Noah.

"I was on your team," Dominic objected, pulling her thoughts back to the conversation.

"You're one of the lucky ones," Nick replied, shifting his right hand and pressing it against his side.

Clint gave them a questioning look as she wet down a napkin and used the mirrored wall behind the bar to wipe some of the dirt from her face.

"To Isabeau, it was definitely a full contact sport," Dominic supplied. "Whenever she couldn't get control of the ball with fancy footwork, she got a bit rough."

"We'll have to teach her rugby," Noah commented, his deep voice drawing her gaze from her own reflection and onto his.

He watched her intently, as he lifted the

bottle of water to his lips and drank. Her gaze lowered, settled on his mouth. Her nerves scrambled, her blood hummed in her ears.

She had to concentrate just to breathe.

"Oh, hell no," Nick exclaimed. "I think I'll pass on that."

Her eyes remained on Noah's hand when he lowered the bottle of water. The memory of his hands on her body as she'd stood before a different mirror engulfed her mind with perfect clarity. Her breath clogged in her throat.

She'd never been touched like that before. She'd never allowed it. Over the years, she'd gotten good at distracting a man with his own pleasure, so that she wouldn't have to endure him wanting to touch her. Up until Noah, no man complained. But Noah was unlike any man she'd ever known. Not only did he not allow her to shift away from his touch, he wasn't so easily distracted. His relentless pursuit of her was proof of that much.

Her reaction to him was different as well, and quite honestly, a bit terrifying. She'd never spent so much time thinking about a man, imagining them together, considering the possibility that there could be so much pleasure in a single touch.

"That's Isabeau for you." Clint's voice barely penetrated the fog of desire that enveloped her. "Whatever she does, she puts everything she has into it."

191

"Like her elbow," Nick suggested.

"Or her knee," Alex piped in.

Noah flashed her a wicked, knowing grin. His eyes reflected the same desire she felt throbbing through her veins.

"Babies," she muttered as heat flooded her limbs, leaving her skin hot and prickly.

Wondering how no one else felt the spark of electricity in the air, Isabeau wetted another napkin and pressed it against the back of her neck. She shifted her gaze off Noah and swept it around the bar. The sudden trill of a mobile phone brought it right back to him.

Noah pulled his phone out of his pocket and pressed the screen. "Yeah?" His smile faded, his shoulders stiffened. "I will," he replied tersely. "Thanks." He closed his eyes and pinched the bridge of his nose.

"Noah?" She reached out, placed a hand on his arm. "Is something wrong?"

"I need to..." His voice trailed off as he stood. "Can I use your telephone, the land line?"

"Of course. Go into the kitchen, where you can have some privacy."

He nodded slowly, then circled the bar and slipped into the kitchen.

"I wonder what that's about?" Nick asked as the door swung closed behind Noah.

"Whatever it is, it's not good," Dom replied.

Isabeau stared at the door, her thoughts

running the same path as Dominic's. Something was wrong. Noah's face was unnaturally pale as he'd slipped from the room, his body taut as a bow.

More than fifteen minutes passed before he reappeared, his already pale face bloodless now. Her stomach rolled over.

Noah stopped just outside of the kitchen, his gaze locked on Dominic. "We need to talk," he said, his voice even, detached. Without waiting to see if anyone followed, he turned and started for the door.

Isabeau flicked her gaze to Dominic, caught his worried frown. He motioned toward the bottles in front of them as he, Alex and Nick all stood. "We'll settle up—"

"Don't worry about it."

Halfway between the bar and the door, Noah stopped and turned back. Unlike his voice, his eyes swirled with emotion as his gaze returned to her. The tension in the room thickened.

"I could use a ride to the airport. Would you—"

"Of course." He was leaving. The knot that had settled in her stomach earlier tightened. Her fingers flexed against her thighs. "I'll take you to the airport."

Without another word, he turned and walked out the door.

CHAPTER TEN

Isabeau ran in the mornings. She logged five miles a day, up and down the streets within a four block radius of her bar, her running shoes slapping against the pavement, ponytail bobbing. She enjoyed the exercise. It calmed her mind, and kept her in shape.

Today she'd left her MP3 player at home, preferring to lose herself in thought rather than drown her thoughts in music. She had enough music in her head without any external source. Enough that she'd already burned through more than ten sheets of composition paper in a desperate attempt to preserve her sanity. So far, so good. In a matter of days the throbbing in her skull had abated. The lingering ache she could deal with, and in reality could have as much to do with sleep deprivation and poor eating habits as with the music itself.

Nearly two days had passed since she'd seen or spoken with Noah. Not since he'd received word that his grandfather suffered a stroke. She'd delivered him first to his hotel room to shower and pack, then to the airport to catch a flight to London. Before he'd left, she'd

194

made a point to program her numbers into his mobile phone in the hope that he would call.

He hadn't. Not for two days.

Forty-eight long hours.

Perhaps if she'd slept it wouldn't eat at her. Yeah, right. She missed him. More than she imagined she could. More than made sense. She might have dwelled on that, but she was too worried about him.

How was he doing? Had his flight been a safe one? Was his grandfather conscious and aware that Noah was with him?

She asked herself these questions at least five times a day when her mind would drift away from work and lock onto Noah. They weren't the only things she wondered when she thought of him. If she were to be honest with herself, she also wondered if she'd crossed his mind since she'd dropped him off at the airport. Or if he'd forgotten about her as soon as she was no longer just down the road from him?

"Idiot," she muttered as she checked over her shoulder for cars, then started across the street at an angle. She wasn't the only one left in the dark. Noah hadn't called Dominic, either.

That was the part that kept her up at night.

The squeal of tires echoed in the still air, followed by the smooth acceleration of a car coming up the road. Isabeau glanced behind her, only to squint as the sun reflected off a mid-sized sedan that seemed to bear down on her with increasing speed. Panic bubbled up the back of her throat.

She shifted to the right, as close to the line of parked cars as she could run. There was time for the driver to correct, room for the sedan to go around her. But as she checked over her shoulder again, she found the car heading directly for her.

Oh, God. Terror brought a surge of adrenaline. Up ahead, about twenty feet, sat an empty parking space—a buffer zone—a way to get off the road and onto the sidewalk where she would be safe. Her tired muscles screamed as she increased her speed. Self-preservation kept her eyes locked ahead when she was desperate to look behind. Her heart beat furiously in her chest. Her side stitched. She continued to run.

Finally she was there. Desperate, she dove for the empty spot. She landed on her forearms, her hands automatically going out in front of her to brace her fall. The skin on her palms tore. Pain lanced up from her left elbow.

Her cry of alarm was drowned out by the growl of the engine as the car zoomed past her, and accelerated down the road.

****

Isabeau sat in water hot enough to turn her skin red and shook. She was in her claw-foot tub, in her apartment, her air conditioning off,

196

her blinds pulled. It had to be close to eighty degrees in here, but at least she was warm.

Okay, almost warm.

The only sound in the room was that of her ragged breathing and the gentle plop of blood dripping off her elbow and into the water. Her abrasions scrubbed and cleaned, arm resting on the lip of the tub, she worked at the final piece of gravel embedded in her left elbow. Her stomach turned when she pushed the fine-tipped tweezers further into her torn skin. Her teeth gritted against the pain.

Another drop of blood trailed down to her elbow, following the same path as the one before it. Nausea surged. Acid crawled up the back of her throat. She closed her eyes, only to snap them open as the pain spiked. Her mind screamed. She increased the pressure on the tweezers, twisting them to get a better hold on the tiny stone, but she made no sound. Not even as the last chunk slipped free.

Isabeau dropped the bloody tweezers on the towel next to the tub and leaned back. She sucked in a quick gasp as her skin made contact with the cool porcelain. Her body shivered. Staring without focus at the ceiling above her, she pressed a cloth against her elbow to stop the bleeding.

Now that her mind was no longer centered on the task of cleaning her wounds, the panic she'd felt during those few minutes on the street returned to grab her by the throat. No matter how many times she told herself the event was unintentional, that the driver had rounded the corner at too high a speed and didn't see her until it was too late, a niggling voice of doubt sounded. How could she believe it was a terrifying accident when the driver steered toward her, not away? When they then sped off and left her lying on the ground, seemingly unconcerned with whether or not she'd been injured.

No, as badly as she needed to believe it was an accident, she couldn't. And that frightened her more than anything else.

She blinked. A strangled sound worked up the back of her throat, but she managed to swallow it down before it could break loose. Her body ached. Her head felt clogged with too many thoughts and more than a little fear. She pressed her palm against her forehead and closed her eyes.

From the outer room came the sound of her mobile phone ringing—responsibility, rearing its ugly head. She had a business to open, a job to do. With a sigh she sat up and removed the cloth from her elbow, checking to make sure the flow of blood had ebbed. Assured that it had, she tossed the soiled cloth on the floor next to the tweezers. She fought a short, fierce battle to pull herself together.

Her mind clear, she stood slowly, pulled

the plug to drain the water, and reached for a towel.

****

Two hours later, Isabeau was setting up the cash drawer when the door opened. One look at Dominic, his usual broad smile absent from his face, and she knew his news was not pleasant. She waited while he settled onto the stool nearest her.

"I just spoke with Noah," he stated quietly.

"His grandfather...he didn't make it, did he?"

"No. He died two days ago."

Two days ago. "Did Noah get to see him before he passed?"

Dominic shook his head. "He was still on the plane."

She pressed her hand into the place in her stomach where pain for Noah and what he was going through settled like a knot. She knew how much Henry had meant to him. Knew from her own life experience, how difficult it was going to be for him to accept that he hadn't made it to his grandfather's side before his death.

"How did he sound, did he..." Her words trailed off as the absurdity of the question struck. She closed her eyes, opened them again. "Will there be a funeral?"

"In a few days. Noah's family is scattered, they'll need time to arrive." His brow furrowed. "Isabeau?"

"Yeah?"

"Your elbow is bleeding."

"Again?" She snatched up a napkin and pressed it to her elbow. "I guess I'll have to bandage it."

"Do you have a first aid kit?"

"Yes. There, under the bar."

Dominic slipped through to her side of the bar. He bent down to look where she had indicated, shoved aside a stack of papers and pulled out the white kit with bright red letters. Placing it atop the bar next to her, he flipped back the lid. "Let me see."

He didn't give her a chance to argue as he cradled her elbow in one hand and used the other to peel the napkin away and expose the injury. His hands were warm, his touch gentle. "It looks painful. What happened?"

She looked into his very blue eyes, and hid her unease behind a smile. "A little mishap this morning while jogging."

"A mishap," he repeated. His gaze moved over her from head to toe before shifting to the first aid kit. He reached for a sealed alcohol swab. "How would you define mishap?"

"I fell." His hold on her elbow tightened minutely when she shifted away from the swab. "Don't you dare try and use that on me, Dominic

Price. It's clean enough. I made sure to wash it good when I got home."

He looked doubtful. "You're sure?"

"I'm sure."

He dropped the alcohol pad and picked up a single use packet of triple antibiotic ointment. She used her free hand to tear the top off the packet when he held it out to her.

"You never answered my question."

"What question?"

Dom sent her a narrow-eyed glance before returning his focus to her elbow. He squeezed the packet, applying a strip of ointment along the worst of her scrapes. "Define mishap."

"I told you, I fell. A car...got a little too close to me. I panicked and fell down."

"You fell down?"

"Yes."

"You?" he questioned, while he taped the edges of the gauze pad in place. "The one who only days ago was sure-footed enough to outmaneuver five seasoned soccer players?"

"Pete, seasoned?" It made her laugh.

He grinned. "Four, then. How did a car get too close?"

She turned her arm to get a better look at his handiwork as he tossed the garbage and washed his hands. She was stalling, she knew it and so did he. But she didn't want to talk about her morning. "I guess they didn't see me."

He studied her, his eyes narrowed in

thought while he dried his hands on the towel she kept near the sink. A few minutes passed before either spoke again.

"I don't like this. The other day your car is vandalized and now someone nearly runs you down? Did you ring the police?"

Nope. And she wasn't going to. They'd failed her too many times in life for her to turn to them the way others did. Besides, she hadn't gotten a good look at the driver or the car's license plate.

He took in her expression. "Well?"

"I'm fine, just a few scrapes."

"Isabeau."

"When is your flight?" she asked, bringing the conversation back full circle. "When do you leave for London?" The look he gave her in place of a response made the knot inside of her grow. "Dom, you're his closest friend, you have to go. You, Nick, and Alex—you all need to be there."

He sighed, stacking both hands atop his head. "It's not possible."

"It has to be. Noah loved Henry. He needs someone to be there for him." Grief swelled. Unable to face the thought of Noah dealing with his loss alone, without the support of his friends and band mates, she turned back to the cash drawer. She began sorting bills into their proper slots.

"You could go," Dominic said quietly.

"Yeah, right." When he remained silent,

she turned back to face him. His eyes caught and held hers. "You're serious."

"Very."

"I couldn't." But it was tempting. So very tempting. "You'll have to find a way around the record company. I'm sure they'd make allowances for something like this."

"Isabeau" His expressive face changed, became almost somber. "We're under the wire here. We meet with the record company in a matter of weeks to show them what we can do. If we aren't ready by then—"

"You'll be ready."

"This record is our last hurrah, our last chance to show we still have what it takes. If we muck this up—"

"The death of a loved one, they couldn't possibly—"

"They can. They will. Noah won't accept that, you know he won't. Getting this right means everything to him. All of us."

She did know. Noah would stand alone, before he'd risk the record. He'd probably told Dom as much—to remain behind and continue working on the demo.

"You could go," he repeated.

A war of emotions waged within her. "Just hop on a plane? Then what, knock on his door?"

"You could."

Of course, she couldn't. "And say what?"

203

"I love you."

"I love you, too, sweetheart, but we're not talking about us."

"Funny." His eyes narrowed as he focused on her so intently that she felt like she stood spotlighted onstage. "You're scared."

"Of course I am," she admitted softly. Searching for a plausible explanation, she grabbed at the first one that came to her. "I hate to fly."

His eyes softened but he did not comment.

She couldn't believe she was actually considering his suggestion. But the lure of seeing Noah, of being there for him during his grief was strong. "What if I get there and I'm the last person he wants to see?"

"Not going to happen, luv."

"You don't know that."

Arching a brow, he leaned back against the cooler.

"I can't believe I'm considering this. I don't even know where to find him. What am I supposed to do, stop someone on the street and ask directions?"

He gave her a smile that was all charm and confidence. Reaching out, he snagged a napkin from the stack near her elbow, and the pen that lay next to the cash register. "I'll give you the address."

Her eyes were intent on his hands as he

began to write. "And if he sends me packing?"

"He won't."

"He could." She rubbed her raw palm over the knotted muscles in the back of her neck. "This is different from jogging across town to the funeral home to show my support. This is..." Her words trailed off as he handed her the napkin. She focused on his chicken scrawl. "This has crazed stalker written all over it."

"What about Noah, spending all that time sitting in the back corner? All those nights he spent watching you, that didn't?" He rested his hand on the bar and leaned closer. "You do realize that was about you and not alcohol, don't you?"

"Wanting someone in your bed and wanting them at your side for a funeral are not at all alike."

Perfect. She'd just said that out loud.

"Go to him, Isabeau. He won't turn you away, I know he won't."

She hesitated, torn by conflicting emotions.

"Aren't you the one who told me 'love is worth the risk'?"

"I did. And I see you took my advice to heart. You haven't even called her have you? Dom, Becca deserves to know you love her. What she does with that knowledge is up to her."

"Noah deserves—"

"Noah knows how I feel about him."

He frowned. His frown deepened when she pushed the napkin back across the bar in his direction.

Regret filled her. She ruthlessly pushed it aside in the same way she pushed her hands into her front pockets. "This insanity is over. If Noah wanted me with him, he would call and ask me to come."

"You're right," he replied, straightening.

A small clutch of pain tightened her stomach.

"You are, because dropping everything, closing your business for a few days so you can jump on a plane and hop the Atlantic, that's not too much to ask." He pushed the napkin back in her direction. "Is it, Isabeau?"

She winced. "He won't call me, will he?"

"Noah has fears, the same as you and me. No one's immune to them."

"He must know I would..." That's when it hit her. Hard. Right between the eyes.

How could Noah know the impact he'd made on her life if she'd only just realized it herself? Right that moment—when she made the decision to face crushing rejection by settling into a little metal box that could fall out of the sky and plummet into the ocean, so that she could be with him.

Dominic gave the napkin one final shove in her direction. "Ring me when you get to

London, let me know your flight went well."

She swallowed hard, but the lump of emotion remained lodged in her throat. "I don't much care for airplanes."

"I know, luv."

CHAPTER ELEVEN

Isabeau's gaze moved between the numbers on the front of the house before her and the numbers on the napkin. Then, for the third time since watching the taxi driver pull away without a backward glance, she checked the street for a road sign. For something, anything that would assure her she was deciphering Dominic's scrawl correctly. It was bad enough she'd failed to have him verbalize the address, but then she'd been so afraid she'd misplace the damn thing, she'd clutched it in her hand the entire flight. As a result the napkin was wrinkled and smudged, and half the ink now colored the palm of her left hand.

This was not her best moment.

Why had she listened to Dominic? She would have been better off getting a telephone number from him and calling Noah. But no, she'd made arrangements for the bar to be closed for a few days, cancelled deliveries and called employees. Then she'd tossed clothes into her carry-on luggage and boarded a plane.

A chill walked down her spine. The greasy ball of fear remained in her belly even though the flight was over. Flying. What could be worse?

Oh, yeah. How about standing before two similar yet detached three-story brick homes on a London street, unable to tell whether the last digit of the address was a four or a nine? To say that she was suddenly questioning the intelligence of her rash decision and last-minute trip would be an understatement.

With a sigh, she carried her luggage to the front step of the house whose street number ended in a nine and reached for the brass knocker centered in the oak paneled door. Before her fingers curled around the knocker, the door swung open.

She stepped back reflexively, knocking over her suitcase in her haste. "Hello, um, I'm looking for the Clark home."

The woman who stepped outside looked to be in her early sixties. Her gray hair in curlers, she scrutinized Isabeau from head to toe and back again in the amount of time it took her to pull the door mostly closed behind her. "Are you expected?"

She did her best not to squirm. "Actually, no. My name is Isabeau Montgomery. I know you don't know me, but I'm looking for Noah." She was stammering, but couldn't seem to stop the flow of words once they started. "Dom wrote out the address for me, but I can't quite make out this last part."

The woman was watching her carefully. Isabeau held out the napkin. "Can you tell me if I'm in the right general area?"

Honestly, she expected the woman to step back into the house and close the door in her face. It was early yet, the sunlight just beginning to rise over the houses at her back and slant across the doorstep. Instead, the woman settled her hand on Isabeau's wrist. "You know Dominic?"

She wasn't used to strangers touching her. She stood there, absorbing the shock and the surprising comfort in the woman's touch. The knot in her stomach loosened a fraction. "Yes. I don't mean to intrude, I—"

"Your hands are like ice, dear. Are you all right?"

"She doesn't like to fly."

The deep, masculine voice drew Isabeau's attention up and over the woman's shoulder. The door remained open a scant four inches. Centered in an archway between the entryway of the house and what appeared to be a formal dining room stood Noah. His gaze locked on her, expression neutral.

"It's more like I'm terrified of flying," she admitted softly. He looked worn-out, his eyes slightly bloodshot and shadowed enough to indicate he hadn't slept much in the few days he'd been gone. The stubble along his jaw remained, thickened now but still unable to

210

disguise the lines of exhaustion at the corners of his unsmiling mouth.

Anxiety warred with an intense relief that she was at the right house.

"Yet you obviously spent the better part of nine hours on a plane," he replied evenly.

Oh God, she wished she could gauge his reaction to her sudden arrival. But his expression gave nothing away.

"About ten actually." There was that hour her plane sat on the runway waiting to take off, while every horrible thing she could imagine going wrong danced through her mind like an in-flight movie. "I had this crazy idea that you might need a friend right about now."

"Did you?"

He didn't tell her she was mistaken. He just looked at her some more.

Her right hand clenched around the strap of her tote, her fingers dug into the supple leather.

"Mum, are you going to let Isabeau in, or did you plan on making her stand out on the street all day?"

Relief filled her. She didn't have to return to the airport. Long Island City. Alone.

Noah's mom blinked, took a quick look at her son. "Isabeau, you say?" She looked back at Isabeau, the most peculiar expression on her face. "You're a friend of Noah's?"

"Yes, ma'am."

211

"I see." Was that amusement shining in her gaze? "Come inside dear, let me take that bag for you. I'll place it in the other room."

"Thank you, Mrs.—"

"Call me Emily, dear, everyone does." Smiling broadly, she picked up Isabeau's carry-on and walked off, leaving her and Noah standing silently across the entryway from each other.

The silence stretched, grew. Unable to take it any longer, Isabeau spoke. "Your mom seems nice."

Noah stood in the archway and drank in the sight of her. He'd been thinking about her all morning, and here she was. In the flesh. In his parent's home. Flustered and so damn radiant in her simple white cotton dress that he damn near cried.

He managed to save himself from that humiliation. Barely. "You're..." He struggled to rein in his scattered thoughts. A part of him wondered if she was truly there, or a figment of his exhausted mind. "You got on a plane? For me?"

"The guys couldn't be here for you. I could."

His eyes began to burn. Damn it. He was going to humiliate himself after all. "What about the bar?"

"I couldn't get hold of Clint before I left, so I closed it." Her fingers clenched and unclenched. As the leather tote she carried slipped off her shoulder, she eased it to the floor near her feet. "Look, if I was too presumptuous, I can leave. Tell me to go."

"Stay," he countered instantly, then swallowed against the tightness that had settled in his throat. How had she known how much he needed her?

Noah spent the last few days in a fog of grief so complete it consumed him. He'd done everything humanly possible to get home before his grandfather died. In the end, he'd missed seeing Henry one last time by a few lousy hours. The ache inside him was total. He needed sleep, desperately, but every time he closed his eyes, the pain of loss swelled. Alone in his bed, he longed for Isabeau. Her touch. Her comfort. She understood grief. She'd lost someone, too. In the dark, he'd reach for the phone and punch in her number.

Only to hang up before the first ring, for fear the sound of her voice wouldn't be enough and he would find himself reduced to begging.

"Noah?"

Here she stood; the answer to his prayers. Every fiber of his being wanted to close the three-foot gap between them and pull her into his arms. He remained rooted in place. What the hell was wrong with him?

He closed his eyes and shook his head in defeat. As the silence settled around him, he feared the worst. Body tight, he waited for the click of the door, the echo of her heels retreating up the walk.

Her cheek settled on his chest, directly above his heart. Arms circled his waist, bringing her body flush against him.

"Isa." His breath left him in a rush. He set his hands on her shoulders, smoothed them down her back, and took up fistfuls of her dress as he buried his face in her hair and breathed her in.

"Are you okay?" she whispered.

The fit was perfect. Her scent familiar. "Let me hold you, for a minute."

"Okay." She shifted even closer and held him, as tightly as he held her.

Minutes passed. Neither moved. Slowly, his heart rate returned to normal. The tension he'd been carrying around for days, eased ever so slightly. He released the tight hold on her dress and smoothed his right hand up her back to cradle her head in his palm. Turning his head, he pressed his lips to the soft tendrils of ebony hair that shadowed her temple. "Thank you."

"You can hold me anytime."

"I meant for coming to London."

She eased back and met his gaze. "I didn't know if I'd be welcome." Her left hand raised to push his too-long hair out of his eyes before cupping the side of his face. "But I needed to see you. I couldn't bear the thought of you going through this alone."

He gazed into her impossibly beautiful eyes and his heart engaged. "You're an incredible woman, Isabeau Montgomery."

Linking their fingers, he shifted her hand from his cheek to his mouth, pressed a kiss into the center of her palm. A ripple of satisfaction moved through him when her eyes drifted shut.

"Hmm, why do you say that?" she murmured.

His thumb caressed the spot his lips had just been, back and forth over her scars. "You're the only person I know who would put her business on hold and her fears aside for me."

An emotion flashed through her eyes, one he couldn't identify. "I doubt that."

"It's true."

"I understand grief. How important having someone to talk to can be. That doesn't make me special."

"Of course it does." A strand of her hair slid along his jaw as his lips brushed her temple, then drifted toward her ear. Her fingers flexed around his thumb.

Rough bumps pebbled her palm. He lifted his head. When he discovered the heel of her hand torn and swollen, he reached for her other hand. It looked only slightly better.

"What happened to you?"

"I took a tumble."

215

He looked her over. Both hands were scraped, and there was a bandage on her left elbow. "How badly were you injured?"

"I'm fine," she assured him. She slid her hands from his and settled them on his chest. Her gaze dropped to his mouth. "A few scrapes. I'm far more traumatized by the fact that you've yet to kiss me."

"Are you?"

"Oh, yes."

He curled his hand around the back of her neck and eased her closer. With his free hand, he cupped her chin, then ran the pad of his thumb along the curve of her bottom lip.

Her lips parted. Her eyes flashed a very pale blue.

He dipped his head, and she met him halfway. A jolt went through him at the first brush of her mouth against his. He stroked his hand down her back, palming her ass as he did his best to inhale her whole.

"Noah, Mum's wondering if..."

Shit.

Isabeau startled, pushing against his chest until he was forced to release her. Over her head, he locked eyes with his brother, Paul. "You always did have rotten timing."

"What can I say, it's a gift." Paul turned his head, his gaze slowly sliding over Isabeau as she leaned down and plucked her tote off the floor. "Maybe if you chose a better place than the front entry to greet your guest, you wouldn't get interrupted."

"Isn't that where you're supposed to greet a guest, the entryway?" Noah watched and waited, wondering how long it would take for Paul to realize the identity of the woman he openly scrutinized. Mum had done it on purpose, of course, sent Paul to fetch them. It was no secret how his brother felt about a young pianist named Isabeau Montgomery.

"I couldn't help myself," Noah said unapologetically. "I'm sure you understand."

Isabeau straightened. She pushed her dark hair over her shoulder and away from her face. Her gaze settled on Paul, her mouth curved in a warm smile. "Hello, you must be Noah's brother, Paul."

Paul took the hand she offered. "I am, how'd..." His jaw went slack.

"You have the same eyes."

"Bugger me!" Paul muttered.

"Excuse me?" Isabeau questioned.

Noah laughed for the first time in days. *Laughed.* He slipped his arm around Isa and pulled her into his side. "You'll have to excuse my brother," he explained as Paul began to stutter. "Mum dropped him on his head when he was a babe."

"I can see that."

"You're...Isabeau Montgomery." Stunned didn't begin to describe Paul's expression.

217

"Yes, I am."

"Wow." Paul blinked. "Wow."

Noah glanced pointedly at his brother's hand. "You can let her go now, Paul."

"What? Oh, sorry." Releasing her hand, Paul straightened. "What are you doing here?"

"She's here for me."

Paul shook his head. He cast an accusatory glance at Noah. "I hate you. You know that, don't you? I've never liked you."

"That's a bit harsh."

Isabeau raised an eyebrow. "Am I missing something?"

"Paul's a fan of yours."

"And?"

"And he's a no-good, stinking rock singer," Paul exclaimed.

Beneath his palm, her spine straightened to its full height—all of five foot three inches. She was going to tear into Paul. And damn if that didn't do something for him. "He's only joking. He loves me."

"I'm not," Paul argued, but his grin belied his words. "You're...what could you possibly see in him?"

Isabeau turned her gaze to Noah. She looked him over, slowly, intensely. A smile curved her lips, warmed his blood.

Paul's brow furrowed. "I don't want to know, do I? Forget I asked."

Isabeau's smile broadened.

Noah tried to laugh, but the sound stuck in his throat. "Come on. I'll introduce you to the rest of my family before Mum sends anyone else looking for us."

****

"I like your family," Isabeau said, a few steps behind Noah as he led her up the stairs to her room for the night. She glanced at the photographs that lined the wall on her right, thinking she should take the time for a closer look. Perhaps tomorrow, after the funeral.

"I believe the feeling's mutual."

"You're a lot like your father."

A bit of an understatement. It was shocking how much like Colin Clark his son was. Not only did they share the same build, the same striking green eyes and charming smile, but both had similar temperaments.

Paul, on the other hand, was a different story. "Your brother is a character."

"Yeah, he is," Noah replied dully.

She glanced up at him. "What is it? What's wrong?"

He stopped in the middle of the second floor hallway, and checked over his shoulder. She did the same, even though she knew everyone else remained downstairs.

"Paul isn't himself. He's not usually so quiet, not like Dad and me."

If today was Paul quiet...wow. He'd

bantered good-naturedly with his younger brother more than once today, getting Noah to laugh. Spent over an hour talking with her about music, his likes and dislikes, and its effect on his life. There'd only been a few times that he had grown quiet, appearing to become lost in thought. "I thought he was very talkative."

"He's usually more like Mum."

"Oh," she replied as understanding struck. Emily Clark was anything but quiet. Kind and gregarious, she was a lady who could talk a person to death. Isabeau already had a great fondness for her. "Your mother's wonderful."

Noah smiled and gestured for her to precede him into the room "I wish I knew what was wrong with Paul."

"Noah, everyone handles grief differently."

"It's more than that. There's something going on between him and Anne."

Yes, there was. And although she'd only just met the couple, she had her suspicions about what that something was.

When Noah had introduced her to his sister-in-law, she hadn't been surprised by the woman's stunning beauty, or the fact that Noah wasn't the only Clark who apparently preferred blondes. She had been surprised that although Anne was genuinely kind to Isabeau, she grew distant whenever her husband was near. Then there were the times Anne would go pale as a sheet and rush from the room. Although Paul showed concern as he tracked his wife's abrupt exit, he never followed her.

"Has she said anything about—" Her words died abruptly as Noah closed the door, stepped past her, and pulled his shirt off over his head. "What are you doing?"

"Getting ready for bed. I'm exhausted."

He looked it, but that wasn't what had her mind blanking. She managed to drag her eyes away from all that naked skin long enough to take in the room more completely. Her suitcase rested atop the full size bed, evidence that she was meant to sleep in this room. However, the black leather duffel bag she'd watched him hurriedly stuff clothes into the other day sat on the floor, next to a dresser topped with a scattering of his personal items. "Is this your room?"

"Yes."

Her gaze returned to him and her breath shuddered out. He'd tossed the shirt carelessly across the chair at his right, and was busy undoing his jeans.

"Oh, no. No, I don't think so." Spinning around, she reached for the handle on the door, gave it a twist and pulled.

He slapped his palm against the door just to the left of her head. The knob slid from her fingers. The door closed with a snap. "Where are you going?"

"I can't sleep in the same room as you."

"Why not?" With his hand above her head, he leaned in, effectively trapping her between his body and the door. His musky scent enveloped her. His warm chest pressed against the back of her arms.

"This is where your mother put my bag? We're not...You can't let her think..."

"That I want you in my bed? I do want you in my bed."

Oh, God. The raw hunger in his voice had her eyes drifting shut. For a moment, everything else faded away as she imagined his weight pressing down on her, those long fingered hands gripping her hips as his hard-as-a-rock body slid over her. Into her.

Heat spread through her belly.

Her nipples.

Between her legs.

He stepped closer. One hand held the door closed as the other skimmed over her shoulder and down her arm. He tipped his head and put his mouth to her ear. "I've been looking at you all day. Watching you smile and laugh with my family. I can't help but think that if things had been different, I wouldn't have to wonder what you look like without that dress." His tongue flicked across her earlobe. "What you taste like."

She let out a helpless moan. Then his

222

thumb shifted from the inside of her arm to deliberately brush across the outside of her breast, and her knees went weak. "You..." She couldn't breathe. She had to drag in oxygen to speak. "You already know what I taste like."

"Not all of you."

"All of me?"

"All of you. Every. Last. Delicious. Inch."

She breathed his name on a ragged sigh. Inside her bra, her taut nipples strained, crying out for his touch. It was a completely new experience for her, to be seduced by nothing but words and the brush of his hand on her arm. She didn't like to be touched.

At least she never used to.

"Turn around, Isa." His voice was gruff, but the hand he placed on her waist only exerted enough pressure to encourage her cooperation.

She turned slowly and came face-to-face with his desire. His skin was flushed. His eyes darkened with need. Against her stomach, he was hard. Very hard.

"Too bad what I have planned for you isn't something I'm willing to do under my parent's roof or I'd lay you on that bed right there and satisfy my curiosity." Without her permission, her eyes darted to the bed. "When I finally get you alone, with no one to interrupt us, and nowhere we need to be...It isn't going to be fast."

"N-no?"

His thigh slid in between hers, pressed at the pulse between her legs. "What I have in mind for you is going to take hours." He had her pinned to the door, their bodies flush. His mouth skimmed the muscle where her neck and shoulder connected. Bit down lightly.

With a gasp, she streaked her hands up, fisted her fingers in his hair and pulled his mouth to hers. A sound of distinct male satisfaction rumbled from his chest when she sucked his tongue into her mouth and rocked against his thigh. Once. Twice.

Caught up in the flood of desire, the whirl of passion, Isabeau didn't think, she felt—the roar of fire through her blood, the clutch of passion deep in her center. Releasing her tight hold on his hair, she reached between them and cupped her hand over his solid length.

He went utterly still. Grabbing her wrist, he lifted her hand and pressed it to the door next to her head.

"Noah?"

Noah buried his face in her neck and swore softly. What the hell was he thinking? He never should have touched her. Never should have given in to the lure of her dark skin against that pale dress. But he'd been watching her for hours. Wondering. Wanting. No way in hell was he going to be able to get any sleep now.

"What are we doing?" he asked softly, then sucked in a sharp breath when she used her other hand to cup him again.

"Do you really want a blow by blow?" she asked, stroking him through his jeans.

Her hair brushed across his chin and her scent wafted up his nose. She tugged to free the wrist he still held. "Isabeau, we can't."

She tipped her head back, her pale eyes filled with emotion as they probed his face. "We won't," she replied, and immediately began working his zipper open. "You will."

"I don't think—"

"Don't think, Noah, feel." Somehow he wound up with his back against the closed door, unable, or perhaps unwilling to stop her as she shoved his jeans down his hips. "You need sleep, and you'll never get it in this condition."

She was right about that. He'd never been so achingly hard in all his life. Her breath came in quick, shallow gasps as her gaze moved appreciatively over his body. Heat followed the same path as her eyes.

"Take them off," she ordered huskily.

He toed off his shoes, stepped out of his jeans.

"Look at you," she whispered as she reached out and settled her hand on his chest. Her gaze following as her fingertips slowly outlined every muscle. Everywhere she touched, she left a trail of white hot sensation. Her hand dipped lower, smoothing over his abdomen, then lower still. He didn't even try to hold back the growl of pleasure when she wrapped her fingers around him and slowly stroked her hand up and down his length.

"Christ, Isabeau."

"Relax," she purred. There was no other word for the sound.

As if he could. He reached out and sank his fingers into the ebony silk of her hair. But when he would have pulled her mouth closer for a kiss, she shifted and pressed her lips to the center of his chest. Her mouth opened, her tongue trailed along the same torturous path her fingers had just taken as she slowly sank to her knees in front of him.

He gathered up her hair, holding it out of the way so he could watch her mouth come closer. The wait was both excruciating and thrilling. Then finally it was over, as she leaned forward and kissed him, pressing her lips against the base of his shaft. He groaned softly as she worked her way up the length of him, felt his knees go weak as she opened her mouth and took him inside.

Wet heat. Torturous. Exhilarating.

His heart pumped harder. His muscles began to tremble.

He closed his eyes and dropped his head back against the door, only to force them back open as the need to watch her pleasure him

226

swelled. She took him deep, sucking, then swirling her tongue across the very tip of him, sending currents of excitement up his torso, down his legs. He swallowed a sharp exhalation as he watched her, the sight of her lips surrounding him damn near as stimulating as her increasing tempo.

She sucked him rhythmically, softly and tortuously. He'd imagined her sexy mouth pleasuring him this way too many times to count, but fantasy didn't hold a candle to the reality. Sensation rocketed through him. His hand flexed and fisted in her hair. His hips jerked.

He was close. So damn close. Her hands circled his hips to close over his ass. As her fingers kneaded his flesh, she took him a little farther into her mouth.

His testicles pulled up. Blood roared in his ears. His orgasm hit him with the force of a freight train, sending a deep shudder throughout his body. He swallowed a shout and pressed his free hand against the door to try to hold himself upright as he exploded in pulsation after hot pulsation. As she lapped at him, taking all of him until he had nothing left to give.

With one final kiss, she smoothed her way back up his body, shifting into his arms. She settled her hand against his chest as she pressed her face into the hollow between his shoulder and neck. His heart hammered violently against his ribs. Easing the hold he still had on her hair, Noah skimmed his lips over her temple.

"Hmm," she murmured, tipping her head to place a kiss on the underside of his jaw. "Do you think you can sleep now?"

"I don't think I'll have any problem," he replied, breathless and spent.

"Good, then let's get you to bed."

That might be a problem.

Somehow he managed to cross the room and set her suitcase aside, to slide under the covers without falling flat on his face. He snagged her wrist when she pulled the cover over him then turned away. "Where are you going?"

"I need to change."

His gaze drifted from her face to her feet and back again. "You're not trying to sneak out and sleep on the couch are you?"

She smiled, then bent down and kissed him softly, slowly. "I'm not sneaking away. I'll be right back."

"Hurry," he replied. Then, with her taste still on his lips, he slept for the first time in days.

****

"How did your hand get scarred?" ten-year-old Robert Clark asked Isabeau the next day as they sat at a table in the large, walled garden.

With the funeral behind them, and most of those who'd stayed to offer proper condolences fed and gone, Isabeau was sitting for the first time that day. She might not be family or have ever met Noah's grandfather, but she knew how to work a crowd and had done her best to assist in every way possible.

She smiled at Robert, who appeared so bored with all the adult conversations that she felt a little sorry for him. "I was in a car accident years ago."

"How many years ago?"

"I was twelve."

His head tipped and he looked up at her through eyes as blue as the sky above them. "Megan's twelve."

"I know."

"How do you know?"

"Your uncle told me."

"Oh." He reached out slowly, and traced his fingers over the scars on the back of her hand. Because he was a child and the move stemmed from innocent curiosity, she let him. "You have a lot of scars."

"I have more on my palm," she replied and turned her hand over so he could see.

"It was bad, then?"

"Yes. My mother died as a result of it."

He frowned. "The way my great-grandfather died?"

The urge to reach out and comfort the boy was strong. Not certain how he would take it, she left her hands where they were. "Yes. Like your great-grandfather."

"Do you miss her?"

"Every day."

The hand still tracing her scars flexed. "I miss Grandpa, too."

Suspecting this was the real reason he started the conversation and that he had something more to say, she waited silently. She didn't have to wait for long.

"So does my dad. He was crying at the funeral."

"A lot of people were. Funerals are for those last good-byes, and people get sad when they have to say good-bye."

"Boys aren't supposed to cry." With his face aimed down at the table and his voice pitched low, she had to strain to hear his words. Her heart bled for him, so young, so unprepared to deal with his loss.

"Everyone feels pain, Robert," she assured him, as a tear streaked down his cheek. "Even boys. Crying is a natural result of that pain."

He swiped the back of his hand under his nose. "Uncle Noah didn't cry."

Her gaze drifted to Noah, at the far side of the garden, deep in conversation with his brother Paul. He'd sat beside her, dry-eyed and stoic throughout his grandfather's service, while those around him wept. She had hoped he would come home, find a quiet place where he could be alone and finally grieve. The rigid set to his shoulders, combined with the smile that didn't quite reach his eyes told her he hadn't.

She sighed. "I know he didn't, but that doesn't make him more of a man, it only makes him stubborn."

She gave Robert a moment to compose himself before turning back to find him studying her intently. "Are you going to marry Uncle Noah?"

Startled by his abrupt shift in conversation, she stuttered, "Um…"

"It would be okay if you did, you're nice and all."

"Thank you," she replied, not knowing what else to say.

"How many scars do you have?"

Wondering where his shifting conversation would go next, she replied, "There are twenty-three scars on that hand."

"Cooool."

"You're such a boy, Robert," his sister, Megan, stated as she sidled up to the table. "It's not cool. It's rather sad, actually." Megan looked like her mother, blonde-haired and blue-eyed. There was a maturity to her, beyond her years. "Dad says you can't play the piano anymore after the accident. But Uncle Noah says you can play, you just don't."

"Your uncle is right. With therapy, I regained the use of the hand, and I can still play the piano. Just not as well as I used to."

"Is that why you quit?"

So most of the world believed. The truth was much more complicated. Painful.

"Megan," her mother chastised as she stepped to the table. "Whatever Isabeau's reasons, they're personal, and you should not meddle."

Megan pursed her mouth. "I love to play the piano," she said to Isabeau. "I could play a song for you sometime."

"I would like that."

"Grandma doesn't have a piano, so it would have to be some other time. I'm pretty good, but I'm not as good as you."

"Keep practicing, you will be."

"I don't think so," Megan stated matter-of-factly. She leaned closer as if she had a secret to share. "I write my own songs."

Isabeau smiled, genuinely pleased by the declaration. "Now that is talent. A person can be taught how to play, but a mind for composition...you either have it or you don't. That's wonderful, Megan."

A flush colored her cheeks. "Thank you."

"Megan?"

"Yeah, Mum?"

"You and your brother go tell your

grandmum and granddad good-bye and collect your things."

"We're leaving? Why?"

"Because your grandparents are probably ready for some peace and quiet," Anne replied. "I know I am."

Megan and Robert muttered good-byes to Isabeau and then headed into the house.

Anne took Robert's vacant seat. "You're very good with kids."

"I love kids," Isabeau admitted. "And you have truly great kids." Not for the first time she noted the circles ringing Anne's eyes, the pale cast to her skin that she'd tried to hide beneath expertly applied makeup. "You're a good mother, Anne."

Anne's gaze darted away at the compliment, and Isabeau knew her suspicions were correct. Anne Clark was pregnant, and she wasn't happy about it.

Pain welled up and grabbed her by the throat. She curled her right hand protectively around her left and struggled to appear calm and unaffected.

Anne cleared her throat. "I apologize if Robert brought up any painful memories. He...well, Megan said it best, he is a boy."

"It's all right," Isabeau assured her.

"You don't have twenty-three scars, do you? I mean, you were exaggerating for the boy, right?"

"I'm afraid not."

Anne leaned forward slowly, and cupped Isabeau's hand in hers in a move that was so maternal, it brought tears to her eyes.

"So much pain," Anne said softly. "You lost so much in that one moment, didn't you? You were so young, just Megan's age. I can't bear to think about it."

Isabeau squeezed her eyes shut and fought to steady herself. It took a couple of seconds for her to regain the ability to speak. "Everything happens for a reason, Anne." She opened her eyes and gazed into the woman's disbelieving, unsmiling face. "We don't always understand why, but there's always a reason."

"How...You can't possibly know."

The kids streaked out of the house, Robert in the lead, Megan hot on his tail. They darted across the manicured lawn circling Noah and Paul at the far end. Unable to look away, Isabeau watched Noah reach out and grab Robert around his waist. The boy squealed in delight, his volume increasing as he was pinned to the ground by his uncle and held there so that his sister could exact her revenge for whatever wrong Robert had done.

Isabeau pressed her hand to her stomach and tensed against the pain that lanced her like a scalpel. "Children are a gift," she managed past a throat that had gone dry. "At any age."

Anne withdrew her hands. Isabeau could

see her mentally struggling to figure out how she had guessed correctly. "It comes with the job," she explained. "I have to be good at reading people."

"Well, congratulations," Anne replied, her words sharp, biting. "You must be very good at your job."

Isabeau went back to watching Noah play with his niece and nephew. He seemed so genuinely happy, so at ease with them.

He had quite a family. Close-knit. Loving.

It made her feel alone.

Next to her, Anne let out a slow breath. "I'm sorry, I don't mean to snap. It's just, I'm too old to start over—the diapers and the tears, the sleepless nights."

"The joy of holding something born of love, the satisfaction of helping to shape a young life. I envy you. Not everyone gets that."

"You're still young. You have plenty of time to..." Her words trailed off as Isabeau turned her head.

Squeals of laughter erupted from the far end of the garden.

Emotion swam in Anne's eyes. "I feel selfish and petty."

"That was not my intention."

"You must believe me horrible."

Isabeau dragged in a deep breath. There were tears in her throat now, tears welling in her eyes. "You're struggling with a major life change. Your feelings are understandable."

"Are they?" Anne asked quietly. "You can't have children, can you, Isabeau?"

She didn't want to cry. She'd accepted her fate years ago, why would talking about it now bring her so much pain?

Shifting her gaze, she stared across the yard at the answer to her unspoken question. Then she said aloud what she'd never told anyone before. "I suffered more than a crushing hand injury in that automobile accident, I also had internal injuries. The damage was so extensive that...I was told I'll never conceive."

"I'm so sorry."

"Everything happens for a reason," she reiterated, then stood and went in search of a quiet place where she could be alone and grieve.

****

Noah finally located Isabeau inside the house, sitting on the stairs. Can of soda in her right hand, she sat on the fourth step from the top, her eyes closed, the fingers of her free hand slowly massaging her temple. For a moment, he stood there and gazed at her, while a kaleidoscope of emotions ran through him. She still wore the simple black dress from the funeral, her dark hair smoothed away from her face and off her neck. But surprisingly, her feet were bare—her customary spike heels kicked off and resting a few steps below.

Watching her, he felt something inside of him shift, something he wasn't ready to look at too closely. All he knew was he liked waking up with her in his bed—nestled against his side. Her face pressed into his neck, hand atop his chest. His right hand had been curled protectively over her left, his other hand buried in the inky black silk of her hair. She'd been wearing the T-shirt he'd tossed on the chair and little else, and although she'd brought him to mind-blowing orgasm a few hours before, he awoke wrapped in her scent, wrapped in her. Aching.

He swallowed. "There you are," he said, climbing the stairs and settling for running his fingers over the smooth skin of her shoulder. "I saw you holding my nephew's hand. Should I be worried that he's planning to steal you away from me?"

She tipped her face to look up at him and his chest tightened. Her lips formed a smile, but there was an intense sadness in her eyes. "Isabeau, what is it?"

She cleared her throat and looked away. "I was looking at these photographs."

"And that made you sad?"

She didn't answer. "Who is this?"

Disappointment filled him, tightened his jaw. Damn, he was tired of the secrets. He wondered how long before she trusted him enough to let him in. Whether he had the patience to wait, or whether he should push her for answers. Uncertain, he followed her pointing finger to the black framed photograph near her shoulder.

"You would pick that one, wouldn't you?" he asked, then sank down onto the step beside her. Barely wide enough for two people, she had to shift in order to accommodate him. He leaned back, resting his elbows on the step behind him, then, because he liked the feel of her skin, he traced the back of his fingers up and down her arm from shoulder to elbow. "That's Danny and me."

"You look like you were causing trouble."

"If Danny was with me, I usually was."

"How old are you there?"

He thought back to the summer it had been taken, remembered it was the year he'd kissed his first girl, Gwen Ryder. A kiss hadn't been all they'd shared that summer. "I was fifteen."

"And?"

"And what?" he asked, sliding the can from her fingers and taking a drink, before handing it back.

"You're grinning like a little boy with a secret, Noah Clark. Don't pretend you don't know what I'm asking."

His grin widened at her comparison. "Let's just say that summer changed my life."

"How did it...oh." Her forehead creased,

her mouth turned down at the corners. "I get it, now."

He didn't mean to laugh. "You're beautiful when you're jealous."

Her frown deepened. "I'm not jealous."

"That's good, because that was a long time ago and you..." His smile slipped away as he came to his own realization. He groaned aloud. "Were you even born yet? I suddenly feel so—"

"Pervy?"

Pervy? He glanced at her, incredulous. "I was going to say old."

She had the audacity to laugh at him.

Her eyes sparkled with joy. The last bit of sadness disappeared from her features as her laughter flowed across his skin, as arousing as a caress. "You've got an amazing laugh."

She sent him a wary look. "Yeah, and an incredible mouth, and beautiful eyes..." She rolled those beautiful eyes and turned back to the photographs. "I changed my mind, you're not pervy, you're slick."

"I meant every compliment I ever gave you."

"Sure, you did," she replied, skeptically. But then her mouth curved, and he knew she was pleased to hear him say it. "What about this one, with Paul. How old are you here?"

Noah allowed his gaze to take in her high cheekbones and full lips, the delicate curve of her jaw and her slender neck. He couldn't recall ever noticing a woman's neck before. Not as a part of her anatomy that he found compelling. "A few years older than you are now. That was taken at Paul and Anne's wedding."

She leaned closer, her fingers smoothing over his image. "Your hair's so long. As long as Dom's."

"Hmm." He skimmed his hand up her arm and settled it at the back of her neck, where he toyed with the small hairs that had worked loose from their twist.

"You look…"

"Half in the bag?" he guessed.

"Tired," she corrected.

"I was. We were in the middle of a world tour. I'd flown in the night before then left again about an hour after that picture was taken." His hand moved higher, working the silver clip loose. Her hair tumbled down around her shoulders, brushed over his arm. Her eyes locked with his as he wove his fingers into the strands and cupped the back of her head. "If I asked you what had you on the verge of tears when I walked up would you tell me?"

"No."

He held her in place as he straightened, easing closer. "What if I asked you to come home with me?"

Her breathing shallowed. "I don't know what you mean."

He settled his free hand on her knee. The aluminum can protested as her hands tightened around it. "To my place, in California."

Her skin flushed. Her gaze settled on his mouth. "Noah," she said, her voice a harsh whisper.

"We can catch a flight out tonight. Spend a day there before heading back to New York." His hand eased up her thigh, slipped beneath the hem of her dress. "You and me. Alone. No interruptions." He tightened his fingers in her hair and tugged her head back, his mouth hovering above hers. "Say yes."

"Yes."

CHAPTER TWELVE

The tension grew inside of Isabeau the closer they got to Noah's house, until it was suffocating. Until she was certain he could hear her heart beating in her chest. He had told her that he lived a little more than an hour from the airport. They'd been driving now for exactly fifty-eight minutes. Of course, there were the ten minutes when he'd gone into the drug store to take into consideration. But thinking about them made her even more uneasy because she knew what he'd gone in to buy, and she hadn't stopped him.

She hadn't stopped him.

Sure, she could rationalize her actions by reminding herself that condoms prevented more than pregnancy, but that wasn't what kept her silent. No, that would be nerves. And a little bit of fear. Easing out a quiet sigh, she closed her eyes and tipped her head back against the upholstered headrest. She realized her fingers were dancing up and down her leg only when Noah stilled the movement with his hand.

The fact that he made the gesture without comment didn't surprise her. He hadn't spoken more than a few words since they'd left the car rental agency at the airport. She glanced across the front seat and tried to figure out what he was thinking behind the dark lenses of his sunglasses. Was he at all apprehensive, did he feel like he could crawl right out of his skin, the way she did? Or was he as calm and relaxed as he appeared?

Seven forty-eight. Another five minutes had passed.

He squeezed her hand in a way she knew was meant to reassure. "Don't worry, we're almost there."

He'd misread her restlessness. Not surprising. After all, her own body couldn't decide if she should be frightened or excited, whether it should flash hot or cold. She knew making love with him would be wonderful, but she'd never given control to anyone before. Never placed herself completely in a man's hands the way she knew he would insist she do with him. Shifting her hand out from under his, she pinched the bridge of her nose as stirrings of uncertainty started low in her stomach.

"There are workmen at your house, aren't there?"

His hand remained on her knee, the individual press of each of his fingers branding her flesh through the lightweight fabric of her dress. "No. I called them after booking our flight and gave them the day off. They won't be back until Monday."

Every nerve ending in her body scrambled as he shifted his hand higher, skimmed his thumb back and forth on her thigh. The acknowledgement that they would indeed be alone once they reached their destination, had her breath shallowing. "Noah?"

"Hmm?" His hand eased up her thigh. "What is it?"

"I'm not sure I can—" She sucked in air on a gasp as his fingers brushed between her legs. Her body jolted, arched. Desperate, she pressed her back further into the seat and covered his hand with her own. "Noah."

Was she asking him to stop, or encouraging him? Even she didn't know.

"Open your eyes, Isabeau. Look at me."

She forced her eyes open, turned her head.

"Relax," he encouraged and stroked her a second time.

She was wound so tight she thought she would break. Her nipples tightened. A pulse had started between her thighs and his advice was to relax?

Not possible. Not anytime soon.

She stared at his profile and wondered...What was he hiding behind his sunglasses? Could it be that she was the only one nervous? Aroused. Anxious. She had to know.

Reaching out, she slid his glasses off. His skin was flushed. The eyes that glanced over full of heat and raw emotion. Her heart thudded. Tossing his sunglasses into the back seat, she reached for him.

"I don't think so," he growled, pinning her hand against his hard thigh. "This isn't about me."

"Of course it is."

"No. We already know you can please a man. I need to know I can please you." His hand tightened around hers, held on as she attempted to pull away. "Remember what I said, Isabeau, it's all about touch."

He made a right, pulling the car into a long driveway and to a halt in front of a three-stall garage. He released his hold on her, shifted into park, turned off the ignition and faced her. Then, as if to emphasize his point, his hand journeyed up her arm, over her shoulder and settled at the back of her neck. He pulled her close.

"What's the matter? Are you frightened?" His warm breath brushed across her lips with every word.

She watched him through her lashes while her breath quickened, while he slowly shifted his head and began to nibble along her jaw.

"A little," she admitted. She expected him to smile in satisfaction, even laugh. Instead, his mouth worked its way down her throat, coaxing a moan from her.

"I know the feeling." He trailed his tongue over her collarbone. "I've never wanted anyone the way I want you."

"You...haven't?"

"No."

When he lifted his head, the truth in his eyes drove away the last of her apprehension. "Noah?"

"Isa?"

"Take me to bed."

Slowly, his mouth curved. Without taking his eyes off hers, he reached into the back seat and retrieved the bag from the drug store. Then he slid from the car, circled to her door, and helped her out.

His hand on her lower back, he guided her up the front path. Thinking only of the pleasure they were about to bring each other, she watched him slide the key into the lock. He pushed the door open and she caught a glimpse of soaring cathedral ceilings, a sea of white broken by gleaming cherry floors, and a panoramic view of the Sierra Nevada foothills, before he pressed her against the door.

His mouth settled on hers, and he kissed her, long, slow, and deep. His free hand cupped her throat. When his thumb stroked the side of her neck, her body began to tremble. Her legs went weak. Pinned between the door and the solid strength of his body, she tugged his shirt out of his jeans until her hands slid beneath the hem. A hum of pleasure broke from the back of her throat as her exploring hands smoothed over his chest.

His mouth left hers to trail kisses along her jaw, then down the column of her throat. He stroked his hands down her back until he reached the curve of her butt. Filling his hands, he hiked her up. The position pressed his erection against her and she gasped, wrapped her legs around his waist. Her dress slid up. Cool air brushed across her skin. Hot, wet heat pooled between her thighs.

She had a vague sense of them moving as she began feasting on his neck. She nipped the lobe of his ear with her teeth, and he sucked in a ragged breath. Her greedy hands raced over his body, touched him everywhere she could reach. Heat pumped through her blood when he shifted his grip and his fingers slid beneath the elastic leg of her panties. He parted her with his fingers, stroking, teasing, until she arched against him.

She needed to taste him. Again. Now. Unable to resist, she fisted her hand in his hair, pulled his head back and planted her mouth on his. He stumbled, knocking them both against the wall. He held her there, as slowly, much too slowly, his fingers slid into her, first one, then two. Moving with intimate strokes, stroking deep, then easing out of her, opening, stretching her—making love to her with his hand.

Oh, God. Her hips arched, urging him back into her. His thumb shifted, circled and pressed, while his fingers continued their tantalizing rhythm. "Wait...I want..."

"You will," he promised, his voice raw. "This is only the beginning."

A roaring filled her head, then pleasure exploded through her like a wave, washing over her, nearly unbearable. Spasms rocked her body, stole her breath as she convulsed and shuddered around him.

Spent, she clung to him as he pushed away from the wall, carried her up the stairs and hung a left, into the master suite. He set her on her feet at the side of the bed. Her knees wobbled, and she let out a shaky laugh. It backed up in her throat as he dropped the bag he somehow still carried, toed off his shoes, and peeled off his shirt.

Holy cow. She wondered if she'd ever get used to how good he looked without his shirt. Lean muscle. Smooth skin. Testosterone oozing from every pore.

He reached for the hem of her dress, drew it up and over her head. Smoothed his hands down her sides, tucked his thumbs in her panties, and eased them off her legs. His eyes, as she stood before him wearing nothing but her silk bra and heels, flashed and darkened. A low growl sounded from the back of his throat as his palm journeyed across her stomach, stirring her back to life. "I knew it."

His breathing had gone uneven.

"What?" She gasped. Her hands slid up his chest, her fingers dug into his shoulders when the back of his thumb traced up her narrow line of pubic hair.

"I saw those bikini bottoms and knew you had something special going on down here." He eased her back so that he could watch his fingers explore her. "Do you have any idea what this does to me? What do you call this?"

His eyes blazed as he stared at her, and she shuddered with excitement. She'd never had a man look at her like he looked at her, like he was starving and she was a buffet. She had to concentrate to breathe. "It's a Brazilian."

"I have to get a closer look at this."

Noah sank to his knees in front of Isabeau, awed by her beauty, completely transfixed by the thin strip of hair above her clitoris. His erection pulsed, strained against his zipper. He'd been hard since the pilot instructed them to prepare for landing. Painfully hard. He didn't think he could get any harder.

He was wrong.

She was bald and smooth, everywhere, but for that landing strip of hair. He leaned in, pressed his face against her then gave her a kiss.

Her hand dropped to the top of his head.

He wanted her in a way he hadn't wanted any other woman—possessively, totally. The need to plunge inside her, lose himself in her heat and take them both to oblivion was almost more than he could resist. But even more than that, he wanted her complete surrender—to possess her in a way no man had possessed her before.

"You're beautiful," he whispered, his lips brushing her with every word. "You smell so damn good." Her fingers tightened, tugging his long strands of hair. "I bet you taste even better."

He stroked his tongue over her and groaned. Incredible. Exquisite.

She arched, cupped the back of his head and pressed against his mouth. He slipped his thumb up into her, his fingers along her folds. He pleasured her with his tongue, reveling in her incredible flavor, as he brought her along slowly, prolonging her pleasure as much as his own.

Beneath his hands, her body began to tremble. Any moment now...

He replaced his thumb with his tongue, and she cried out his name.

Every cell in his body burning for her, he stood, unhooked her bra, and eased her down onto the bed. He lowered down beside her.

Eyes luminous, she pushed his hair away

from his face, cupped his jaw. "Noah, I can't...take much more of this."

He fastened his mouth on one of her breasts, drew in the rigid tip of her nipple and suckled. He used his teeth, his tongue, and his lips to excite, while his hands skimmed over her. "You can," he answered, nipping his way to her other breast. "Trust me."

Her back came off the bed. Little sounds slipped up her throat, half whimpers, half sighs, driving him crazy. Leaving her breasts, he trailed higher, up the column of her throat until he found her mouth. Her tongue stroked his, and he wondered if she found her taste as pleasing as he did.

He smoothed his palm along the inside of her thigh, then back to her hip, making sure to brush between her legs in the process. From her hip, he skimmed up her body and cupped her breast, teasing at her nipple with his thumb as he continued to feast on her mouth.

She moved restlessly beneath his hands. A tiny moan slipped up the back of her throat before she tore her mouth from his. Her fingers fought with the button on his jeans. "No more. I want you inside me. Now."

Now was good.

He left her long enough to remove his jeans and grab a condom. Her legs opened for him in invitation as he moved over her. Her hands smoothed over his chest and held onto his ribs as he braced his weight on one arm and used the other to guide him to her. Christ. The sound she made when he pressed against her entrance nearly sent him over the edge.

He hissed out a breath as her muscles clenched around him. Tight, she was so damn tight. He watched her face as he rocked his hips, slowly thrusting into her, easing his way one slow inch at a time until he was buried to the hilt.

He swore softly and tangled his fingers in her hair. "Are you okay?"

She arched against him, wrapping her legs around his hips and pulling him deeper. She raised her hands to the sides of his head and brought his face to hers. "Don't stop," she whispered against his mouth.

As if he could.

He kissed her long and deep as he moved over her, slowly sliding in and out of her with a rhythm that grew in speed and urgency. Driven by insatiable hunger, he slid deeper. Moved faster. Harder. Her hips moved in time with his, arching up to meet his every stroke.

Reaching up, he removed her hand from his face and positioned her arm over her head. Their fingers linked, her nails bit into the back of his hand as he drove them both higher. A helpless little moan slipped from the back of her throat. Her head rocked back into the pillow as her sheath clamped tightly around him.

The look of her, hair tangled, cheeks flushed, and pale blue eyes dazed and locked with his pushed him over the edge. His vision blurred when her body clenched and convulsed around him. He rode her through it, unable to slow down as he buried his face in her hair and surrendered himself to her.

****

"Welcome back," Clint called out to Isabeau as she strode through the front door of Izzy's wheeling her luggage behind her. "Did you have a good trip?"

Exhausted, aching in more places than she ever thought possible, she responded shortly, "Except for that whole 'death of a loved one' thing, yeah." She sidled up to the bar and dropped her tote atop it, then pressed her fingertips against her throbbing temples. "I'm sorry."

"You know I didn't—"

"I know," she assured him. "I'm sorry, Clint. I'm tired, my head is killing me, and I just got off a plane. You know how I feel about planes."

"I know how you feel about planes."

Reaching above the bar, Clint pulled down a glass, filled it with ice, and set it before her. With his other hand, he reached into the cooler near his knees and pulled out a can of cola, popping the top and placing it next to her

253

glass.

"You look like you could use the sugar," he explained. "Actually you look more than tired, you look exhausted. Although there is something else..." He squinted his eyes and stared at her a moment before stepping back. An emotion she hadn't seen before flashed across his face. "Never mind."

"He's in love with you, Isabeau". Could it be true?

She didn't know what to say. She suspected that she did look a little more than tired. After all, she'd spent the entire time she'd been in California making love with Noah. They'd had exactly twenty-four hours together before they'd had to catch their flight back to New York, and they'd used every second of it. Even she couldn't believe how many times and in how many different ways they'd come together, stopping only when their bodies demanded refueling. She could feel the effect their time together had on her emotions, as well as her body. It was entirely possible that someone looking at her could see it.

By the look on his face, Clint certainly had.

She closed her eyes and sighed, hoping this didn't make things awkward between them. As the fizz and crackle of cola pouring over ice penetrated, she opened them.

He placed the full glass back down in

front of her. "Drink it. There are also a few leftover pieces of the pizza I ordered for lunch in the kitchen. They should still be warm."

"You're far too good to me, you know that?"

He smiled.

Slinging her tote back over her shoulder, she stood and picked up the cola. "What's with the boarded up front window? Kids again?"

"Um, not exactly."

"What exactly?"

He cleared his throat, then glanced around the bar to make sure no one needed him before he answered. "Someone threw a brick through the window, but it wasn't kids."

"How do you know?"

"Because there was a threatening note attached to it."

A shiver skittered down her spine. "Let me see it."

"Can't. I don't have it anymore. I took the liberty of notifying the police when Pete called to tell me about the window. While I had them here, I told them about everything else, too."

"What do you mean?" she asked, momentarily confused.

"For one thing, how about the car that tried to run you down?"

Her breathing grew shallow as a ball of fear lodged in her stomach. "I forgot about that."

"You forgot?" he asked, incredulous. "How

the hell do you forget something like that?"

Okay, she didn't exactly forget. She'd pushed it to the back of her mind where it remained until now. "Who told you about the car?"

"The one with the accent."

"They all have accents, Clint." Except Alex.

"I don't know his name. The one with the long black hair."

Dominic. Of course. He was the only one she'd told. Absently, she wondered who else he'd felt the need to share his knowledge with.

Shit.

"They want to talk to you."

"Who?"

"The police."

Double shit.

Clint turned to the cash register. He pressed his finger to the touch screen, lifted the tray when the cash drawer slid open and removed a business card from beneath. Closing the drawer he faced her again, his hand out in front of him. "Officer Jake Ryan would like you to call him."

She took the card without looking at it. "I'll call him tomorrow. I'm getting some sleep first." She was already in the kitchen, when she thought of one last thing. Stepping back through the swinging door, she called out to Clint who was busy washing glasses at the other end of the bar. "I thought I closed this place before I left."

"After the brick, I took it upon myself to open back up. I figured it might deter further incidents."

"Thank you," she said and meant it. "Remind me to give you a raise."

She meant that, too.

Finished with the glasses, Clint dried his hands on a towel. "I'll do that. Now off with you before I get in trouble with the boss for neglecting customers."

Isabeau smiled and pushed back into the kitchen. Her smile faded once she passed through the door at the top of the stairs and dropped her carry-on luggage in front of the washer/dryer. With no one around to see her, she didn't have to pretend that fear wasn't rushing through her veins, making the pounding in her head that much worse. Alone, she could press her hand into her stomach and worry that the instances against her were piling up and the possibility that someone wanted to hurt her, was no longer just a possibility. It was fact.

Shaking with a combination of fear and exhaustion, it took three tries before she got the key inserted into the lock. Pushing into her apartment, she dropped her tote, flipped the deadbolt, then crossed the room to turn on the air conditioner, stripping down to her bra and

257

panties along the way.

On her return trip across the room, she bypassed the bed, easing instead into the corner of her leather couch. She took a slow, deep breath to try to counteract the icy panic that clawed at her stomach. Why would someone want to hurt her? She didn't understand it. Not any of it.

Dropping her head to the back of the couch, she closed her eyes and pressed unsteady fingers against her temple. When five minutes later her body continued to tremble, the ache in her skull throb, she gave up the idea of rest. After all the time she'd been with Noah, she needed sleep, but she needed something else even more.

Resting her notepad on her lap, she began to compose.

CHAPTER THIRTEEN

With the sun hanging low over the sky and the clawing heat of the day ebbing, Noah stood in front of the recording studio, his back propped against the building. His mind wasn't on the song they were laying down, the sleep he never seemed to get enough of anymore, or even the fact that Alex had been hungover the last three days in a row.

His thoughts were on Isabeau.

Although he'd been with her last night, he wanted her again. Wanted to sit in the same room as her and drink in her beauty. Hold her against his side and absorb her heat, her scent. Forget everything as he lost himself in her.

Suddenly, painfully aroused at the thought of her, he shifted, looking for a more comfortable position where none could be found. All along he'd believed that once he had her, once he sated himself, the ragged edge of desire would ease, allowing him to concentrate on why he'd come to New York in the first place. But if anything, his desire had only grown stronger now that he knew the way her body responded to his touch. The flush that darkened her skin, the bite of her nails on his back and that sexy little whimper that broke from the back of her throat every time he slipped inside her.

Now he knew the sound of her laughter in the dark of night, the weight of her body across his, as they lay tangled together and talked until dawn.

Sighing, Noah admitted he was in trouble. Not because he was like an addict and she was his drug. Not even because he recognized how easy it would be to lose his heart to her.

No, he was in trouble because of those other things he didn't think much about whenever thoughts of her consumed him. Like his goal, his dream and the upcoming meeting with the record company. There was more than just himself at stake, there was also Nick, Alex, and Dominic. More than just his dream riding on his ability to stay focused and get the job done, but their dream, as well. As the one the guys looked to for direction, he needed to stay focused. He couldn't allow his growing feelings for Isabeau or his desire to be with her to distract him from the real purpose for their being here.

Recording a demo.

Proving they still had what it takes.

A police cruiser drove by while he waged his internal battle. Absently he watched as its brake lights flashed, and the car slowed. He straightened away from the wall when the cruiser came to a stop in front of Izzy's, and a uniformed officer slid out from behind the wheel. Curious and admittedly a bit worried, he watched the officer, noting that nothing about the man's actions appeared casual as he positioned his cap atop his head and stared up at the building before him.

He wasn't there for a hot meal. He was a cop there on business.

His thoughts on Isabeau and how she might be in trouble, he was already ten feet away when the door at his back swung open and Alex stepped out. "You wanted to talk to me?"

Shit. Hadn't he just been telling himself he needed to remain focused?

Once again he'd been distracted by thoughts of Isabeau, forgetting his true purpose for hanging out in front of the studio. He had to stop doing that. Somehow, someway, he needed to shake loose all thoughts of her so that he could concentrate.

Shoving a hand through his hair, Noah cast one last glance down the street. Then he pushed all thoughts of the ebony-haired bartender to the back of his mind where, this time, he hoped they would stay, and faced Alex.

Alex Morgan, the youngest of the group. They'd brought him in to fill the hole Danny's death had left. Blonde-haired and blue-eyed, he looked more like a surfer than a drummer, but drumming was his talent. Too bad women seemed to be another talent of his. A bit of a playboy, Alex spent all of his free time cruising the nightclubs of Manhattan. It was beginning to show.

The irony wasn't lost on Noah as he said, "Alex, we need to talk about how you're spending your evenings and the effect it's having on the band."

****

"He's like a bear with a sore paw," Dominic said, with a shake of his head. "Seriously, Isabeau, I don't know how much more of him I can take. Can't you do something?"

One look at Dominic's face and Isabeau knew he wasn't exaggerating. His eyes appeared troubled, his customary smile absent. "What would you have me do?"

His eyebrow arched as he met her gaze.

"You want me to take Noah to bed?" she asked incredulous.

"Luv, you can take him in the lounge at the studio for all I care, just make the man happy before I'm forced to take him out back."

She couldn't hold back the laughter that bubbled up. "I'm sorry, but the imagery…" Holding her stomach, she laughed long and hard. Until Dom's expression soured. Then, she sighed.

Truthfully, she'd been afraid this would happen. Over the past week, she'd seen no signs that Noah had accepted his grandfather's death, nothing to indicate that he had faced his grief. Since he'd gone these last two days without coming to see her, she'd chosen to give him his space. Hoping against hope that he remained absent from her life because he was dealing with emotions he didn't feel comfortable expressing in front of her. It appeared that wasn't the case.

"Look, as appealing as your suggestion is, it won't solve anything. Noah's problem is that he has yet to properly grieve for Henry. Until he does, nothing we do is going to help."

Dominic closed his eyes and shook his head. "That's not what I want to hear."

"I know," she replied, then covered his hand with her own.

"He's going to force me to take him out back and kick his arse."

"Please don't."

"Come on, Isabeau, I promise not to hurt him too badly. Can't I knock some sense into him? Every day he gets worse."

Before she could reply, the door swung open and Noah stepped into the bar. His spine was stiff, his shoulders rigid. Dark circles ringed his eyes and a tiny nick marked his left cheek. Her throat tightened. How long could he go on like this before he broke?

263

The need to slip out from behind the bar and hold him was intense. She would have done it, if she hadn't caught a flash of something cold and dark in his eyes. Noted how his balance shifted as he looked from her to the top of the bar where her hand remained atop Dominic's, and back again.

His hands clenched against his thighs. "Don't you two look cozy? I hope I didn't interrupt."

Dominic shifted, the muscles in his arm flexed.

"Don't," Isabeau warned. She recognized the look of someone spoiling for a fight. She'd seen it enough times, both in her childhood and at the bar. What surprised her was that Noah was the one wearing the look. "That's what he wants."

"Then I should oblige."

"Dom," she said, only to be ignored.

Dominic turned and faced Noah. "Is that the best you've got?" he asked, his voice low, challenging. "Bullshit insinuations? Don't hold back, Noah. You want to have a go at someone, let's go. I've had it with your foul attitude."

Noah's long strides ate up the distance between them. Isabeau barely made it out from behind the bar before they squared off. She pushed between them and settled a hand on both chests, exerting just enough pressure to encourage them to separate.

264

"What is wrong with you?" she asked Noah.

"He's a bloody prick, that's what," Dominic replied.

Noah's lip curled.

Isabeau sighed. "Knock it off, both of you."

"No worries, I'm off," Dominic said, the edge of anger in his voice. His face was grim when he looked down at her. "I'll see you later."

"Sure." She waited until the door swung shut behind him to face Noah again.

"Give me a dark lager," he stated then leaned against the bar in a way that was deceptively casual.

She narrowed her eyes, welcoming the flare of temper that moved through her. At least it blocked out the want. She wanted so many things when she looked at him. Offering comfort was only a small part of it. "Funny."

"I'm serious."

He was. That was the problem. A fist tightened around her heart. "Is that your answer? You don't want to feel, so you plan to numb the pain with alcohol?"

"It's a thought."

"Are you sure you want to fall back into that cycle?"

The muscle in his jaw flexed. "I can handle a few beers."

"Can you?"

He gave her a caustic smile. "I have before."

"Yes, but you weren't trying to deny your grief then." She stepped closer, cupped the side of his face. Her heart was bleeding for him, for what he needed to accept, but continued to fight against with everything he had. "He's gone, Noah. I'm sorry."

Something flashed across his face. For a brief second, she caught a glimpse of the pain inside of him, but then it was gone.

He jerked away from her touch. "Damn it, Isabeau, give me a beer!"

"No," she replied with a shake of her head. "What if you're wrong? What if you can't handle it? Are you willing to risk your career, your comeback?"

He shoved a hand through his hair. "That's not—"

"Of course you're not, that's why you came here. Because you know I won't serve you."

A strange light glinted in his eyes as he stared down at her. He shifted, backing her against the bar and pressing his body against hers. His hands settled on either side of her, pinning her in place. "Is that why I'm here? Are you sure?"

The press of his erection against her belly shocked her. Even more surprising was the realization that if she could see even the

266

slightest bit of heat in his eyes, anything other than that ice cold glint, she would lock the doors and take him upstairs. She was that far gone over this man.

She swallowed with difficulty. "That won't help either."

"Don't bet on it."

"Noah..."

"Is that a no?"

"You need more than—"

"What's the matter, Isa? You find someone else to warm your sheets?"

His suggestion was so cliché it was almost laughable. Almost.

The trembling started in her knees and worked up her body. Her hands had a fine tremor to them. She curled her fingers into her palms and clenched her teeth. Damn him, she wouldn't give him the satisfaction. "I won't fight with you, no matter how insulting you are."

"No?"

"No."

"And you obviously won't fuck me either."

She pushed against his chest until he backed away. "Not when you're acting like this."

"Then why did I bother to come here?"

His words were razor sharp—cruel and biting. And they hit their target.

"That's a good question, Noah. Was it to hurt me? Was that your goal?" Imagine that. She could sound cool and collected even as she

267

bled inside. "Well, congratulations, your trip was a success. Your callousness hurts. Do you feel better now? Does my pain somehow lessen yours?"

Needing distance, she sidled down the bar and slipped to the other side. "Go away. I have to prepare for the lunch crowd."

He opened his mouth as if he had something he wanted to say then closed it without comment. His jaw clenched tighter, a muscle jerked in his cheek as he stared at her. He didn't budge.

"Get out, Noah. Come back and see me when you can be civil."

Isabeau didn't know what hurt more, the fact that he'd felt the need to lash out at her. Or that his face remained a cool, emotionless mask even as he turned and walked away.

****

After Noah left, Isabeau was so angry that she called Clint and told him to take the night off. If he wondered why she chose to work from open to close behind the bar, he didn't ask. He just thanked her for freeing up his evening and promised to be on time for his shift the next night.

It was a long, exhausting day. Exactly what she needed to keep her mind occupied and off the sandy-haired singer she didn't know how to help. Unfortunately it didn't seem to be enough to guarantee sleep.

Isabeau overturned the chairs onto the tables, mopped the floor, washed the glassware, and cleaned the bathrooms. She disinfected every surface in the kitchen, checked and double-checked the locks on the doors and even did her liquor inventory. Still, sleep continued to evade her.

In case her problem had to do with the chill in her apartment, she crawled out of bed. Using the light from the streetlamp outside her front window to guide her across the room, she adjusted the temperature. Then, because she was already up, she wandered to the window to watch the storm roll in.

She loved storms. Even as a child, when most kids her age were terrified by the rumble of thunder and the flash of lightning, she'd been enthralled by it. She couldn't remember how many nights her mother had gotten out of bed to check on her during a storm, and found her awake and standing at the window—engrossed in the power and the beauty of nature's symphony.

The first few times, her mother would coax her back to bed, but Isabeau never remained there. By the time she was eight, her mother no longer bothered. Instead, she would stir long enough to make certain Isabeau was inside the house, not standing in the middle of the sidewalk in the rain as she'd been found a time or two. Then, with a parting kiss atop her head, Nicole would head back to bed.

By the time she was twelve, her mother was gone, and no one cared enough to do that much for her.

Frowning at the painful thought, Isabeau turned her head to the right and looked out over the city, in the direction of Noah's hotel. She couldn't see it from her location, but as the lightning flashed across the sky, she wondered how he was doing tonight. If he was any better than when he'd stopped by, or if Dominic had been forced to carry through on his threat to knock some sense into him.

She wrapped her arms around herself against the chill that still hung in the room and continued to gaze out the window. After about five more minutes of storm watching, she finally felt like she could get some rest, so she crawled back under the covers and allowed the music of the rain against her roof to lull her to sleep.

Only to awaken barely an hour later to someone pounding on her door.

Startled, she bolted upright in bed, her hand pressed against the frantic beat of her heart in her chest. A glance at her alarm clock told her it was thirty-six minutes after four. The incessant pounding told her whoever stood at the outside of her reinforced steel security door wouldn't be ignored.

Wearing nothing but her silk robe, she

crossed to the door, paused to peer through the peephole. She blinked to clear her eyes and looked again. With a gasp of shock, she threw the lock and pulled the door open.

Lightning flashed, illuminating Noah as he stood with his hands braced on either side of the doorway. Water ran in rivulets down his handsome face to soak his clothes to his skin, but he didn't seem to notice. In fact, he didn't seem to be aware of anything but her as he looked down at her.

Where earlier today his eyes had been emotionless, tonight they were anything but. Her skin flashed hot, her breath caught as deep green eyes filled with longing and desire locked on her. He didn't say anything, he didn't have to. His intent was obvious.

Before she could absorb the shock of his arrival, he used his left hand to push the door open wider. His right curled around her waist and pulled her against his wet body. Sensation overwhelmed her—the damp chill that immediately saturated her robe, the hot press of his mouth against hers and the heady combination of pleasure and pain as he fisted a hand in her hair and tugged her head back.

She realized in an instant that this was not going to be like any coupling they'd shared before. His lips were hard and demanding, his muscled arms like steel around her. He kicked the door closed as he feasted on her mouth,

271

devouring, arousing her with his teeth, his tongue. And far from shying away from it, she fisted her hands in his shirt and begged for more.

He tasted like rain. He tasted like aroused man. Desperate to touch him, she trailed her hands down his chest and slipped them under his shirt. Beneath her palms, his body vibrated. Whether it was from restraint or emotion, she wasn't certain, but she knew it was important for him to work through it. She was more than willing for him to do it with her.

She rocked against him, shuddering as his heat and strength radiated through their clothes. A groan rumbled out of his chest, and he lifted his head to come after her from a different angle. His kiss was voracious, starving. Rough and demanding. She wanted more.

His arm tightened around her waist and he lifted her off her feet. She braced her hands on his shoulders and arched her back in pleasure as his mouth closed over her breast. She sucked in air hungrily, greedily as he suckled her through the fabric, scraping his teeth across her budded nipple—moaning against the exquisite pain, sobbing his name. Shifting her, he treated her other breast to the same beautiful torture until she felt an orgasm building inside her.

His free hand skimmed over her body, slid down the outside of her thigh then up beneath the robe to cup her bare cheek. Her breath left her in a rush as sensation streaked through her. She lifted her knees and hugged his hips. The action separated her cheeks and his fingertips brushed along the division of her buttocks.

"Noah!" she gasped.

"Tell me to leave," he growled as his fingertips continued downward, following the intimate curve until his long fingers eased between the lips of her sex and his thumb pushed into her in one devastating plunge.

She clamped tightly around him as a contraction exploded inside of her. "Stay."

"What I said to you—"

"It doesn't matter." But his grip loosened. His thumb eased out of her and her body started the slow slide down his until she stood on her own two feet.

"It does. This is a bad idea."

She couldn't stop the whimper that escaped as he removed his hands from her and stepped back. Now as damp as he, she shivered at the sudden loss of his heat. "No. No, it's not." His eyes were locked on her, highlighted by the strobe of lightning outside her front window. Desperate, she tugged the sash of her robe free, then lowered her arms and allowed the material to slide off her shoulders and pool at her feet. "Stay with me, Noah."

"You were right, I was angry and hurting.

I..." His words trailed off as he brushed his fingers along her collarbone then down, stopping above her nipple. "I shouldn't be here. I'm not feeling very civil right now."

"No?" She grabbed the hem of his shirt and pulled it up and off. It landed on the floor near her robe.

"I tried to stay away from you. I tried, and I failed."

"I don't want you to stay away from me," she said hoarsely, then reached down and cupped him through his jeans.

He jerked, his breath hissing out of him. "Isabeau."

Heat emanated off of him as she stroked him. Up, then down and back again. She pressed herself close, welcomed the surge of electricity as her nipples brushed his chest. Pressing her lips against the underside of his jaw, she whispered, "Take what you came here for, Noah. If you want it hard and fast, take me hard and fast. You can have me however you want me. I'm here for you."

He came alive at her words—beautifully, gloriously alive. Making a feral sound, he rocked his mouth over hers, mindless, desperate. His chilled, damp hands skimmed over her body. He cupped her breasts, pulling at her nipples until she felt the rush of wet heat flood her. Every nerve in her body came alive, eagerly responding to his crazed urgency.

Her fingers fumbled with the button on his jeans. Because he was soaked to the skin, it was more difficult than normal to work the button free, ease the zipper down. She slipped one hand into the front of his jeans and closed her fist around him, while the other pushed and tugged at the wet denim.

He swore and scooped her off the ground. Encouraging her legs to circle his waist, he crushed his mouth to hers, positioned himself at her opening, then thrust up as he pushed down on her hips. A sob eased up her throat as her body opened for him inch by torturous inch, the sensation intense enough it set off a series of small orgasms.

Every cell in her body singing out with pleasure, she bit down on his bottom lip then slicked her tongue across the injury. His hands flexed, holding her tightly against him as he strode across the room to her bed, his every step rubbing her sensuously against him, driving her farther up that slippery path of desire. They settled on the edge of the bed, her astride him, him reaching around her to shove his jeans off.

She shifted so that her feet were flat on the mattress, fully seating him deep within her. Then she raised herself up, nearly off him before sliding back down. His hands clamped onto her hips, fingers dug into her flesh as he encouraged her to repeat the action. Again she raised herself up, where he held her as his hips

275

hammered upward in deep, powerful thrusts before he pulled her back down.

God, she was more excited by this side of him than she imagined she could be.

He was looking down, watching his body slide out of her as he lifted her almost all the way off him, then slammed her back down. Heat gathered between her legs, spread across the tightened muscles of her stomach. Gasping, shaking with need, she released her tight grasp on his shoulder to take up a fistful of his hair and drag his head back. Their gazes locked. The carnal gleam in his eyes pushed her over the edge.

"Not enough," he groaned as wave after wave washed over her. "It's not enough."

He flipped them over and drove into her, her vision graying as the change in position caused her orgasm to continue rippling through her like nothing she'd ever experienced before. He took her like a man possessed. Demanding and desperate and she loved it. He plunged into her again and again, as her heart crashed like the thunder outside her building.

Bracing himself on one arm, he slipped his hand behind her knee and pulled her leg higher, sliding deeper, increasing her pleasure. She murmured his name, nipped his shoulder. Beneath her hands, the muscles in his back bunched and rippled as he moved within her.

His breath sawed in and out of him as he

pressed his face into her neck. He moved faster, harder, pumping into her again and again until his body tightened. The hand he'd pushed into her hair fisted as he buried himself to the hilt and growled with completion.

Slowly, his body began to relax, his full weight settling down upon her. When she could no longer take a deep breath, she pushed against his chest. He responded instantly, rolling to his side and taking her with him. His body trembled with what she expected was more than the aftereffects of a powerful orgasm. She slid her eyes open, noted the devastating need of a few moments ago was gone. In its place was a deep sadness.

"Noah," she sighed, then pressed her lips against his. She kissed him softly, soothing him the only way she knew how. Cradling his face in her hands, she feathered kisses across his cheek, up to his eyes, his temple. "You can't stay strong forever, Noah. Let it out."

His eyes remained closed as he whispered. "I'm sorry, Isa." When they refocused on her, they were wet with tears. "I'm so sorry."

"It's okay." Her fingers smoothed his wet hair away from his face. She kissed him again and this time she could taste his tears and knew that finally, finally, he was grieving. "It's okay now."

The arms he held around her flexed, pulled her tighter against him. She went

277

willingly, molding herself to his body, pressing her cheek against his chest. She held him as he shook in her arms, as quiet sobs tore from his throat. She ached for him, stroking her hands up and down his back, offering him the comfort of her body, of not being alone in his grief. Gradually his emotion ebbed, and he drifted to sleep.

It was only then that Isabeau acknowledged what she'd expected all along. She was in love with him, and she didn't know how she was ever going to let him go.

CHAPTER FOURTEEN

The incessant beeping of his mobile phone's alarm pulled Noah from sleep. His first thought as he opened his eyes was that he needed an aspirin. His head hadn't hurt this badly since his younger years when he would wake hungover from a night of too much drink. His second thought was where the hell was he and how did he get here?

Panicked for a moment, he feared that he may have fallen back on his old ways, gotten drunk and passed out. Then it all came crashing back to him...

The storm.

His grief.

A reckless, all-consuming need to see Isabeau.

He recalled his walk through the slashing rain, the icy chill of the night air that did nothing to cool his blood, and Isabeau herself— in his hands, his mouth, crying out as he took her in a frenzied rush.

Bloody hell. He'd never known anything like the desperation he'd felt last night. Thankfully she'd been with him every step of the way. Still, he feared he'd gone too fast, was too rough. He should have taken more care with her, but he'd been a little crazy.

Had he hurt her? Caused her pain in any way? If he had, he would never forgive himself.

As the alarm continued to chirp, he tossed the sheet aside and rolled out of bed. It wasn't until the chill of the room washed over his skin that he realized not only could he not locate Isabeau anywhere in the apartment, but he couldn't find his clothes either. He crossed to where his phone and wallet rested atop the kitchen counter and turned off the alarm. Then, comfortable in his own skin, he stepped onto the landing of the interior staircase leading to the bar and pulled open the door. Relief filled him at the sound of someone moving around in the kitchen below.

"Isabeau?" he called out, his voice pitched just above normal range.

She appeared at the base of the steps. Her eyes skimmed down the length of him, lingering on his groin before returning to his face. A mischievous smile blossomed. "I bet you're glad it was me down here and not Clint."

He cringed.

Her smile widened. "While I could happily gaze at your magnificent body all day, you might want to get dressed. I have a delivery truck scheduled to arrive any minute."

"I can't find my clothes."

"They're behind you, in the dryer."

Of course. He'd been soaked to the skin when he'd stripped them off.

After a quick shower, Noah dressed and wandered back to the kitchen to retrieve his phone and wallet. He clipped the phone to his waist then flipped open the wallet and removed the magnetic key card to his hotel room before heading down the stairs.

Isabeau talked to the delivery man while he leaned against the counter, taking the signature pad and signing her name on the form affixed to it. Then she offered the pad back to the man, took the box he held and turned.

"Hey." She set the box on the counter, pulling each item out and setting it aside after a brief inspection.

Vegetables. Organic, if his memory was correct. "Hey, yourself."

As he'd stood beneath the shower's hot spray, waiting for the heat to clear the cobwebs from his head and ease the ache behind his eyes, he had done some thinking. Made a few decisions about their relationship. Now that she stood before him, he wondered how much of what he'd decided she was going to want to hear.

He pushed off the counter and crossed to stand at her side. But when he looked down at her, he was suddenly reminded of how much smaller she was than he and the knot of guilt returned. "I didn't hurt you?"

"Of course not."

"You would tell me if I did?"

She turned to face him, placing her hand in the center of his chest. "You didn't hurt me."

"Good." He closed his eyes and released his breath in a rush. "That's good."

"I'm glad you came to me last night, Noah. That you let me comfort you."

He should probably be embarrassed by the way he'd broken down in her arms. He wasn't. Of far greater concern was that she understood he would never knowingly harm her. "About that...Isa you do realize that I didn't use a condom last night?"

"I wasn't worried," she admitted, then shifted her gaze over his shoulder. "Noah, you—"

"I had a complete physical in March of this year," he assured her. "I was tested for everything from the flu to HIV. I'm clean, Isa. I wanted you to know that."

Her gaze shifted again, this time to the center of his chest. "Okay."

He hooked a finger under her chin and forced her gaze back to his. "Why won't you look at me? Are you sure I didn't hurt you?"

"You didn't hurt me."

He lowered his head and pressed a kiss to her temple. Her skin was a haven of warmth beneath his lips as they slowly journeyed to her

282

cheek, then her mouth. He kissed her softly, slowly, showing her the gentleness he hadn't shown her last night. He teased her lips open with his tongue and tasted the rich flavor of her morning coffee.

Reaching up, he wrapped his hand around hers, ran his thumb across her palm. "I'm sorry about yesterday."

Her breath hitched as he replaced his thumb with his lips. "You don't need to keep apologizing to me."

But he did need to explain. "I was angry. It wasn't just my grandfather's passing, it was also...I thought if I stayed away from you, I could concentrate on the demo more. It's not right yet, and we're running out of time. But all staying away did was make everything worse. It turned my grief to anger, anger I took out on you."

With his hand still wrapped around hers, she cupped the side of his face. "Not just on me. Dominic was pretty upset with the way you were acting."

He sighed. "I know. I'm surprised he managed to refrain from slugging me." He turned her hand over and pressed the magnetic key card into her palm. "Will you come to me tonight after you close?"

She curled her fingers around the card. "I'm not scheduled to close tonight, but if we get busy, I may need to stay."

"I don't care." He nibbled on her bottom lip, drawing it into his mouth to softly suckle. "I need to talk to you. I need to be with you."

"It..." A tiny shudder worked through her. "It could be quite late...before I get there."

His lips roamed over her cheek, then traced a path to her jaw. "I'll wait up for you."

****

"It needs a piano," Noah said, giving voice to the one thought that had been gnawing at him all morning. That the song they'd been working on for days still wasn't right because it was missing an important element—one that no one in the control room had the talent to provide.

Straddling the chair to his left, his arms draped across the top of the chair back, Nick agreed with Noah's conclusion. "He's right, that's what is missing."

"You can't slip something like that into a song without reworking it," Alex argued fervently, his eyes clear, indicating he hadn't been out drinking the night before. "We don't have time to rework it."

Dominic leaned forward in his chair, his gaze scanning each occupant in the room. "Can we afford not to?"

Nick cursed under his breath.

"What do you think, Pete?" Dominic asked, drawing the man into the conversation.

With anxiety tightening his gut, Noah closed his eyes and pressed his fingers against his lids where a pounding ache flared anew. He knew where this conversation was headed but it was too late to go back now. Too late to change what he'd set in motion.

Pete turned his back to the mixing console. "I know of a few skilled pianists in the area. However, if you want it done without having to start over, there's only one."

"No," Noah stated as the pain in his skull intensified. "No way."

"She's got the skill," Pete continued. "Hell, something on this small a scale wouldn't be difficult for her at all."

"Who?" Nick asked.

"I'm confused," Dominic said as he pushed his hand through his hair. "I thought after the car accident—"

"It wasn't her injuries that stopped her from making music."

Noah shot Pete a questioning glance. The man obviously knew more than he was saying.

Alex leaned in and repeated Nick's question, "Who?"

Dominic turned to Noah and regarded him for a moment. "She might do it for you."

"I'm the last person she'd do it for."

"Will someone please tell me who we're discussing?" Nick asked, his irritation evident.

"Isabeau," Dom answered, openly

285

studying Noah.

Although Noah couldn't decipher the look in Dom's eyes, he found it was enough to make him uncomfortable. It was all he could do to keep his features neutral.

"Izzy plays the piano?" Alex asked, clearly taken by surprise.

"Not anymore," Noah stated, but no one appeared to be listening to him.

Nick blinked, surprised. "Is she any good?"

"You can't imagine," Pete replied.

Abruptly, Noah pushed to his feet. He crossed to the opposite side of the room, suddenly feeling like the walls were closing in on him.

"How do you know this?" Nick asked Pete.

"She recorded all four of her albums here, in this studio."

Nick shook his head. "Four? How come I'm the only one who didn't know Izzy played the piano?"

"I didn't know," Alex interjected.

"Four?" Nick continued, "Izzy, Noah's Izzy, has recorded four albums?"

"Yes," Pete replied, a broad smile on his face. "Isabeau Montgomery was a true virtuoso. She was six when she recorded her first album, and rumored to be the best pianist in the world."

"Six?"

"So small she couldn't reach the pedals

without an extension, but you should have seen her. Lord, could she play. She was a sight to behold."

"Ask her," Alex said simply. "What have we got to lose?"

Noah shook his head. "She doesn't play anymore. She won't do it."

"But she could," Dominic surmised.

"She could," Noah confirmed.

Alex shrugged. "Then I don't see that we have any other choice."

Noah pushed off the wall he'd been leaning against and began to pace. A line formed between Dominic's eyes as he tracked his movements from one wall to the other and back again.

"You don't have any other choice," Pete stated bluntly. "There is no one else. Not in this area and definitely not in your time frame."

"We need this one," Nick said matter-of-factly. "And a piano would make the song everything it can be."

"You'll have to ask her, Noah," Alex persisted.

Expelling a heavy breath, Noah rubbed his hand over the tight muscles in his neck.

Dominic gave him a dubious, narrow-eyed look. "What's going on here, Noah? What aren't you telling us?"

Noah slid his hand in his pocket and glanced around the room, taking notice that all eyes were looking to him for an answer. "She hasn't played since her mom died," he stated, choosing to give them the simplest answer, instead of the one that was tying him in knots. "She can, but doesn't."

Averting his gaze, Pete went back to the mixing console. No doubt about it, the man knew something. Something he wasn't sharing.

"I don't see the harm in asking," Alex exclaimed.

"She knows how important this demo is to us," Dominic stated. "To you, Noah."

Noah retraced his steps and lowered himself onto his chair. "She'll think it's a set-up. The words won't even be out of my mouth, and she'll already have shot me down."

His gaze landed on Dominic, his best friend. Dom had formed a friendship with Isabeau immediately, earned her trust faster than even Noah had been able to do. If Dom asked her for help, she would know the request was sincere, their need for assistance genuine. Noah needed her to at least hear the song before she made up her mind, and if he went to her, she would never give it a listen.

Because one look at him and she would know what he had done.

Noah scrubbed a hand over his eyes and sighed. "You'll have to ask her, Dom."

"All right. You mind telling me why? Last I knew we were just friends. I'm not the one intimately involved with her."

"That's exactly why it needs to be you, Dom, because you're not the one intimately involved with her."

****

The instant Dominic strolled through the double doors, Isabeau felt a strange sense of déjà vu. He smiled in greeting as he eased onto his stool, but for the second day in a row, the usual glint was missing from his eyes.

"What's the matter?" she asked, automatically wiping a cloth across the bar before placing a napkin before him.

He sighed while he spun the napkin with his fingers. "I could use a beer right about now, Isabeau."

"Sure." She turned to the cooler, retrieved a bottle and removed its cap. Hands unsteady, she settled the bottle atop the napkin. "I thought you would look a little happier than yesterday. Noah's doing better, isn't he?"

"Noah's fine," he replied, then took a long swallow of beer.

She breathed a sigh of relief and filled two more orders. It was only two o'clock, and already they were at half capacity. She got the feeling it was going to be a long, busy night, and she didn't need the extra strain that worrying about Noah would bring. While she waited for Dominic to say more, she did a quick survey of the patrons, making certain that no one appeared to need anything.

Assured that she could take the time to talk, she glanced at Clint. He nodded at her, his signal that he would watch things, then went back to his own conversation with a customer.

She took up her customary position directly across from Dominic. "Spit it out, Dom, you're beginning to worry me."

"We need your help."

She couldn't begin to imagine what he was talking about. "What kind of help?"

His intense blue eyes locked onto her as he took another drink. Apprehension filled her.

"Help with the demo."

"How could I possibly help with the demo?"

As he turned his head, she followed his gaze to the opposite side of the bar where two businessmen stood talking, ties loosened, shirtsleeves rolled up. They'd been here for thirty minutes and both were on their second beer. But she knew it wasn't the men Dom was focused on. It was the upright piano against the wall at their back.

The tight clenching of her stomach was automatic and instinctive. "No," she said softly, adamantly.

As he reached for her hand where it rested atop the bar, she snatched it away and straightened. He didn't need to know that she was shaking. That her stomach had soured and bile was already working its way up the back of her throat.

"We need you, Isabeau. Without you, our chance of getting this contract...it won't happen."

"That's a bit melodramatic, don't you think?" This couldn't be happening. Even more painful for her to consider, it couldn't be a coincidence. "Did Noah put you up to this?"

"He said you'd think that."

"He was right." Her heart crawled into her throat. The knot in her stomach tightened. "You go back there and tell him his ruse won't work. Try again."

Dominic's eyes held hers, but he didn't move. Didn't slide off the stool and out the door now that she'd figured out the game, and called an end to it.

A customer walked up to the bar to place an order, providing her with the perfect distraction. She leaned in to catch the man's order.

Dom still didn't move.

Pulled down a pitcher and started to fill it.

Nope.

Was it possible he was telling the truth?

Momentarily distracted, she turned her attention back to Dominic. She noted his body language, the lack of spark in his eyes and the thin set of his mouth. The dread inside her built.

The pitcher overflowed, causing beer to flood the drip tray beneath it and spill down the front of her jeans. She cursed under her breath and grabbed for the cloth at her right. Eyes burning, she swiped at the mess, but only succeeded in making it worse.

"Let me do it."

Clint's voice, directly beside her, caused her to startle. She looked at his hand outstretched before him then the concern in his eyes. He'd obviously picked up on the fact that she was upset.

"Go get cleaned up," he said, taking the cloth from her. "Take a break."

She needed a break.

Turning, she headed for the kitchen and the staircase to the apartment. On her way, she stopped alongside Dominic. She dragged in a jagged breath. "It is a ruse, isn't it?"

"It's not a ruse. We need you."

She pushed through the door and hurried up the steps. Dominic's slower, steady pace followed. Grabbing a pair of jeans off the top of the dryer, where Noah must have placed them that morning when he'd been looking for his own clothes, she threw open the door to her apartment with enough force it slammed into the wall. She didn't slow down until she'd rounded the corner and stood in the center of her bathroom.

Her hands shook as she struggled to work the metal button fly of her jeans open. If she had been thinking clearly, she would have sat on the edge of the tub to remove the jeans. The damp denim stuck to her skin. She wiggled and shimmied, finally managing to pull one leg out. Her second foot got hung up and she lost her balance. Grabbing the sink kept her from falling. It also knocked the coffee mug she'd left there onto the floor where it shattered, spraying cold coffee and broken pottery everywhere.

"Isabeau, are you all right?"

Blinking back tears, she stared down at the mess.

"Isabeau?" Dominic rounded the corner and stopped abruptly. "Whoa, sorry."

"Wonderful, that was my favorite mug." She dropped the beer soaked jeans that still hung from her fingers and reached for the dry pair. "What kind of song are we talking about?"

Having learned from her near fall, she perched on the lip of the bathtub and pushed her legs into her jeans. It took a minute for Dom's unnatural silence to penetrate. She glanced up at him. He quickly averted his gaze.

"Earth to Dom. What's wrong with you?"

His eyes returned to her momentarily before skittering away. "What?"

"I asked you what kind of song it was." She eased the denim over her hips as she eyed him. "Are you blushing?"

"Hell, no!"

"They're cotton boy shorts, Dom. My bathing suit covers less. I thought you Englishmen were supposed to be comfortable with nudity and sexuality?"

"You're sleeping with my best friend. I don't think either of us wanted me to know about the love bite you have on your inner thigh."

"I do not!" she exclaimed, a bit embarrassed and more than a little tempted to look. Wait a minute. "You looked?"

"You dropped your trousers in front of me."

"I did not. You walked in on me. You shouldn't have looked."

He flashed her a wicked, naughty grin. "I'm a man. Men always look."

She started to laugh. She looked at Dominic, standing in her bathroom, with his black hair, blue eyes and easy smile, and she laughed. She laughed because if she didn't, she would start to cry. She was going to miss him, his sense of humor and bluntness. She was going to miss all of them. It suddenly occurred to her just how much she would lose when they left.

"Noah's gonna kick my arse," he muttered, and she laughed even harder. Her laughter died abruptly when he answered her previous question. "The song is a ballad. Noah wrote it."

"Noah wrote it?"

"Yes. It's a great song. It's just...missing something."

"Something only I can provide." Her voice wavered.

So did her heart.

"Isabeau?"

Pain washed over her. The fact that Noah had written a song that conveniently needed a piano was verification of what she'd feared all along. She wasn't enough for him. His interest was in Isabeau Montgomery, the musician. Not Isabeau Montgomery, the woman.

"I don't play anymore," she whispered.

"I know. I don't know why you stopped, but I believe you still possess the skill—"

"Find someone else."

"Pete says there's no one else who can do it."

She pressed unsteady fingers against her stomach and blinked back tears. She'd given Noah her heart, and it still wasn't enough. Standing there in her bathroom, she finally got it. She and Noah were only temporary. Not because his time in her city was limited, but because he couldn't accept her the way she was.

Her chest imploded right there. Absently she wondered how Dominic couldn't see that she was falling apart. Her legs gave out, and she sank to the edge of the tub.

"Come to the studio and listen to the song, Isabeau. You'll agree it's the hit we need to secure our comeback."

****

"You manipulative son of a bitch," Dominic growled, the moment he stepped in front of Noah. "You played her, and you used me to do it."

Leaning against the front of the studio in a pose that was far more relaxed than he was, Noah studied his friend. Dominic was so angry he was vibrating, as he paced back and forth, both hands stacked atop his head.

He refused to feel guilty. "What did she say?"

"What did she say? Aren't you even going to try to deny it?"

What was the point? Dom was right. He wrote the song for Isabeau, knowing all along she could provide them with the proper accompaniment. But then when it came time to ask for her help, he'd chickened out and sent Dominic in his place.

"Who are you?" Dominic asked.

Noah didn't have an answer for that, either. He pinched the bridge of his nose between his thumb and forefinger. Plotting, then worrying over the outcome had stirred his headache back to life.

"Do you realize what you're doing to her? Did you know that at the mention of playing, all the color drains from her face? She was shaking like a leaf at the thought of sitting at a piano again. Shaking, Noah. Did you know that?"

"No." Unease moved through him. "I didn't know any of that."

The anger in Dom's eyes turned to wariness. "Has Isabeau ever told you why she stopped playing?"

"No. What about you?"

Dom shook his head. "After today, watching her try not to fall apart...I'm not sure I want to know."

He didn't understand. He'd heard her that first night, seen with his own eyes that she still had the skill. The music she could wring from that sorry excuse for a piano that sat in her bar was astounding. Why would she throw that away? "Her reaction, it was that bad?"

"You can't imagine."

Somehow they'd changed positions. Dominic now leaned against the building, his head tipped back, eyes closed, while Noah paced before him.

"We need to rethink this, Noah. There has to be another way."

Noah muttered a curse. "She's incredible, Dom."

"Yes, she is."

"I mean as a pianist. I've heard her.

Maybe not as smooth as before the accident, but still...incredible."

"I know what you meant."

His stomach tightened. "She's wasting her talent running that bar."

"There are people all over the world, more talented than you and me, who go through life without ever realizing their potential," Dominic pointed out. "It happens every day."

Frowning, Noah rubbed a hand across his jaw. "I know that. I do, but I'm not..."

"You're not what, Noah? You're not in love with them?"

He let out a slow breath and shook his head.

"You didn't plan on that, did you? You saw something you wanted—Isabeau—you went after her. You thought you would swoop in, save her from herself, and walk away unaffected."

"I can't," he admitted softly. Dominic was right. He loved Isabeau. "I can't walk away."

"She may never play again," Dominic had to point out.

"I don't care."

"Of course you do, you wrote a song for her."

He didn't care. She was the only woman he wanted to be with. She made him laugh. Hell, she made him cry.

"Let me ask you something," Dominic said, his eyes grim. "Have you considered the risks of this plan of yours? What if it backfires?"

"Backfires, how?"

"You push her into this, you force her to play when she doesn't want to, isn't ready to…it doesn't matter that your heart is in the right place, she may not thank you. In fact, she could wind up hating you." Dom settled a hand on his shoulder. "Trust me, Noah, that's a place you don't want to be."

CHAPTER FIFTEEN

Clint's voice trailed off the moment Thomas pushed through the doors and slid onto the stool at Noah's right. By the way the bartender straightened away from the bar, he felt the same thing from Thomas as Noah. Something was wrong. Very wrong.

No one had seen or heard from Isabeau all day. Not since yesterday, actually, when she walked out of the studio and broke into a run. Thinking about it sent nausea lurching into Noah's stomach. Dom had been right; he hadn't wanted to know what the thought of playing again did to her.

Now he not only had the grave misfortune of knowing, but being unable to shake the image loose. Every time he closed his eyes he saw her, pale and shaken. She'd stood in the control room, refusing to look at him, at any one of them, as she listened to the song. At the song's completion, she turned to Pete and informed him that they didn't need her. What they needed was to record the song with a few strings backing them. Once the suggestion was made, he had to admit that she was right. But as Pete was quick to point out, they only had a few days left in which to finish the demo.

At Pete's comment, she'd finally looked at him. The pain in her eyes cut him to the bone.

For the rest of the day, he held on to the hope that she would come to his hotel room as planned. She didn't. He didn't begin to worry until on his way to the studio this morning, he'd swung by the bar and found it locked up tight. The way it remained until Clint's arrival late in the afternoon. When all his calls to her went unanswered, his worry increased.

Isabeau was angry with him, Noah understood that, but the longer she went without contact with anyone, even Clint, the more afraid for her he became. And so he'd staked out her place, hanging out with Clint long after closing time. Which was why he was still here as Thomas came through the door, pain and anxiety evident in the lines on his face.

Desperate fear seized Noah's heart, easing only slightly at the creak of the floorboards as someone moved in the apartment above them.

Before the thought to go check on her was even complete, Thomas settled his hand on Noah's forearm, effectively keeping him in his seat. "Scotch please, Clint, three fingers. Then leave the bottle and make yourself scarce."

Clint's mouth settled into unhappy lines but he did as Thomas ordered; placing the

Scotch atop the bar before slipping out the door.

Noah waited, muscles tight, body prepared for a blow. He felt it in the air, in the very essence of the room. Thomas was here to offer the missing piece in the puzzle that was Isabeau. Or, at the very least, some insight into where that piece lay hidden.

He could only hope he was prepared to hear it. "Is she okay?"

Thomas released Noah's arm, lifted the glass to his lips and sipped. "If you mean is she hurt, then the answer's no. But she's hurting."

Hurting because of him, and what he'd asked her to do. "Has she been with you all day today?"

"Only since early evening."

That left nearly twenty-four hours unaccounted for. Where the hell had she been?

Thomas kept his gaze focused on a point in the distance while his fingers turned the glass clockwise. "Have you heard Izzy play?"

"Once," Noah admitted, "but only briefly."

"I haven't heard her play in thirteen years. For all I knew, she couldn't. Not after the accident."

The emotion in Thomas's voice had acid swirling in Noah's stomach.

"I always hoped...she seemed to be able to use her hand normally, but the dexterity? I didn't know if it was there. All I knew was she never touched the piano again, not after her

302

mother died. Even so, I've kept hers tuned for all these years, with the hope that one day..."

Letting his words trail off, Thomas drained the glass, refilled it and offered the bottle to Noah.

Noah shook his head. "No, I don't drink hard liquor anymore."

"It's not something I often do myself."

That bit of information only increased the amount of acid churning in Noah's gut. He shifted uncomfortably on the wooden stool.

"She used to play all the time, day and night. Some days, I thought it would never end. Then she would go on tour with Nicole, and I'd miss it." The glass continued to turn as his gaze focused on something only Thomas could see.

"I was finishing up with a customer. It was about five...that's when it began. The opening bars were strong, unmistakable. From her last tour, her final performance. I heard her practice for that tour enough times, I'd know her music anywhere," Thomas admitted, then lifted the glass to his lips and drained it a second time. "One song bled into another with little or no pause. She played the entire set—the whole show—played for over an hour while I sat in that tattoo parlor and cried like a child."

Propping his elbow atop the bar, Thomas pressed his fingers against his closed lids. Noah didn't move. He didn't turn to witness the emotion of the man at his side or reach for his

303

own glass, even though his mouth was suddenly dry. He sat there and absorbed.

"Then the final note rang out and there was silence—a few minutes of total silence before the most pain-filled sound I've ever heard. That instrument did not like what she was doing to it. I crept up the back stairs to witness her pound on that piano. With her fists, her arms, all while a godawful sound broke from her throat."

When his hands began to tremble, Noah fisted them against his thighs.

"I tried to stop her, but she wouldn't let up. I can't believe she didn't break something— not the piano as much as herself. When she finally stopped, she drew her knees up to her chest, curled her arms over her head and cried. She curled into the smallest ball possible, like she was trying to disappear. That's when I knew." Thomas shook so hard, the scotch splashed onto the bar as he attempted to refill his glass. "I suspected. All these years, I suspected. Now I know."

"I'll go—"

Again, Thomas stopped him with a hand on his arm. "There's something you need to know."

"It can wait." What he'd already heard had been difficult enough to sit through, Noah didn't think he could handle much more. He wanted to go to Isa, hold her and believe he had the power to ease her suffering. He didn't want to know that what she was suffering was more than he could fix.

Thomas began talking again without pause. "The day they took her from me...that was a pain like no other. Nicole, she was my heart, but Izzy, ten years she called me daddy. Ten years I called her daughter. Then because I didn't have a piece of paper to tell me I was allowed to love her like I did, I was labeled a—"

Thomas took a deep breath and didn't say aloud what he'd been labeled. "They took her away from me and gave her to him."

"The devil incarnate," Noah supplied, the knot in his stomach twisting painfully.

Slowly, very slowly, Thomas turned in Noah's direction. "She said that? Izzy called him that?"

Noah closed his eyes. "Yes."

"What else? Has she ever told you anything else about him?"

She hadn't meant to reveal even that much to him. And when she had, he'd been too afraid to ask what she meant. "She doesn't talk about him. She'll only talk about you, her true father."

"Some father I turned out to be. I failed her, Noah. When she needed me most, I failed her. John Whitehorse was a miserable excuse for a human being. He filled her head with lies, stripped her of her self-confidence. She ran from him more than once. The last time, she was fourteen. She came to me all coltish looking—long limbs and eyes bigger than her face. One look at her and any fool could see that when those gangly teen years were past her, she was going to be beautiful. That's not what he told her."

Thomas' knuckles whitened as his grip tightened around the glass. "She spent three days with me that last time. I could tell there was more going on in that house than she would say, more than just the emotional cruelty. I didn't know what to do. I had no power to help her. In the eyes of the law, *I* was the criminal."

"Because she kept running back to you."

"Yes. A young girl and a grown man. The law saw only one reason she kept coming to me. "

He didn't need to explain. Noah knew what the authorities thought of Thomas's relationship with Isabeau.

"She was starting to open up to me, beginning to tell me what life with him was like when Whitehorse arrived with the men in blue. He gave me three days with her, knowing how much more it would hurt having had the time. He was right, of course. The pain in her eyes as they snapped the cuffs on me—it was like the courthouse all over again. Only this time, Izzy didn't cry."

Thomas lifted his glass, spoke before

draining it. "I knew then that I wouldn't see her again. And I didn't. Not until Whitehorse died."

"She was protecting you."

"I should have been protecting her, damn it!"

His hands had been tied. Literally.

Thomas released a ragged sigh. "I should have fought them, begged them to listen, to see what I could see. But the minute he walked through the door, she closed up. That was the most painful thing of all. She didn't argue, she didn't say anything. She gathered her things and left."

She'd definitely been protecting him. Noah knew enough about her personality, as well as her love for Thomas, to say with certainty that young Isabeau realized by running to Thomas, she was hurting him. And because she didn't wish to hurt him, she stopped running.

He turned his gaze to the ceiling. The silence of the apartment above them made him uneasy. There was no sound of music coming through the floor, no echo of her feet as she walked around. He could only hope she was still up there, that she hadn't disappeared once again. He needed to see her, hold her. As much for his own peace of mind as hers.

"Izzy was seventeen when Whitehorse managed to send himself to an early grave. I hadn't seen her in three years when one day the door to my shop opened and there she stood, suitcase clutched in her hand. I cried then, too. Then I reached for her..."

"She shifted away from you, didn't she?"

"She was right there, then she wasn't. It broke my heart. She stood there, with this blank expression on her face. Disconnected. Then she went up the stairs to her old room and unpacked."

Taking a deep breath, Noah gathered his courage. "What had he done to her?"

"That son of a bitch took a beautiful, confident, outgoing, and loving child who gave affection freely and often, and turned her into a skittish woman. With walls and barriers she allows no one past. Not even me."

"Do you think he abused her?"

"I know he did," Thomas hissed through his teeth.

Acid climbed up the back of Noah's throat. He closed his eyes, gathered his courage. "Sexually?"

Thomas' gaze locked with his. He made no reply. He didn't have to.

Noah's denial was total, instinctual. No way. Not his Isabeau. It couldn't be true, he wouldn't accept that.

"Jesus Christ." He scrubbed his hands over his face. Thinking about Isa suffering something like that tore at his insides, froze the blood in his veins.

"She'll talk to you," Thomas said softly.

Noah slipped from his stool, tipped his head to the ceiling and struggled to breathe. "I'm not so sure."

His body trembled, his heart split apart as he pictured the little girl from the courthouse photo—so tiny, so terrified. So lost. She was no match for a grown man. No child was.

He had to force back the nausea that surged up the back of his throat.

"You're the catalyst, Noah, you started this. It was only once you came into her life that she began breaking out of whatever hold Whitehorse still held on her. You got past her aversion to touch. I believe somehow you drove her to that piano today."

"Thomas—"

"Ask her about those years, Noah. She needs to let go of them, share them with someone. There's too much pain for one person to handle alone."

****

Isabeau sat on the floor of her living area, frantically transferring the music from her head to the composition paper before her. The lights were dimmed, the stereo silent. Although was chilled, she didn't stop, even for the few minutes it would take to retrieve her robe from the end of the bed or a blanket from the back of the couch. She couldn't stop, not until she got it all out, until the music was silenced. It haunted her, the melody that played over and over through her mind. Unnerved her in a way no melody had done before.

Dominic was right, this was the song to secure them a contract with the record company. It was also the song that insured Noah would leave her.

The song was spectacular—different to everything else out there in both lyric and composition. Not that the concept expressed was anything new, for love was timeless. But the depth of emotion behind the words, the way the music seemed to amplify that emotion, these were what drew the listener in. What made them experience the song instead of just hear it.

Closing her eyes, she couldn't help but wish that she had never heard it. It had played through her mind endlessly since she stood in the studio, slowly dying inside. Somehow she'd managed to make it out of there without anyone seeing the pain. The heart-wrenching agony of discovering that while the song may have been written for her, it most definitely had not been written about her.

Noah's ballad.

Black Phoenix's future hit.

The story of a man and the feelings invoked in him by a woman he loved unconditionally.

As tears threatened, she closed her eyes.

She was tired, so tired—physically drained, emotionally exhausted. She didn't want to feel right now, she wanted to be numb. But she hadn't been numb since Noah strolled into her life, bringing with him the relentless, unavoidable waterfall of music, constantly flowing through her head.

The music that was suddenly louder than normal.

Her head came up. She blinked to bring her eyes back into focus, absently wondering if she'd remembered to turn the lock on the door leading down to the bar. Aside from the fact that she didn't want to see anyone right now, she didn't worry about the identity of the person who turned the knob on her door in an attempt to get it. She didn't have to. The only person to ever make the music in her head louder was Noah.

He'd called her a few times today. More than a few. Enough times that she'd turned off the ringer on her mobile phone. She didn't want to talk to him. The truth was she couldn't. Not now. Not yet.

A quick glance to where the phone rested on the table near her elbow told her that he hadn't called again since the last time. Why would he, she wondered, when it was obvious he'd been staked out in her bar. It didn't matter that it was long past closing time, Clint wouldn't kick him out. Not when he would have been as worried about her failure to open today as anyone.

"Isabeau?"

Noah's voice drifted through the door to wash over her.

"Isabeau, open the door, I need to talk to you."

She glanced in the direction of the door, the pain in her chest so intense she was amazed that she could breathe at all. She had nothing to say to him, nothing left to offer. She'd given him everything she had and it wasn't enough.

"Please, Isa," he continued, his voice lowered with intimacy and touched by emotion. "I need to know you're all right."

Pulling her legs up to her chest, she wrapped her arms around them and rested her cheek atop her knees. Her lungs were burning, her body shaking uncontrollably. She wasn't all right. At the moment, she wondered if she would ever be all right again.

Noah fell silent, but she knew he remained outside the door. The knob turned again, remained locked, and he sighed. Immediately the image of him pushing his hand through his hair the way he did when things weren't going his way sprang to mind.

The pain in her chest intensified.

"I'm sorry, Isabeau. I'm so damn sorry."

So was she.

Noah didn't speak again. A few minutes

later, he left, and she went back to work. She didn't answer the phone when he called an hour later, even though she was still awake and composing. She didn't answer it the next morning either. Only once did she pay the telephone at her elbow more than a passing glance, and it was when she called Pete and told him to expect her at noon.

CHAPTER SIXTEEN

Noah came to an abrupt stop the moment he caught sight of the piano centered in the recording booth. He scrubbed his hands over his face, wishing he'd gotten more than an hour of sleep and his eyes didn't feel like they were filled with sand. Then he focused on Pete, taking up his customary position at the mixing board.

"You've heard from Isabeau?"

"She called first thing this morning," the man replied as he leaned back in his chair and glanced at the clock on the wall above Noah's head. "I expect her any time now. She told me she'd be here by noon."

"How did she sound?"

Pete arched his brow, rubbed his hand over his chin. "Is there a way she was supposed to sound?"

"She's pretty upset with me right now, for pushing her into this. No one has seen her for the last two days." Just Thomas, who brought her home after her breakdown and then told him enough about her past to have Noah tossing and turning all night. "We shouldn't have done this."

"We?"

"I shouldn't have done this," Noah corrected. "I shouldn't have pushed her. But damn it, I thought I was helping her."

"I've known that girl her whole life," Pete admitted, smiling broadly. "She was such a sweet little thing. Friendly and outgoing."

His smile dimmed, his brow furrowed, telling Noah he knew something that didn't make him happy. "You are helping her," he stated bluntly. "But that doesn't mean she'll thank you for it."

"Now where have I heard that before?" Dominic asked as he stepped into the room. Then, like Noah, he stopped abruptly and stared through the glass into the booth. "She's coming in?"

"I guess so," Noah replied.

Dom gave him a questioning look. "You haven't talked to her?"

"No. She called Pete."

"Who called Pete?" Alex asked, stepping into the room, Nick right behind him.

"Isabeau," Dominic answered.

"Here she is," Noah stated, as he stepped closer to the glass and drank in the sight of her.

She was wearing those incredible jogging pants of hers, the ones that rode low on her hips and hugged her amazing ass. Above those pants, and the two-inch gap of flesh that got his blood up, she wore a tank top. The kind with skinny little straps the only thing holding it up. Her hair was down, tumbling past her shoulders, reflecting the lights from the ceiling above her.

His stomach clutched at the dark circles beneath her eyes—eyes as colorless as her skin as she walked directly to the piano and sat, without ever looking toward the booth.

With the way the piano was positioned, Isabeau's back was to them all. As Noah stared at the uncompromising set to her spine, he found himself silently urging her to turn around.

Pete pushed the button so that his voice projected into the booth. "Hey, sweetheart, how are you?"

"I'm ready."

She didn't bother to place the headphones over her ears. In fact, now that he thought about it, Noah noticed there wasn't a pair out for her. He glanced at Pete to see that the man didn't have the song cued and ready for her to listen to as she played.

"Give me a scale, would you, sweetheart?"

Back straight, hands steady, she positioned her fingers above the keys and began to play. He could only watch, transfixed as her fingers began to move up and down the keys, at times so quickly his eyes couldn't make out their individual movement. Then she slowed down, and he recognized the first few measures of *One*

Last Breath.

The song she was here to record.

"Thank you," Pete stated as he made a few adjustments on the sound board. "Damn, it's good to hear you play again."

Though he hadn't thought it possible her back straightened a bit more.

Pete didn't seem to notice. "Whenever you're ready, sweetheart."

This time when she lifted her hands out of her lap, they shook.

Noah clenched his jaw.

The nerves that made her hands tremble didn't have an effect on the skill with which she played. Isabeau played her addition to the song through once, from beginning to end without stopping. Perfectly, from start to finish. Without any errors. When she was done, she placed her hands in her lap and waited.

"Turn around, Isa," he whispered, his voice pitched so no one could actually hear him. "Turn around and come in here."

"Damn!" Alex exclaimed. "I didn't think she could do it."

"I still don't believe it," Nick said. "She heard the song once, only once."

"That sounded perfect," Dom agreed.

"It was," Noah assured them. It would blend perfectly with what they had already recorded. He didn't foresee any changes that would need to be made.

He kept his eyes on Isabeau's back, waiting.

"Someone tell me how she did that," Nick exclaimed.

"How did she perform nocturnes at five years old?" Pete asked, checking the playback. "Izzy plays by ear. That's her talent. Once is all she's ever needed to hear something." He pushed the button so that she heard his next comment. "That was perfect, like always."

In the booth, Isabeau stood. She turned for the door, took two steps and stopped. Reaching out, she settled her hand atop the piano's cabinet. Then she walked away without a backward glance, her hand pressed against her stomach as if she were in pain.

"What have we done to her?" Dominic asked quietly, from his spot behind Noah's left shoulder.

They hadn't done anything. All of this was on him. He'd gotten what he wanted—her; playing the piano—but at what price?

Suddenly struck by a very real fear of losing her, he pulled open the door and stepped out into the hall. "Isabeau."

Already halfway to the outer door, she flinched. She stopped walking, but kept her back to him as he closed the distance between them.

His need to touch her, to comfort was so overwhelming, he reached for her, only to have her jerk away. She turned to face him after shifting out of his reach. Her eyes were shadowed. Overflowing with pain.

His stomach clutched. "Why did you do it? Why play if you knew how this was going to affect you?"

"It's what you wanted," she replied simply. "You've made that pretty clear right from the beginning."

He opened his mouth, but with nothing to say in his defense, closed it again. There was no denying the truth of her words. He hadn't kept his desire for her to play again a secret. It had been his goal from the beginning. At least until he realized what he was asking of her. By then, it was too late.

"You never asked what I wanted. You stormed into my life and embarked on this heroic effort to save me from myself, but you never asked me if I wanted to be saved. You didn't care."

She stepped back as he reached for her, expertly staying an arm's length away. "Isabeau—"

"I don't want to perform again, Noah." She squeezed her eyes shut, opened them. "I never wanted to. I hated going out there, being put on display like some sideshow freak."

"You're not a freak."

"A child that hears music in the blowing of the wind, the rustle of the leaves on the trees?

319

A little girl not yet of school age who can play Chopin after hearing it only once?" She hugged her arms around her middle. "It doesn't matter. None of this matters."

"It matters." God, he wanted to touch her so badly he ached. "Let me in, Isabeau. There's a wall around you that you won't let me past, an entire part of you that you won't let me be a part of."

"I can't."

"Why?"

Her lips trembled. "Nothing's enough for you. I'm certainly not."

"That's not true. I want you to—"

"What about what I want?" she asked, her voice pitched so low he had to strain to hear her. "No matter what I give, you always want more. There's nothing more for you."

"I don't believe that."

"It doesn't matter what you believe. Your life is somewhere else. What's between us— whatever else it is—is temporary. You know that. I know that."

His throat tightened painfully. A burning ache settled in his gut, crawled up his chest. "I'm asking you now. What do you want?"

"I want to be important to you."

He took a step closer. "You are important to me."

"Because of who I was, who you believe I could be again. The woman I am isn't enough for you."

"That's not true."

She was inching away from him again, moving closer to the door at her back. If she thought he was going to let her walk away from him, she'd better think again. After talking with Thomas last night, Noah had a better understanding of what motivated her to keep people at a distance. But he wasn't having any of it. Not anymore. He wanted past that wall of hers. He wanted her to share her secrets with him. All of them.

She gazed up at him, her eyes gray and shiny with unshed tears. "I wish I could believe that."

"Believe it."

She cupped his face in her hands, brushed his cheeks with her thumbs. Then she turned and walked away.

"Isabeau, wait!" He pushed through the door, squinting as the afternoon sun struck him in the face. "What happened to you during those years with John Whitehorse?"

She froze with her hand on her driver's door. Her spine straightened. A small sound of distress slipped up the back of her throat. "Why would you ask me that?"

"What did he do to you, Isabeau? Why the walls? Why won't you let anyone in?" If possible, she went even paler. "I know he hurt you. What I want to know is if it was more than

321

emotionally. The physical abuse—"

"Don't do this."

"—how far did he take it?" Throat raw, palms sweating, he took a step closer. "Is Thomas right? Did John Whitehorse sexually abuse you?"

She started to shake. "He thinks that?"

"It's a logical assumption."

"The hell it is!"

"Your time with John changed you."

"Please stop."

He couldn't. He had to know. "You closed off, shut down, and began to draw away from even the most platonic touches."

Covering her face, she stood there, body vibrating with emotion. "Thomas told you this?"

"Yes."

"When?"

"Last night. After he brought you home, Thomas came into the bar where I sat waiting for you. He told me about the last time you ran away from John."

"I was fourteen," she whispered, through her fingers.

He pulled them away from her face. "There was something you would have told him then, if John hadn't shown up with the police. What was it, Isa?"

"All these years...How could he believe this and never say anything? He should have asked me."

"I'm asking you. Isabeau, did John Whitehorse sexually abuse you?"

"No."

Noah released his breath in a rush. As she continued talking, he realized his relief was misplaced.

"John would have had to see me as a human being to do so, and I was never that to him. I was a machine, his money-making machine. That's why he fought for me—to cash in on the curiosity. John had dreams of becoming a very rich man. What he didn't realize was that everything I ever made was tied up in a trust fund that I couldn't touch until I turned twenty-one."

She looked up at him, her eyes unreadable. "He didn't molest me, Noah. He said vile, cruel things to me. He routinely left more than his fair share of bruises on me, and once, once he beat me so badly he damn near killed me. Is that what you wanted to hear?"

Sick to his stomach, he shook his head. "Not really. You never told this to anyone?"

"I told no one, especially not Thomas. There wasn't anything he could do. The court had turned his love for me into something indecent. I couldn't go back to him, and I refused to put him through any more. His life was torn up enough."

"Damn it." Anger coursed through his blood. "What about your life?"

"I survived."

"Is that what you call this, survival?" As he took a step forward, she took one back. It only increased his anger. "How much of you survived and how much was sacrificed? Your gift? Your desire to create music? Your ability to trust?"

"You can't possibly understand."

"Help me to understand. Christ, Isa, you can't give me bits and pieces and expect me to see the whole. You're angry with me for not being happy with you, but how could I be when you kept that person from me? I don't know you, not because I didn't ask the right questions, but because you never trusted me enough to let me in." Because he couldn't help himself, he trailed the back of his fingers down her cheek. "You're right about me, I want more. I want all of you."

She shifted minutely so that he had no choice but to drop his hand. "I can't give you that."

"You mean you won't."

Turning her back on him, she opened the driver's door of her SUV and reached inside. When she faced him again, there was a manila file folder in her hand and a tear streaking down her cheek.

"What's this?"

"My entire life, people have always referred to my music as a gift. But it's not a gift, Noah, it's a curse. It took away my mother and gave me to a devil in human form. And it will take you, right back into a world where I no longer belong." She wiped away her tears with an angry swipe of her hand. "You're going to do it. You're going to get your record deal."

He took hold of her elbow as she tried to climb into the SUV. "Wait!"

Her eyes slid closed and she sighed. "Noah, let go of me."

"I can't," he replied softly. "I can't let you go."

Her eyes slid open as she jerked free from his grasp. "You have to. You don't have a choice."

Hand fisted, Noah stood motionless while she drove away. He opened the file folder, certain its contents would change everything.

He was right.

The wind picked up. Papers rustled, lifted. He slapped his palm down and held them in place as his mind struggled to process what he held. Good-bye, that's what it was.

He began to swear long and loud.

****

Everyone was still in the control room when Noah returned. His gaze swept over each of them as he crossed to Dominic and dropped the folder into his lap.

"What's this?" Dominic asked, his brow wrinkled in confusion.

325

Noah pressed the palms of his hands against his eyes. "A gift from Isabeau."

Surprise raised Dom's voice. "Is this what I think it is?" He didn't need to open his eyes to know that Dominic was now paging through the papers, his disbelief growing with every sheet he uncovered. He'd done the same. Not five minutes after Isabeau walked out of his life.

Yesterday she'd advised them to record the song with strings backing them. Today she provided them with the means to make it happen. Inside the folder he handed Dominic was the accompaniment's music. The title of each page, written in her precise script, was the name of the song she'd recorded the piano portion of.

"Isabeau composes?" Nick asked.

Finally Noah opened his eyes to find Nick and Alex looking over Dom's shoulder.

"Izzy has the kind of skill you don't see often," Pete informed them. "A skill that extends beyond the piano."

"She composes?" Noah repeated, earning him a questioning look.

"Of course. Didn't you listen to her albums?"

"I did."

"Then you know she wrote every song. It's right there in the album sleeve." Pete frowned. "She's a talented composer. She always has been."

Noah's gut tightened. He swore under his breath. "I didn't know."

He'd never thought of her as a composer, never even considered it. He'd been so hung up on her skills as a pianist that he'd been blinded to any of her other talents. And because of it, he'd pushed away the best thing to ever come into his life.

CHAPTER SEVENTEEN

Noah stood in the studio in his basement. He'd known before he left New York to fly back and meet with the record company that the studio was completed. He'd kept it to himself. There was no sense in getting anyone's hopes up before he saw it with his own eyes, made the final inspection.

Unclipping his mobile phone from his belt, he pushed number two and activated speed dial. Dominic picked up on the third ring.

"It's ready," Noah said without preamble. "Get things started."

"Have you met with the record execs yet?"

"Tomorrow afternoon. I met with Tony this morning." Tony was the band's manager, as well as a loyal friend of Noah's. They'd seen each other through many tough times. "He's confident we'll be offered a contract."

"Yet you don't sound pleased at all," Dominic pointed out, then disconnected.

Noah sighed wearily. Dominic was right, he wasn't pleased. He didn't feel a sense of excitement over a new beginning or relief that something he worked so hard for was finally within his grasp. He couldn't seem to feel much of anything besides the ache in his gut that grew a little larger every day.

Isabeau.

Standing in his bland, colorless home it became clear to him how much he'd lost. Damn it, everywhere he looked, even here in the studio, all he could see was her smile. All he heard was the laughter she'd brought with her during their time here on their way back from London.

Shit, if he closed his eyes and tried hard enough, he swore he could smell her. It wasn't possible, he understood that, yet it was something he kept finding himself doing, as he stood in the very spot he'd stripped her clothes from her body and made love to her. What had he been thinking, to take her in the studio, the one place he needed his concentration most? From now on out, he would forever equate this room with her—her scent, her taste. The feel of her flesh sliding atop his.

Swearing viciously, he closed his eyes. He'd had his share of women, most of them during the height of his musical career. They lined up, all but lay at his feet. He'd been young back then, awed by all the attention, and he'd taken advantage. But only Isabeau made his blood pump hot and fast in his veins. She was the woman he couldn't keep from touching, the woman who caused him to lose control of his sexual urges. All he had to do was breathe in the scent of her, and he was hard as a rock.

He'd loved before. He'd loved Beth, but she'd never made him feel the way Isabeau made him feel. It wasn't just need and desire, it was a sense of coming home. A sense of completion that had been there since that fateful night he'd wandered into her bar. The night he'd looked up into the palest eyes he'd ever seen and fallen.

She'd become everything to him.

His heart.

His oxygen.

His future.

He couldn't let her go. Life without her was as empty as this house. Standing in it, with the silence settling around him, he came to a conclusion. It meant him asking something of her again, something he wasn't certain she'd be willing to give. But he had to take the chance.

Heading for the stairs, he ascended them two at a time. Hurried, driven by a need to have everything ready before he flew back to find her, he crossed to the front door and his Aston Martin parked in the driveway. He needed to get back to Sacramento before the stores closed.

He needed to see a man about a ring.

****

Heat.

After being cold for days, Isabeau was

finally warm. She sighed in her sleep and rolled over, expecting to be pulled against Noah's solid chest. It was a moment before the pull of sleep eased enough for her to realize two things. One, Noah wasn't in her bed. He hadn't been for days now, and no matter how many times she awoke in the middle of the night reaching for him, she always came up empty. Her pain was all consuming. Her lungs heaved. Her chest hurt. The second realization came to her, this one far more terrifying than the thought of spending another night without Noah.

Her building was on fire.

It wasn't the pain of loss that tightened her chest, but the chokingly thick black smoke that surrounded her.

"Oh, God," she mumbled, only to start coughing.

Simultaneously she reached for the cordless telephone on the nightstand and rolled to the floor. Her eyes teared as the dense smoke burned more than her lungs. Blindly, she pushed a button on the phone and lifted it to her ear. She stabbed again, frantic when the dead phone wouldn't turn on.

She scanned the room, checking for flame, searching for her way out. Fiery sparks danced in the air. A terrifying roar sounded just before the windows near her bed burst and flames licked in over the sill.

Frozen in fear, she watched as they ate

their way toward her mother's photographs. How could this be happening? Why hadn't her sprinkler system turned on, her alarm sounded? Without thinking, she lunged off the floor and toward her wall of memories. Her bare feet became tangled, the floor rose to meet her. Her arms shot out in front of her to protect her face as she skidded across the wood toward the theater chairs.

The flames licked closer. Blinding pain shot up her arm and she screamed. Rolling off her stomach, she scrambled back, away from the wall. Reaching out blindly to tug at whatever had tangled itself around her ankles. The building groaned. Downstairs, glass shattered. But the smell was the worst, like nothing she had smelled before. And the pain in her arm...

Nausea surged. Forcing it back made her cough harder. Panic built as she tugged at the leather around her ankles. Finally freeing her legs, she fisted her hand around the strap and began to crawl. Smoke filled the room, blinded her. She followed the rug that ran the length of her home, moving in the direction of her outside door. It was the darkest part of her apartment, indicating the fire had yet to reach that side of the building.

Her lungs burned, her throat ached. Gasping for breath, she crawled a little faster when the heat of the floor penetrated her sweatpants. She didn't have much time. She couldn't stop coughing, and her body felt strangely disconnected.

Stay on the rug. Stay. On. The. Rug. Without the ability to see clearly, she couldn't risk veering off in the wrong direction.

Body sluggish, limbs clumsy, it seemed as if she would never reach the opposite wall. She coughed steadily now. Her entire body ached, her head throbbed. The fire was loud, louder than she could ever imagine as it devoured the building around her.

Her body cried out for her to stop, to rest a minute and allow her to catch her breath, but she recognized it for what it was. She was starving for oxygen. She wasn't going to make it. Already she could feel her lungs shutting down, her airway swelling shut.

She could feel consciousness slipping away.

Suddenly, her hands came down on something cool and she breathed a sigh of relief. She was at her door, and it wasn't hot like everything else in the room. Reaching up for the knob, she twisted and pulled.

Nothing happened.

A bubble of fear worked its way up the back of her throat and she cried out. Then her muddled thoughts cleared enough for her to remember to turn the lock.

On her knees now, she reached out with her left hand and twisted the deadbolt, with her right she pulled on the door. The dense black smoke cleared for a moment, then the room behind her howled in such a way that she stumbled out the door in a rush. She was weak, clumsy, and moving much too quickly for her legs to keep up. About halfway down the back stairs, her legs gave out completely.

Pain.

It exploded throughout her body as she tumbled down the stairs, desperately tucking herself into as tight a ball as possible. She landed hard on her hands and knees, the jolt that shot through her limbs enough to make her gasp. But she didn't stop. She couldn't. Now that she was on the ground, she was even closer to the flames. The wall next to her moaned, and she scrambled away as quickly as she could, dragging her leather tote behind her.

She gained her feet about ten yards from the building. Her shoulder ached, her forehead stung, and she was pretty sure it wasn't sweat that she kept blinking out of her eyes. But it was the pain in her right arm that had her cradling it protectively against her body as she stumbled, coughing and choking her way toward the street.

Red lights were flashing everywhere. Men in turnout suits were swarming out of fire trucks. One of the men saw her and grabbed her shoulders, causing her to cry out. He said something, but she couldn't hear him over the roar of the fire and the noise of the sirens as more emergency vehicles pulled up.

Isabeau shook her head, trying to communicate. Her vision grayed, her knees weakened, and he tightened his grip when she would have fallen over. She couldn't breathe, couldn't draw enough oxygen into her lungs. Gasping, she put up no resistance when he scooped her off her feet and carried her to the nearest ambulance.

Then, everything went silent as she slid into darkness.

****

"You do recall there's a three-hour time difference?" Noah stated, as he groggily answered his mobile phone. "I just got to sleep."

Silence was the only reply. Complete and total silence.

"Dom? Are you still there?"

"There's been a fire, Noah. Around three o'clock this morning. At Izzy's."

He sat bolt upright in bed as panic brought him full awake, his every sense alert. "Isabeau?"

"There's not much left. The place is...a burned-out shell."

Crippling fear froze the oxygen in his lungs. His chest felt like someone stood on it. "What about Isabeau?"

"I don't know."

"What do you mean you don't know? You must know something!"

"Fuck, Noah," Dominic rasped. "I don't know anything. Pete's making some calls right now, trying to find someone with information."

Noah climbed out of bed, frantically stuffing clothes into his leather duffel bag. She was fine, she had to be. He'd know if something had happened to her, he would feel it. Wouldn't he?

"Wait a minute," Dom said, his voice grim, cold.

Straightening, he waited. Voices sounded from the other end of the line. Not loud enough that he could make out the words. "Dom? Dominic?" His chest tightened. "Damn it, Dom, talk to me!"

"A news report came on the telly. There were two people injured in the fire. One didn't make it."

There was a big black hole yawning at his feet, and he felt like he was being sucked down into it. He gathered his courage and asked the question he didn't want to hear the answer to. "Who didn't make it?"

"They didn't say," Dominic replied, his voice thick with emotion. "They won't say until a positive identification is made, and the family is notified."

Noah swallowed down the bile crawling up his throat. "I'm coming back," he said, his voice strangled. "Call Tony, let him know he's on his own today."

"Sure."

He refused to accept that she was dead. Because then, he would never see her face again, hear her whisper his name. "Dominic?"

"Yeah?"

Pain screamed through him, growing louder, stronger with every ragged breath he took. His knees crumbled, and he sank back onto the bed. "You'll let me know if you hear anything else?"

"I'll let you know."

Noah stared at the mobile phone in his hand. He swallowed past a throat that was much too tight, rubbed his hand over a heart he couldn't believe still pumped. She had to be all right. She had to be. He couldn't let himself think about her any way but alive—smiling and laughing.

He couldn't consider how frightened she must have been, trapped in a fire, struggling to breathe while heat and flames nipped at her. He couldn't wonder if she'd thought of him at all, in those last moments. If she had any idea how important to him she was.

Or if she'd died, never knowing how much he loved her.

Standing abruptly, he rushed to the bathroom, bent over the toilet and vomited.

****

Isabeau's throat was on fire.

She lay in the hospital bed, the blankets pulled to her chin, shaking, cold even though she'd been trapped in a burning building. Her entire body ached, throbbed, from her multiple injuries. Her right shoulder was scraped raw, her forehead cut. There were tiny little welts, dime-sized burns she'd been informed, all along her back where bits from the ceiling fell on her as she crawled along the rug. The largest of her injuries was the second degree burn on her right arm. At the moment, she couldn't decide which hurt worse, her arm or her throat.

But at least she was alive.

Unlike Clint.

Tears welled in her eyes when she thought of Clint, trapped in the hell she'd managed to escape. Of the panic he must have felt as he choked and gagged on the thick smoke.

Unlike the police who'd just left, she believed Clint to be an innocent victim. She didn't care that there were signs the fire was intentionally set. Even if the evidence showed it originated from inside the building, she refused to believe Clint had anything to do with it. Not Clint. Dear, sweet Clint who'd been her employee for years. Her friend.

Of course, if it wasn't Clint, then there remained someone out there who wanted her dead. Someone angry and twisted enough, that they were willing to hurt others, in their quest to get her. Nausea and fear churned in her belly.

Suddenly uneasy, she rolled to face the door, cringing when pain knifed across her back. No position was comfortable, but at least if she remained still, the discomfort was kept to a minimum. A nurse had been by earlier and offered her a painkiller. She'd turned her down. She didn't want numbness or sleep. She wanted the doctor to come and listen to her lungs again so she could leave.

Her pain was extensive, her loss complete, and her emotions much too close to the surface for comfort. If she was going to break, which with every minute longer she waited she feared was closer and closer to happening, she preferred to do it in private. She didn't want any witnesses to her grief. She wanted her own bed and Noah.

Her eyes slid closed. Her heart clenched. Loss consumed her.

She wanted what she no longer had. Her home and business had been lost to fire therefore she had no bed to curl up in. And Noah, he was in California, working on his future.

A future she played no part in.

She couldn't, she admitted, even if she wanted to. Because her livelihood was not the only thing lost to the fire. She'd also lost the music that had been with her for as long as she could remember—even when she hadn't wanted it.

A constant, ever present piece of her.

Gone.

Leaving behind nothing but silence.

Unable to hold it off any longer, Isabeau curled in on herself and wept.

CHAPTER EIGHTEEN

"How long ago did you get back?" Dominic asked as Noah sank into the overstuffed chair in the corner of Dom's room.

"What time is it?" Noah glanced at the digital clock on the bed stand. "Three hours ago." He leaned back in the chair and rubbed at the stubble on his chin. "Have you seen her, Dom? Spoken with her?"

"No. I'm sorry."

"I can't find her." Noah sighed, pressing his fingers against his eyes. "I have to find her."

Exhaustion pulled at him, combined with the fear already coursing through him. He'd been searching for her since he'd gotten off the plane and discovered the voice mail message left by Dominic. The message that assured him that Isabeau had survived the fire. After eight hours of desperately trying to get back, of believing the worst, all he could think of was holding her. The only problem was no one seemed to know where to find her.

"I even went by the bar..." A shiver worked through him. A horrific sight that added fuel to his futile search for Isabeau, there wasn't much left of her home and business. The fire had spared nothing, not even her SUV. Parked in its usual place along the back of the building, it had been too close to escape the intense heat and flames. "I can't believe it's the same place."

"Have you checked with Thomas?"

"I went there first. The tattoo parlor was locked up tight, as was the entrance to the apartment above. No one answered."

Dominic leaned forward, resting his elbows on his knees. "I assume you checked the local hospitals as well?"

Noah groaned. "You don't even want to know how many there are. The most I could get out of them was that she wasn't on any of the floors, and even that bit of information wasn't easily gleaned."

It wasn't until the last place he'd gone that he discovered she'd been treated and released. Information that sent him back into Manhattan, to Thomas's again, where his knocks had gone unanswered a second time.

He tossed his arm over his eyes. Where the hell was she?

"Noah?"

"Yeah?"

"Have you spoken with Tony since you left California?"

"He left me a message while I was in flight. I haven't rung him back."

"He says the offer is fair."

Noah shifted his arm off his eyes and placed it across his lap. He stared up at the ceiling, trying to work up enough energy to go back to his room and make the necessary telephone calls. "I'll ring him later."

Dominic shifted positions, leaning back against the headboard. He pulled one foot onto the bed, resting his arm on his bent knee, while the other foot remained on the floor. "You know that Nick left?"

He hadn't known, but the news didn't surprise him. Were he in Nick's shoes, with a wife and kids waiting for him back home in California, Noah would have skipped town already, too. "I don't blame him."

"Yeah."

They fell into a comfortable silence, a silence Dominic finally broke. "Noah?"

Dom's change in intonation brought Noah's head up. He focused on his friend, half sprawled atop the bed, his head tipped back and slightly angled.

"How many places do you think you looked for her?"

"Too many. Why?"

"Did you check your room?" He gestured with his thumb toward the wall at his back.

"What are you—" Water. Running through pipes. Out of all the hotels in all the cities in the world Noah had stayed in, there wasn't a single room where the sound of water

343

running in the next room wasn't audible through the wall.

He stood, heart in his throat. "It's most likely the maid."

"She came through this morning."

Scooping up the duffel bag that lay near his feet, Noah was out the door and standing before his room in the space of a heartbeat. He fumbled for his wallet and the keycard he kept inside. On the third try, he finally got the green light and pushed the door open.

Isabeau.

In one piece. In his room. Sporting blue surgical scrubs a few sizes too big for her frame, and a gauze wrapping that circled her right forearm from wrist to elbow.

Her hair was pulled back in a ponytail, her feet bare. Her face was pressed into one of his shirts—a poor substitute for the comfort she'd come to his room seeking. "I can offer you something better than an old shirt."

Her head came up, her eyes locked on him. She was pale, her face drawn. Dark rings of fatigue circled pale gray eyes.

He'd spent eight long, agonizing hours not knowing if she was alive or dead. She had never looked more beautiful.

He pushed the door closed, turned the lock and placed the duffel near the closet. Then, he crossed the room and removed the shirt from her hands. Dropping it atop the dresser, he wrapped her in his arms. "I've been searching all over the city for you."

She sagged against him, fisting her hands in his shirt to keep him close. "You're supposed to be in California."

"I'm supposed to be right here. What's the matter with your voice?"

"Smoke inhalation."

He could hardly bear to think about what she'd been through. And how much worse it could have been.

"Noah, are you shaking?"

"Like a leaf," he admitted. "I need a minute. Just...give me a minute." He closed his eyes and pressed his cheek to the top of her head—relishing the feel of her in his arms, breathing her in. He caught the hint of smoke beneath her shampoo and another tremor moved through him. "Are you all right? Were you hurt?"

She eased back enough to look up at him. "A few scrapes and bruises."

He touched her, tracing his fingers lightly around the cut on her forehead. Her eyes drifted shut as he leaned down and pressed his lips near the mark. "I heard about Clint. I'm so sorry, Isa." He cupped her face in his hands as tears welled in her eyes. "I thought it was you. When Dom called and told me about the fire, I thought..." He had to clear his throat to go on. "I didn't know whether or not you were alive. Not

345

until my plane landed."

"Noah," she whispered.

He couldn't stop touching her, her face, her throat, her hair. She reached up and pulled the elastic band from her hair and he pushed his fingers through the silky strands. Then he kissed her, her face, her throat, he pressed his lips against hers and drank in the familiar taste of her. A taste he'd feared he would never experience again.

"How did this happen? Do they know?"

"They're looking at Clint. They believe he may have gotten trapped after he started the fire."

"No way, I don't believe it." You didn't look at a woman the way he'd seen Clint look at Isabeau, and then try to burn her alive. "You don't think Tommy—"

"No. He wouldn't do this."

He slid his hands down to rest atop her shoulders, wondering if he was ever going to stop shaking. Someone had intentionally set her building on fire, knowing two people were inside? "How do you know?"

"He wouldn't, couldn't have, he's in rehab. Thomas convinced him to go, and I—"

"You what? You're paying for it, aren't you?"

"Yes." She gazed up at him, her eyes soft, sincere. "I'm doing it for Thomas, to give him a better chance at a relationship with his son. He deserves that."

Emotion tightened his throat. Noah brushed his hand down her hair. "Yes, he does."

She was the most unselfish woman he'd ever met. He wanted to take her to bed, make love with her, and then hold her while she slept. Long enough for the shadows to clear from her eyes. He wanted his hands on her—all that smooth, soft skin—wanted to hear the quick hitch in her breathing as he explored her body, reassuring himself that she was all right.

Sliding his hands off her shoulders, he smoothed them down her back.

Her spine went taut, her body arched away from his. The hands fisting his shirt tightened as she drew in a quick shuddering breath.

"What's the matter?" She'd gone pale. Tears filled her eyes. "Isabeau?"

"I'm okay."

He could tell she wasn't.

Slowly the tension left her spine. Her hands opened, her palms settled against his chest. "I'm okay, it's...my back is burned."

Burned?

She hadn't said anything about being burned. He dropped his arms to hang at his sides. "You only mentioned scrapes and bruises."

"There are a few sore spots."

He might have believed her if her gaze

347

hadn't shifted away. "Let me see."

"No." She stepped back. "It's fine, my arm is much worse."

"Your...arm..." For some reason, it hadn't occurred to him that the gauze on her arm might cover a burn. He sank onto the bed as nausea climbed up his throat. He scrubbed his hand over his face. "What else are you hiding?"

He didn't know how much more he could stand. Every second that passed turned his nausea to white hot rage. The son of a bitch that did this to her better hope he never got his hands on him. He wanted to tear him limb from limb, beat him into a bloody pulp.

His fingers curled into tight fists.

"This isn't the first time that he's tried to harm me," she admitted softly.

"What are you saying?"

"There was the morning when I was jogging...someone tried to run me down with their car."

He hadn't thought it possible, but his stomach clenched even tighter. Swearing softly, he put his head in his hands. "Let me guess, I was in London and when I asked you about it, you said you 'took a tumble?'"

She knelt in front of him. Her hand brushed through his hair. "I'm sorry."

He straightened, cupped her face in his hands and gazed into her eyes. "You should have told me."

She shifted closer, splaying her hands on his chest. "I know."

"Tell me you at least told this to the police."

"They think that was Clint, too."

"No," he mumbled, but he was no longer certain. He couldn't think straight, couldn't seem to clear the rage and helplessness enough to concentrate. What else hadn't she told him? "Isabeau..."

Her hands began inching his shirt up his body. Reaching over his head, he fisted his hands, pulled it off. A hum of pleasure moved up her throat as her hands smoothed across his chest. She settled her open mouth over his nipple.

"Isa."

"I'm so tired," she murmured against his flesh. "I can't sleep when you're not beside me. I keep reaching for you, waiting for you to pull me against your side." Her hand trailed to his other nipple and her mouth followed.

He slid his fingers into her hair and cupped the back of her head. "You need to rest. I'm here now."

"I need you to touch me," she argued, and tugged at his nipple with her teeth.

Pleasure shot through him as every nerve came to life. He had the fleeting feeling that there was more going on than what she was telling him, but it was forgotten the moment she pushed the scrubs over her hips and off, immediately followed by her top.

Her naked body took his breath away. The warmth of her skin as she took his hands and placed them over her breasts arrested all thought.

"Make love to me, Noah."

****

Isabeau had no idea how long she'd been standing at the window. With the sheet draped around her body, hanging low in the back so it didn't brush against her burns, she stared out across the city. Her mind was in turmoil; her thoughts a jumbled mess. The one thing that stood out from the rest, the only thing she knew for certain, was that this was the only place she wanted to be.

Right here, with Noah.

The rest of her life had become one big nightmare, but here, with him, she felt a sense of peace. As if somehow, everything would work out.

Which didn't make a lick of sense, because the future was still up in the air. There were things she could never give him, even if he would want them with her. Secrets between them, things she'd kept from him in a vain attempt to save herself from revisiting the pain. And for what, she wondered as she watched the sun dip low over the city? It hadn't worked.

Refusing to give voice to her past did nothing to keep her from remembering, from dreaming and aching. In the end her silence saved her nothing. In fact, it could quite possibly cost her something that had come to mean everything to her.

Noah's affection.

Fighting tears, she closed her eyes and tried to find music in a room that was uncomfortably silent. She startled when Noah came up behind her, swept her hair aside and pressed his mouth to her uninjured shoulder.

"You should be asleep," he whispered, settling his hands on her hips. "Why aren't you?"

She had been. Exhausted and sated she'd drifted to sleep in his arms, only to wake barely an hour later. Suffocating. Believing she was back in the fire and the smoke. She'd untangled her fingers from his, eased out of bed and after phoning her father and letting him know she wouldn't be needing her old room after all, stood staring out at the city ever since. Her body was still exhausted, but her mind wouldn't shut off.

"I keep thinking. About the fire and how the police are wrong about Clint. I keep thinking about my life. I used to love this city. Now I look out there, and I wonder who started the fire and where they are. I wonder what I did to make someone hate me so much."

She turned, shifting so that he no longer

351

touched her. "I look out at the city, and I'm afraid. I'm tired of being afraid, Noah. I've been afraid most of my life."

"Afraid of what?" he asked, his green eyes locked on her face.

"Afraid someone would discover my secret."

"What secret?"

She closed her eyes for a moment, then made herself open them and meet his. "You're right, I keep things from you."

He took a step forward, his mouth a thin line. "Why?"

"Because you mean too much to me."

"You're telling me you keep things from me because you care about me?"

Her throat was so tight, she wasn't sure she could answer. With an effort, she swallowed. "I don't just care about you, Noah. I love you."

An emotion she couldn't identify flashed through his eyes. He reached for her, but she stopped him with a hand to his chest. "I thought if I held back, as long as I didn't give you all of me, I could survive you leaving."

"Isabeau—"

"Let me finish, please." She could feel the tears coming and knew that if she didn't get this out now, she wasn't going to be able to. He needed to know the truth.

He deserved the truth.

"I've lied to you. I've lied to everyone,

even myself. The music never died. It's always been there, an ever-changing melody in my head." Until now. It wasn't there now. She fought back a sob. "A tune so clear I never understood how others couldn't hear it. My gift, my mother always said, and in my naiveté, I believed her. I loved to play the piano. It was like...breathing. Something a body, my body, couldn't survive without."

His hands tightened on her shoulders. "You're shaking. Let me hold you."

She kept her arm a firm barrier between them, even as her tears broke free and trailed down her cheeks. "I would play to the music in my head, and I was happy. Even after my mother died, I would play, and she would come back to me, sit with me. Smile and tell me how gifted I was."

A shudder moved through her. A sick trembling settled in her stomach. "John Whitehorse thought I was gifted as well—gifted enough to make him a very rich man. I was young, but far from stupid, no matter what he said. I refused, refused to play for him, or anyone else that came around expecting me to. I told them all I couldn't, not after the accident, after losing Mom. And they believed me."

It had been so simple.

Until it wasn't.

She raised a trembling hand, pressed her fingertips to her lips. A sob bubbled up the back of her throat, broke loose.

"The hell with this." His arms wrapped around her, pulled her against his solid chest. One hand cupped the back of her head, the other rested low on her back where she wasn't burned.

Hot tears spilled down her cheeks. Tears for everything she had already lost and everything she was sure to lose yet. And all the while he stroked her hair, soothing her with words, whispered words she didn't understand, but that she found comforting.

Once she could speak, she continued her tale, her voice shaky, uneven. "I didn't care that John told me every day, in every way he could, what he thought of the daughter he'd spent a small fortune fighting for, only to have her refuse to make him rich. I could handle that. What I couldn't handle was not playing."

Cradling his big hand in hers, she ran her fingertips over his palm, his calloused fingers. God, she loved his hands. The shape and size of them. The way they moved across her body. Caressing. Pleasuring.

Never hurting.

"I couldn't handle not playing," she repeated. "So one day, on my way home from school, I went to the studio. I went to Pete, and I played. With no one else around, I walked into the booth and I played. What he must have thought that first time, having believed I no longer had the ability. But he never said anything, just made sure that the studio was empty for me every day after school."

Fighting a fresh swell of tears, she found comfort when Noah eased her a little closer, held her a bit tighter. "Of course John found out. I got careless. I allowed the draw, the lure of the music to distract me. He followed me one day. That's when the beatings began. If I wouldn't play for him, I wasn't allowed to enjoy playing."

"I'm sorry," he murmured. "I'm so sorry."

"I tried. I tried so hard. I begged and pleaded with God every day to make the music in my head go away, the need to create stop. It never stopped, I...couldn't stop. And John...John didn't stop."

His arm tightened around her in reflex, setting off an ache across her back. She didn't care. The discomfort was nothing compared to the agony she was recalling.

"John would punish me with silence. He would take away my radio, smash my CDs, all in an effort to force me to play. And when that wouldn't work, he would hit me some more. Once, he kicked me so hard he left a bruise in the shape of his boot on my back. I thought he'd kill me. I prayed for it."

"God, Isabeau."

"Instead I learned. Finally, I learned. Not to enjoy it, not to love it. I learned to ignore the music and to lie."

The words came easier now. She pulled her face out of his neck and released his hand. She wiped her tears from her cheeks, took a deep breath and looked up at him.

"It worked for me. Right up until the moment you walked into my life. You changed everything, Noah, that night you stepped into my bar. You turned my world upside down. Suddenly the music was louder. So loud I couldn't ignore it or drown it out." She cupped his handsome face in her hands. "I know it sounds crazy, but it's true. I even checked behind the bar to make sure one of the customers hadn't messed with the stereo volume. Then I looked up and there you were, smiling at me. And it was so obviously coming from you that..."

"What?"

"I panicked. I was mean and hurtful and I pushed you away because you were a threat to this carefully constructed lie of mine. If you get hit enough, just the thought of playing will bring the fear, the pain. Every once in a while the lure returns, and it's strong enough to smother the pain, at least for a moment. But it never lasts, and it never ends well."

"That's why you were playing later that night, when I returned?"

"It wouldn't go away, even after you left. It remained so powerful I couldn't concentrate. I even forgot to check the door after the last employee left. I never forget when I'm alone after close."

He skimmed the back of his knuckles down her cheek. "You were trembling. I thought you were frightened of me."

"I was," she whispered. "Frightened of how you made me feel. All I could think about was getting you out of there. You needed to get away from me so I could breathe. It never occurred to me that you would come back."

His mouth skimmed her temple. "I did come back."

"And I tried to fight it. I tried not to be drawn to you because you wanted something from me I couldn't give you. It was never about performing, Noah. I never enjoyed that. The joy was always in playing. After John, I couldn't even do that without throwing up."

"Yet I forced you to do it, anyway." He bent close then kissed her, deeply, thoroughly, his fingers furrowing through her hair. "I'm sorry for that," he said, and kissed her again. "I'm sorry for ever making you feel like you needed to play in order to have my affection."

Drained, she rested against him, relying on his strength now that hers was gone. Slowly, the chill left her body as his warmth began to penetrate. Her eyes drifted shut.

"Isabeau?" One of his hands cupped her throat, tipped her head up.

"Hmm," she asked, forcing her eyes open.

Discovering a look in his eyes she'd never seen before, she tilted her chin. "What's the matter, what is it?"

His thumb stroked the hollow of her throat as he continued to gaze at her. The look faded, a smile curved his lips. "It'll keep," he said softly. "Right now you look like you're going to fall over. Let's get you back to bed."

CHAPTER NINETEEN

Isabeau stood over the bathroom sink, drying her hair with the hotel-supplied hair dryer. With nothing else to wear, she'd pulled on the scrub bottoms, but traded the uncomfortable top for one of Noah's older, softer T-shirts. Her ears rang, her body ached like someone who'd fallen down a flight of stairs, and showering without getting her gauze-wrapped forearm wet had been interesting, to say the least.

Her reflection in the mirror confirmed she looked as bad as she felt. The stark white of the butterfly bandage on her forehead stood out against the dark purple bruise that had formed around it. A long, thin scratch graced her right cheek. And even cold compresses hadn't been enough to help her eyes. Already swollen and irritated from smoke, her crying jag last night had puffed them up even more.

She looked bad, she felt even worse, and because she still couldn't speak above a raspy whisper, she hadn't been able to order breakfast and a bottle of aspirin from room service the way she wanted to.

If she could keep her concentration

359

focused on what she was doing, her hair would be dry and she could sneak down to the lobby gift shop and settle for whatever she could find. But her mind kept wandering to Noah, wondering when he was going to tell her that they'd gotten their record deal.

He was at the studio now, a sure sign that things had gone well in California. He never went into the studio this early, not before noon. And he never shut off his mobile phone, as he'd done last night, before taking her to bed. Put those things together and she only came up with one thing.

He didn't fear missing a call about a contract offer because one was already on the table.

She tried to be happy for him. Okay, she *was* happy for him. But tangled up with it was also the harsh reality that he was leaving. Soon.

There was nothing to keep him in New York.

Emotion welled in her throat, settled into a knot. She turned off the hair dryer, closed her eyes, and curled her arms around her middle.

The light click of the room door closing had her snapping her eyes open. She glanced over her shoulder, out into the part of the room someone would have to pass through upon entering. It was empty.

"Noah?" she called, then shook her head when his name came out more of a croak than anything. Slipping out of the bathroom, she stepped into the main room. She froze.

A man stood at the foot of the bed, muttering under his breath as he rifled through her leather tote. Confused she watched as he popped the snap on the back section, reached in and pulled out the sheet music she kept there— her music. The expression on his face shifted from frustration to rage as he clenched the papers so tightly they wrinkled. Then he turned and looked directly at her.

Icy fear washed over her in waves as she noted the madness in the hardened green eyes that locked with hers. Not Noah's eyes, but Gregory Howard's.

"You bitch! I knew you were at it again."

In the seconds it took to get her terrified body to turn for the door, Gregory was on her. He grabbed her by the hair and pulled, stopping her forward momentum and knocking her off balance. Her back slammed into his chest with enough force she cried out.

His fingers twisted in her hair, tightened and she froze as memories of past abuse slammed into her like a fist. Gregory cupped his free hand around her throat, under her chin and pulled her head back painfully.

"Don't have much of a voice left after that fire, do you? That's good."

His voice was lowered, his mouth pressed against her temple in such a sick facsimile of intimacy that she shuddered with revulsion as much as fear. A whimper crawled up the back of her throat, struggled to break free.

Don't give him the satisfaction. Never give them the satisfaction of knowing you're scared.

"You couldn't stay dead, could you?"

"What—" His fingers tightened around her throat, cutting off her words. She grabbed his wrist and pulled, but to no avail. His hold didn't loosen. The ringing in her ears grew louder.

"You always thought you were so much better than the rest of us, didn't you?"

He clenched his fingers tighter in her hair and yanked viciously. Her stomach rolled. The door. The door was so close, yet so far away. John Whitehorse's insults swam through her mind, coalescing with Gregory's.

"Momma's little girl, so perfect, the child prodigy. The world loved you, the stuck-up little bitch. You loved to make the rest of us look bad, didn't you?"

What?

Gasping, she shifted her fingers from his wrist to his hand. She couldn't breathe, she wasn't getting enough oxygen, and it was starting to affect her ability to process speech. That had to be it; otherwise Gregory wanted her dead because she was a better pianist than he? It was so ridiculous that she started to laugh.

Then, she began to cry.

"I got rid of you once. Cutting off your mother's car was a stroke of genius. She wasn't supposed to die, you were, but it worked anyway. It shut you up."

Her body bucked from the shock of his admission.

"It was fate that brought you to me that night. I knew I had to get rid of you, I just didn't know how. I was drunk and feeling sorry for myself. My fame, usurped by a child. A spoiled little brat. Then while sitting at the red light I glanced over, and like an answer to my prayers, there you were."

Bastard! She'd lost everything because of his petty jealousy?

Lungs heaving, she began the struggle to break free. Her fingernails dug into his hand, clawing, tearing at his flesh. Her legs kicked at his shins, his knees, whatever she could hit even as pain shot up her heels.

"Bitch!" His hand tightened on her neck purposefully, cutting off the rest of her air. "You've been lucky so far. Somehow, you survived the car accident and the fire. Well you won't survive this. I can't have you composing and performing again. I can't have you taking the attention off me. I won't."

And she wasn't going to die without a fight. She was no longer a child, she didn't have to stand there quietly and take the abuse. She had to do something. She had to get away from

Gregory. He was insane. He wanted her dead because he was afraid she would begin performing again and take away his success? Because of some twisted obsession to be the best?

Working her fingers beneath his, she pulled. She fisted her hand around two of his fingers and she pulled as hard as she could. Bending. Forcing them back at the knuckle. His scream was followed by the sickening snap of his fingers breaking.

His hand fell away from her throat, his grip on her hair eased. She sucked air greedily into her lungs and took two stumbling steps toward the door.

A heartbeat later pain exploded in her back as cursing and swearing, Gregory kicked her. She pitched forward, landed hard on her palms and knees. Gasping, whimpering, she reached for the door. Her fingers brushed the handle at the same moment he grabbed her hair and jerked her head back.

"You'll pay for that," he spat out, bracing himself with his legs apart, his feet alongside her knees. "You'll pay, and no one will hear you scream."

Squeezing her eyes shut, she fought back the panic, struggling to formulate her next move. Weak and exhausted, she slumped, dropping her hands back to the floor. When he refused to release her and instead followed her

364

movement, bending down to spit obscenities in her ear, she reacted.

Bucking, she drove her head back and smashed it into his face. Stars burst in front of her eyes and the room spun.

Gregory groaned. His grip loosened.

She drove her head back again, then once more. Another crack, this one not as loud and a little wetter, and she lurched out of his hold. Frantic, desperate to get away, she yanked open the door and bolted down the hall, her bare feet soundless against the carpet.

She didn't take the time to glance behind her until she was in front of the elevator, stabbing the call button over and over with her thumb. Air heaved in and out of her lungs. Terror clawed at her, and pain washed over her in waves.

The stairs were off to her left, but she was too shaky. The chance of stumbling, falling down another flight of steps was too great. Unless he came out of that room, she was choosing the safer route. The one where his longer legs didn't give him the advantage. Where she could face both the door and the threat, instead of risking it sneaking up behind her.

The elevator chimed, marking its arrival. Eyes still on the room down the hall, she jumped for the doors. With no room to spare, she slipped through and collided with someone waiting to step out. Hands settled on her shoulders, and she screamed. She screamed louder when she realized she could barely hear herself over the pounding sound of her blood in her ears.

"Bloody hell," a familiar voice exclaimed.

"Isa? Isabeau, what happened, what's the matter?"

Noah. Noah was holding her, his eyes full of confusion and fear. Dominic stood behind him.

"In the room," she croaked. "He's in the room."

"I'll go," Dominic stated, his long strides carrying him down the hall. "You ring the police."

"Did he hurt you?" Noah asked. He pulled the phone off his belt and punched in the numbers. "Are you injured?"

She pressed against him, buried her face in his neck as he cupped the back of her head with his free hand and held her tight. Her stomach turned. Her legs wobbled. And no matter how hard she tried, she wasn't able to catch her breath.

"Send an ambulance," he barked into the phone after giving their location to the emergency dispatcher on the other end of the line.

"No. I don't need one."

"You're bleeding."

The waver in his voice brought her head up. There was blood on his hand, the hand he'd been stroking her hair with. "It's not mine."

"Whose is it?" he asked, still holding the phone to his ear. "Who did this to you?"

Coursing, followed by a groan. Sputtering, then a deep, accented voice saying he'd gotten off easy. They both turned as Dominic hauled Gregory out of the room by the scruff of his neck. Blood poured beneath the hands Gregory held to his nose, and even from this distance there was no mistaking that two of his fingers were broken and bent at an awkward angle.

The hallway suddenly became too warm. Nausea surged up the back of her throat. "Gregory...did it all. He...ruined...my life." She pressed her face back into Noah's neck and closed her eyes. "He killed my mother."

CHAPTER TWENTY

Two days later, as Noah showered in preparation for their dinner out, Isabeau paced the floor of the hotel room. She'd already showered, piled her hair atop her head in an elegant sweep and applied her makeup. The choker that covered her fading bruises and matched the dress she'd bought specially for this occasion, was around her neck. The only problem—she was having second thoughts about going.

Restlessly, she roamed around the room, the silk of her robe brushing against her legs with every step. Her body was healing, most of her pain gone, but it wasn't a desire to keep her injuries hidden that had her pacing. It was the fact that over the last two days, Noah had never once brought up the future.

Which could only mean one thing: there was no future for them.

A knock sounded at the door. Spotting Dominic through the peephole only tightened the knot in her stomach. She turned the lock, undid the chain, and pulled the door open. Her feet rooted to the floor and her eyes burning, she stared at him, standing there in the hallway with his luggage clutched in his right hand.

"Wow, don't you look pretty," he said, stepping into the room as she moved back.

She forced a smile. "Thank you." She looked at the luggage he placed on the floor near his feet. "On your way to the airport?"

"Yeah."

Her stomach clenched tighter. If it was this difficult to see Dominic go, how was she ever going to be able to let Noah go?

"You're…" She cleared her throat. "You're going to call Becca, right? Like we discussed?"

"Sure."

She could tell by the look on his face he wouldn't. "Dominic, what am I going to do with you?"

"Give me a hug. My taxi's waiting."

She put her arms around him, settling against him as he pulled her into his embrace. It was an odd feeling, being held by a man other than Noah or her father—not unpleasant, just different. "I'm going to miss you, Dom."

"You'll see me again, soon."

She didn't think so. She tightened her hold on him minutely. "No one makes me laugh like you."

"I'll take that. The last woman I held in my arms I made cry."

She was pretty certain she was going to cry as well.

A rush of humid air brushed over her as the bathroom door opened.

"Uh-oh," Dom stated. "It's a good thing you're wearing more than your knickers this time or I'd surely be in trouble."

He flashed her a grin as he eased away from her and she laughed as she knew he wanted her to. There'd be time for tears later.

"Take care of yourself, luv," he said then tipped his head at Noah, picked up his luggage, and walked out the door.

She turned away before the door closed behind him, but that left her face-to-face with Noah. Standing outside of the bathroom, towel hanging low on his hips, as he watched her steadily.

"I'll go get dressed," she whispered, then slipped past him.

Once inside the bathroom with the door closed tightly behind her, she leaned against the sink and closed her eyes. She couldn't do it. She wasn't going to be able to sit across the table from him, in the nicest restaurant in town, and pretend she wasn't falling apart.

What was the point? She loved him and he was leaving. She didn't need a romantic dinner to remember him by, she would never forget him.

She was never going to get over Noah Clark.

"Oh, God," she whispered, as pain

wrapped around her heart.

Straightening away from the sink, she pulled the bathroom door open. Stepping out, she found him near the dresser. He was wearing his dress slacks and white shirt. The shirt hung open as he worked the buttons of the cuffs through their corresponding holes. As it did every time she looked at his body, her breath caught. Her hungry eyes drank in the smooth muscle of his chest, before dropping to the dark line of hair that trailed from his navel to the waistband of the slacks.

She forced her gaze back to his handsome face. "I can't do this."

His head came up. A tender smile curved his lips. "Do you need help with your dress?"

"No...I...Just say it."

Confusion wrinkled his brow. With his cuffs buttoned, he crossed to her. "What?"

"Tell me," she urged, wrapping her arms around her middle and holding herself. "Get it over with. I don't want to have to pretend anymore."

"Isabeau, our reservation is—"

"You can't expect me to sit in that restaurant and pretend I don't know what you're planning to say to me."

His face registered surprise. "I can't?"

He looked so unaffected, perhaps a touch nervous, but nothing like she felt—like a hole was opening up inside of her.

Until the first tear slipped free. Then he paled.

"Say it."

"Isabeau—"

"You know what, I'll say it. You're leaving. There, see, that wasn't..." She turned her back on him before she embarrassed herself further by sobbing. But the move had her facing the bed. The bed they'd just gotten out of. The bed where he'd made love to her slowly, passionately. Never taking his eyes off her as if he wanted to memorize her face, imprint her on his memory so he never forgot her.

She knew that was what he'd been doing, because she'd done the same thing.

A cry of pain broke free and she crossed to the door. Shaking, she struggled to remove the chain and turn the lock.

"Whoa." He pressed his palm against the door to prevent her from opening it, trapping her as he'd done in London.

She closed her eyes as the memory burst to mind. It seemed like so long ago now, when she didn't yet know him intimately, hadn't experienced the way it felt when his body joined hers and their souls touched.

"Where are you going, Isa?"

She needed out of the room, away from him. Where every breath didn't bring his scent into her lungs. "I need some air."

"You can't leave," he stated matter-of-factly. "For one thing, you're not dressed."

She was panicking. She wasn't being rational or fair or even remotely adult about this, but she didn't care. She'd thought she was prepared for him to walk away.

She wasn't.

"Please, Noah, I...let me go."

"I can't, Isabeau." His right hand still holding the door closed, he reached out with his left and ran the back of his fingers down her cheek. "I can't let you go."

Her eyes drifted shut.

"It tears me up inside, the thought of leaving you."

Dragging in a ragged breath, she slipped under his arm and away from him.

He leaned against the door, blocking her only means of escape. "I wish I could stay here with you. I know how much you love this city. But my life is in California. My house. The band."

"Your future," she supplied, closing her eyes against the pain.

"I hope so," he whispered, as his hand cupped her cheek.

She hadn't heard him approach. For her heart's sake, she needed to back away. Instead, she pressed her cheek into his palm.

"I hope you'll come to California with me." He took a deep breath. The fingers he held against her cheek trembled. "When I was in

California, alone in my empty, colorless house, I knew then that I couldn't live without you—that I didn't want to live without you. Then Dominic called to tell me about the fire."

Pulse hitching, she raised her hand and pressed it against his.

"Not knowing if you were alive or dead...I've never known pain like that before. I kept wondering how I was supposed to live without you. I kept thinking how you had died upset with me. Hurt, and not knowing how much I love you."

"You...love me?"

"You know I do."

"How would I?"

He leaned down, narrowing the distance between them until his mouth hovered over hers. "I told you."

"No."

"Yes. The only way I knew how—in a song."

Her breath hitched as her heart rolled over. "The song you wrote for me?"

"The song I wrote about you."

Her knees gave out, and she sank onto the edge of the bed. In no time at all, her world had shifted. She cupped her left hand in her right and stared down at the scars. She knew better than anyone that in one moment, one second, everything could change.

Noah shifted, planting his knees on the

floor and digging his right hand into his front pocket. After retrieving what he was looking for, he covered her hands with his. Between his thumb and forefinger, the ring glinted in a beam of sunlight. A princess cut diamond, set in a platinum band. It was beautiful. It was simple but elegant and absolutely the most beautiful thing she'd ever seen.

Except for the man offering it to her.

"Isabeau, you are my future. I can't offer you much. You said it yourself, there's nothing nine-to-five about the music industry. It's long hours in the studio followed by months of touring, living out of buses and drab, institutional hotel rooms. It's not an easy life. But if you agree to share it with me, I can promise to love you, every day for the rest of my life, and to hold you every night as you drift to sleep."

Her heart climbed up in her throat and stayed there, making it hard for her to draw her next breath. She'd wanted to talk about their future, but she'd never expected this. Not this.

Trembling, she wrapped her arms tight around her middle and struggled to draw oxygen into her lungs.

"Breathe," he urged softly. "Breathe, Isabeau."

"I can't...Noah, I can't..."

He cupped her face in his hands, leaned forward and kissed her. A long, thorough kiss that lazily explored her mouth, demanding a response without holding anything back.

Startled, she wondered why he would choose to kiss her when she couldn't catch her breath. Within a matter of seconds, she knew. Her heartbeat slowed, the pressure in her chest eased. He kissed her temple, her cheek, and her jaw before returning for one last gentle press of his lips to hers.

"Better?"

"I can't marry you."

He jerked. The raw emotion in his eyes sounded in his voice. "Why not?"

"I can't give you what you want."

"You've said that from the beginning, but you're wrong. You're what I want."

"I can't give you children."

Keeping his gaze locked with hers, he lifted her left hand and pressed a kiss into her palm. "I don't care about that."

"Of course you do, you love kids."

"I love you." He turned her hand over, watched as he slid the ring on her finger. "I love you, Isabeau. More than you'll ever know."

A symphony of sound exploded in her head as her music returned to her in a rush. She lifted her face to gaze into his incredible green eyes—eyes that saw everything, even her.

"Marry me. Build a life with me, a future."

The music shifted, changed to a gentle

melody. It swelled inside of her the same way her love for him swelled. She took a trembling breath and drew in his scent, bringing with it a desperate need to lose herself in his arms. "Yes," she whispered. "I love you, Noah. I'll marry you on one condition."

"What condition?"

Smoothing her hands up his chest, she cupped his face in her palms. "That you include in your promise of forever, the promise to never stop touching me."

His smile was slow, intimate. "I can do that." He slipped his hands between their bodies and pulled the robe's sash free. Parting the silk, he settled his hands on her ribs. "Let's start working on that one right now."

Her breath caught as his hands began their ascent, gliding up to cover her breasts. When he pressed a kiss to her shoulder, she sighed. She'd found everything she'd ever hoped for and never thought she'd find.

Threading her fingers through his hair, Isabeau sank into him as he eased the robe down her arms. "Let's," she said, before pressing her lips to his.

A sneak peek inside
MIDNIGHT HEAT
Black Phoenix #2

Chapter One

"Forty year old male involved in a T-bone MVC," the medic called as he and his partner pushed the stretcher through the doors and into the emergency department. "SUV versus semi. SUV rolled multiple times before stopping on its passenger side."

Adrenaline surged through Dr. Rebecca Dahlman's system, revving her pulse, pushing away the fatigue of an overly long shift better than the half pot of coffee she'd already consumed.

"Upon arrival, patient was unresponsive. We were able to get the c-collar on him right away, but had to wait for rescue's hydraulic equipment to extricate."

Gown and gloves in place, Rebecca ran her gaze over the man strapped to the backboard with orange belts as they swung into room one and transferred him to the ER's bed. Her team moved efficiently around the patient, cutting off his clothes with trauma shears.

The medic continued feeding her pertinent information as she began her assessment. "Blood pressure is one-twenty over seventy-five, pulse ninety-five. Pulse ox is one hundred percent. Pupils – dilated, equal, and reactive."

The guy was a bloody mess. Blood covered his face, soaked the left side of his head and shoulder of his shirt. He had a laceration on his left upper arm, deep enough to require sutures, and some bruises were already beginning to form at his left shoulder and right hip from the seatbelt doing its job of holding him in place. Even more troubling was the bruise forming on his right side, a sign of rib trauma. Ribs weren't the only common injuries from impact with the center console. The ones she couldn't see were what caused her the most concern.

"I want an ultrasound of the abdomen," Rebecca stated automatically as she shifted closer and listened to her patient's chest. Lungs clear, no abnormal heart rhythm. She looped her stethoscope around her neck and leaned in, searching the man's scalp for head trauma. "Get me a cross-table C-spine, chest and pelvis x-ray. Draw a trauma panel, type and cross, and a tox screen."

Karmen Williams, Rebecca's best friend and charge nurse for the night, pulled the man's wallet from the pile of clothes on the floor.

Directly above his left ear Rebecca uncovered the source of all the blood. Pushing her fingers into his hair, she palpated the injury site. The wound immediately began to bleed again.

"Rebecca."

"No skull fracture that I can detect."

"Rebecca."

"I'll want a CT scan of the head and neck."

"Rebecca." Karmen's voice was tight and pulled her attention. "It's Dominic."

For a moment, a heartbeat really, the words didn't make sense. Then, she looked closer. As if in slow motion, Rebecca dragged her gaze up the torso, locked it onto the face partially hidden behind long, blood-soaked black hair. Her breath snagged in her throat and she froze, the echo of her pulse beating in her ears. It was a struggle to keep her hand steady as she pushed his wavy hair away from his face and focused on his mouth, those lips, the bottom one slightly fuller than the top, the thin, straight nose.

"Stud," she whispered, her voice torn.

His eyes were closed, ringed in thick black lashes. Were they open, she knew they would be the color of the sky just after a cleansing rain.

Her world tilted.

No. It couldn't be. This wasn't Dominic. Dominic didn't have a goatee or a scar across his right clavicle. Dominic wasn't in California, he was in London. Safe in London.

Not unconscious and bleeding in the

middle of her ER.

About the Author

As a young girl **Sarah Grimm** always had a story to tell. At times they were funny, other times scary, but they always ended with a happily-ever-after. Sarah spent years scribbling in notebooks, filling the pages with partial chapters and the margins with titles and story ideas. She told friends the characters spoke to her, and that she was compelled to get their stories on paper. Eventually, she sat down at a computer and wrote her first tale of dangerously sexy suspense.

Sarah lives in West Michigan with her husband, two sons, and three rescue dogs. Between mom's taxi service, her day job, and keeping the books for the family marine repair business, Sarah can be found curled in her favorite chair, crafting her next novel. Visit her online at http://www.sarahgrimm.com